The Secret Diary of a PREGNANT BENGALI

HALIMA KHATUN

A HAYAT HOUSE book
First published in Great Britain in 2024 by Hayat House.

ISBN: 978-1-9163183-5-9

Cover design by Felix Diaz de Escauriaza

A CIP Catalogue record for this book is available from the British Library

This isn't your average romcom...

Thank you for buying my book and joining me on this author adventure. As a token of my appreciation, I'd love to give you more... so read on to the end for how you can be a part of this very unique series.

28th July, Tennis?

"So, when do you want to play tennis?" asks Julia, sipping on her frothy mocha.

"Tennis?"

"Yes. I've been thinking about what you said about how we should start playing tennis again, like we used to. It'd be a nice addition to our repertoire of activities, which at the moment revolves around eating."

I take a bite of my panini and a rogue cheesy mushroom falls out of the side, landing on the dining bench. Julia pretends not to notice.

Of course, tennis! It feels like a lifetime ago that I broached the subject of playing again to Julia, yet it's only been a matter of weeks. Since then, my world has changed. I am now with child. I can't tell Julia, though. It's far too early.

"It's not like we only ever eat out. Look at us now. We've just finished a game of crazy golf." I gesture towards the fake grass mounds, windmills and many a beer-clutching amateur golfer.

Julia raises an eyebrow. "We played for ten minutes as you raced through each course to get to the diner. Technically, I'd still park this under a food-based activity."

I'm eating for two, I think to myself. "Yeah, we should do tennis at some point," I say, rather noncommittally.

"Great. To prove I've got time for you, as you're always complaining about how I'm a busy lawyer, I took the liberty of checking online and there are some tennis courts near you. It's £5 for a one-hour session."

"£5! It used to be free in Manchester when we were growing up. Since when did they start charging to play tennis out in the open? It's not like they'll be providing a bat and balls."

"It's London, my love. Nothing is free."

"True, but... can I let you know? I'll see how my weekends are."

Julia looks at me quizzically. She knows full well I never plan my weekends in advance. The only constant in my calendar is a monthly trip back up north to see my parents and in-laws. Even then, that's rarely set in stone and we can cancel at a moment's notice.

"You were quite keen last time we met," she says. "Remember, we were discussing how engaging in some sort of leisure activity may help us de-stress and lead to some magical fertility?"

My nervous laugh kicks in. "Well, I'm not sure about the fertility bit but it would be great fun. Let me double check and get back to you." I didn't mean that to sound quite so official.

"You do that but bear in mind, the courts will get busy over the summer, so the sooner we book, the better."

"I'm sure it'll be fine." I attempt my most relaxed exhalation, though it's short, raspy and doesn't appear relaxed at all. "Did we ever struggle to get a tennis court when we used to play as kids?"

"That was a different era and a completely different place." Julia sips her mocha, leaving a smidge of froth across her top lip. Very un-Julia like. "As I say, this is London."

Bloody London.

The temptation to spill all to Julia is huge. She's my best friend. I've known her since I was five. But I can't tell her. I haven't even told my family yet. I'm waiting to tell mum in person and she can then pass on the news to dad. Either that, or he'll figure it out when I get a big belly.

I'm also scared of jinxing myself by getting too excited. After all, I haven't had the best luck getting pregnant and staying pregnant. I'm glad I've got my doctor's appointment soon. Then, I can get it signed in blood that I am actually expecting and will feel a little more reassured. At least I'm hoping so, anyway.

Exactly as big sis advised months ago when I had my first phantom pregnancy, I am walking extra slowly and carefully, to the point of being ridiculous. Therefore, I think thrashing a ball around a tennis court will be off the cards.

Julia and I say goodbye, getting caught between sharing a hug and an air kiss (these days she alternates between both so I never know what she will go in for).

"I hope you've still got your tennis whites." She elbows me in the ribs. "It'll be like the old times."

"I never had tennis whites. It was you that was kitted out for Wimbledon. I had a mismatched tracksuit. Though you're right, it will be like the old times."

"Well, mismatched is hipster-chic in London, I think." Julia squints, as she's too prim to know what is hipster or chic. "I'll check in with you next week, shall I?"

"Sure."

I guess I'll have to keep making excuses until I feel ready to tell her.

8th August, Another day, another doctor

I don't know if it's all in my head (in fact, scratch that– of course it is) but I already feel very pregnant. There's a heaviness in my abdomen. This is hilarious in and of itself given that, according to Google, if I am carrying a baby, it will be the size of a peanut right now.

I'm exhausted, too, but that could be down to my questionable iron levels. I'm also more achy everywhere. I could chalk that up to the mammoth walk I did the other night from Holborn all the way back to Aldgate. The buses were taking ages so, in a moment of madness, I decided that Holborn isn't much further than my usual commute from Cheapside. It was a major miscalculation. I've never walked so much in my life.

However, even though most feelings can be accounted for, it feels like something is brewing.

Luckily, I've got my doctor's appointment today, to verify things either way.

As I walk towards the tube station, my least favourite place, I wonder whether I should have the special seating. The thing is, I'm not officially pregnant yet. I haven't got that coveted Baby on Board badge that will afford me a seat, no matter how crowded the carriages. I should've planned this better. Surely the whole point of having my own business is that I can schedule my appointments around the quieter times of the London Underground? Never mind, I'll do better next time.

Just as expected, there is a carriage full of commuters. Three men in grey suits have taken up the space near the doors. They have the cockney geezer vibe about them and are bragging about some client they've landed. Apparently said client is going to change the game for them. Stood near them is a girl wearing a lilac blazer, which I suspect she bought in the sale. It's not really a common colour for workwear.

I barely manage to rest my back against the glass divider, when the Tube pulls away. An older man is sat with his eyes closed, as if in meditation, while the carriage judders from side to side. He's got the right idea. Perhaps it's the best way to get any peace down here. I should do the same. Maybe it'll help me silence the bothersome thoughts about crashes, technical faults, and the story from two decades ago about the bombing on the underground that mum reminds me of to this day. If there's ever any doubt where I got my worry-wart ways from, look no further than the one who birthed me.

A lady with choppy black hair is wearing a coat with such oversized shoulder pads that she is taking up more space on this claustrophobic carriage than necessary. I spy a blonde girl in denim overalls staring down at my outfit. Is she admiring my dress? It is a daring shade of fuchsia, with a cowl neck that's not low enough to show cleavage, but chic enough to make me look a little fancier than usual. Her eyes focus on my belly. I'm not sure if I'm already showing signs of being pregnant, or it's just bloating. I did have lamb curry and rice for lunch. It's tricky to avoid such delicious meals when my co-worker, Neetu, is right there in my office, selling it.

As the Tube pulls up to Aldgate East, hordes of passengers pour out, rushing past me on either side. One guy knocks my bag off my shoulder, with a half-arsed sorry and not so much as a glance backwards. Why is everyone in such a hurry? Don't they know there might be pregnant people on board? That *I* might be pregnant? Oh yeah. They don't. As it's too early to say.

The walk from the station to the surgery seems like a marathon. Does it normally take this long? Or am I walking at a snail's pace? I'm just so tired. Why did I offer to meet Julia in Chancery Lane for a coffee again? Why do I always offer to meet Julia near her work? I have work, too. I have a business to run. So why is it always at her convenience? It was an awkward meeting at best as I'm still keeping mum about my potential pregnancy. And yes, she brought up tennis. Again. Damn tennis.

She'll have to come to me from now on, either at Saint Pauls, or Aldgate. Maybe not Aldgate. I'm slightly embarrassed about my urban surroundings. Perhaps Liverpool Street, or something. Yes, I'm going to suggest that next time.

I have two minutes left before my appointment. I hope M is already there. Though it's unlikely. Punctuality isn't his strong suit.

Just a few more steps. A couple more blocks. Right, I've reached the butchers. Now I'm heading past the thoroughfare of restaurants. Nearly there. Blooming heck, there's another block yet! Curse me and my lack of spatial awareness and sense of direction.

Okay, now I'm really, nearly there. Yep, this is definitely it. The doctor's surgery is unmistakable. It looks locked in time, with its dated fascia, dated decor and even more outdated magazines. The only thing that's new about the place is the touchscreen which allows me to check in without having to report to reception.

I settle myself opposite a lady carrying her baby in a sling, when my phone pings. It's M:

2 mins away babe x

He'll be here in five, then.

The woman with the baby carrier catches my eye roll and smiles.

"Hubby's running late, as always," I say, surprising myself by making small talk with a stranger. Obviously, you can take the girl out of Manchester, but you can't take the northern friendliness out of the girl.

Thankfully, the woman replies with: "It's always the way," while pulling strands of her long, auburn hair from her baby's mouth. The baby reaches for her hair again, grabbing a clump with its chubby fist.

"How old is your..." I'm about to say boy but stop myself as I can't tell what gender the baby is. He or she is bald and dressed in neutral yellow. No clear clues there. "How old is your baby?"

The lady laughs, giving in and sacrificing a lock of hair to be chewed by a small person. "Oh, he's not mine. I'm his nanny. He's eight months old now. Teething like crazy, hence the hair snack."

The baby gnaws away, burrowing his head into her chest. I'd have never guessed he's not hers.

I have so many questions. How many days does she have him? Does the mum work full-time? Does she work from home? Is she around when the nanny is, like a rich celebrity? If not, how does she know the baby's being looked after?

By the looks of it, the baby is very comfortable in his current company, which satisfies my nosey/irrational/old-fashioned concerns. Given that I'm about to be called in for my consultation any minute now, I decide to stick with pleasantries.

"He's adorable." I smile and the baby offers a gummy grin in return.

The lady strokes the baby's cheek. "Yes, you're a little charmer, aren't you, Felix? I had him at mine for the bank holiday weekend as his mum and dad went to Florence, and he had my kids wrapped around his little finger."

"Did he?" I gasp, absorbing the fact that his trusting parents handed him to someone else, a paid stranger at that, for three whole days.

Having been brought up by one woman, and one woman only, as dad was mostly working away at a restaurant in my infancy, I don't think I could do it. I've certainly entertained the idea of having a nanny when I have kids. However, I envisioned the kind of set up where I'm around all the time, while my baby is in another room being taken care of but still within close proximity.

Just as I'm left with more questions around attachment, bonding, safeguarding and boundaries, M parks himself next to me.

"Sorry, babe. I was just about to leave work and then Lucinda called me over. She was checking over one of the projects I submitted. She could've done it ages ago but obviously decided to leave it to the last minute like she always does. It does my nut in. She started talking about all these pedantic changes I should make. In the end, I cut her short, telling her I've got an appointment and need to get going."

M looks at me, waiting for a pat on the back, a shiny gold sticker, or a high five. I don't have anything of the sort to offer. I've got this terrible habit of zoning out when M talks about work. I don't mean to but, to this day, I couldn't explain in detail what he does. It's finance, you see. It's boring. Number crunching. Spreadsheets. Pivot tables. Things that I struggled with in school and I still struggle with now when I have to do my End of Year accounts. It's not like my work, getting clients in the media. Finding the story behind the story. Now, *that* is interesting. That is sexy. Couple my confusion about his career, with the hormones that accompany pregnancy, and it completely went over my head that Lucinda is M's new boss.

"Did she know you had an appointment?"

M huffs. "Course she did. The worst bit is, she was like: '*It's not your appointment. It's your wife's, right?*' Making it sound like I shouldn't bother going. That's what she does. Every time. She tries to dictate what appointments we should and shouldn't attend. It didn't bother me before as she was working in the other team and I only had to deal with her once a quarter. Since she transferred over last week, I have her on my case all the time. She loves staying late and leaving things last minute but then why wouldn't she? She gets paid way more than the rest of us."

"That reminds me of my old boss, Maggie. She used to give dirty looks to anyone that left the office before 6pm. Her life was work and she expected us all to be the same. But it's hard to have the same work ethic when you're on about 30 grand less. Is this Lucinda giving everyone grief?"

"Pretty much, though Kamran's just announced he's moving on."

"Is he?" I ask, half-heartedly. I'm less enthused about tales of Kamran, after he ghosted my friend, Bushra.

"Yeah, he's going to be contracting with a Swiss finance firm. He'll be raking it in."

"Good for him. You should do the same if work's so annoying."

"Maybe I will."

I look at the time. Why is it that when you rush like crazy to get to your appointment by the skin of your teeth, the doctor is running late? However, you dare be a minute late, and you're taken off the list? It doesn't make any sense. It's not even like it's a packed surgery. There's only M and I, plus the nanny with the baby.

Felix starts crying and his nanny expertly sways him in a gentle, dancing motion.

"They love movement," she tells me, with a smile that suggests she knows she's imparting well-heeded advice. I smile back, as if in collusion. It's like I'm part of a secret gang, in a parallel universe, of mums, mums-to-be, and mums who look after other children as well as their own.

The crackly tannoy summons me to my appointment.

"Good luck," says the nanny as M and I stand up.

Flipping heck, that's presumptuous. Is she a baby witch?

"Thanks," says M as we leave the waiting room. "Did you tell that lady you were preggo?"

"No, as if! You know how scared I am of jinxing it. She just made an educated guess, that's all."

"A very educated one. You should have thrown her by saying you've got diarrhoea."

"You're so childish." I glare at him, though I secretly love his immature sense of humour.

"I might as well be childish while I can. It'll be proper adulting after this." M laughs, leading me to the consultation room.

I hope it's Dr Wong. She's the GP I saw last time, who advised me to chill the hell out to improve my chances of getting pregnant. It would be nice to see her and thank her in person for her no-nonsense advice. Honestly, had I not seen her that day I'd probably still be pissing on ovulation sticks and fretting about it all.

It's not Dr Wong. Instead, a thin man, with a severe widow's peak and thick-rimmed glasses, is hunched over a keyboard. I sit on the chair next to him, while M has to lean against an examination bed as there's no more seating.

"Hi, I'm Dr Fraser. What brings you here today?"

Dr Fraser's smile is warm and in sharp contrast with his stern look.

"I... erm... so I did a pregnancy test a couple of weeks back, and it was positive. I've not done one since to double-check. So I've just come to get properly checked. To make sure I am actually pregnant."

Another smile from Dr Fraser. "You say you've had a positive pregnancy test?"

"Yes, I have."

In the corner of my eye, I can see M. He can't hide his excitement and delight at potentially being a dad.

"Well, if you've done a pregnancy test and it's been positive, then you're pregnant. Congratulations to both of you!" Dr Fraser swivels his chair to include M in the celebration.

My husband's smile turns into a goofy grin.

"But do you need to do any more tests?" I ask. "Like a blood test, just to be sure?" I thought there was more to this.

Dr Fraser pushes his glasses back up his nose. "Nope, if you've had a positive pregnancy test, that's proof enough that you're pregnant. We'll take your word for it."

Dr Fraser asks a couple more questions around when I last got my period, which is hard to work out. I'm terrible with tracking my cycle. He then takes my weight and height measurements and that's it. That is literally it.

He gets up to show us the door, which is unusual practice for a GP, at least in my experience. It's as if now I'm officially pregnant, I need extra care, and have people open the door for me, even though I have a husband right there that would've done it. M also holds the door open for longer than usual as I pass through. It's like he's imagining I've got a huge belly already.

The appointment is surreal and, dare I say, anticlimactic.

"I think he was more excited than we were," says M. "I bet our own parents won't be as happy about the news."

"That was nice but he was ever so trusting," I say, as we walk down Commercial Road. "No extra tests? I assumed he'd at least take a blood sample or something. I thought they had more accurate equipment to detect pregnancy."

"True. Like, what if you made it all up? When would they figure it out?"

"I'm guessing at the scan. When there's no baby in my belly."

"Oh yeah. And when would that be?"

"I think it's at 12 weeks."

"So you could lie for three months! That's crazy, especially if you could get free vitamins and stuff. Anyway, no need to lie, because we're having a baby." M squeals and does a dad-style happy dance, not even stopping when we pass two Bengali men who are smoking in the street. He's losing all of his usual coyness. "Does it feel real now?" he asks.

"It does."

"Just as well. There's no turning back now."

M grins widely while I offer a half smile, as there are a million thoughts going through my head. Mainly: *Oh my God, I'm having a baby. Oh my God, I'm having a baby! Woo hoo! But also, shit. But also, woo hoo! But also shiiiit.*

10th August, To tell or not to tell

"Can I have one of those samosas, mum?" I ask, reaching for the flowery saucer before mum pats my hand away.

"No, this for *damand.* I save you some here." Mum points towards a rather bleak colander with two crispy samosas nestled on an oil-soaked tissue. One even has a bite taken out of it. Who'd do that? Probably one of my nieces or nephews, I suppose.

"I know the *groom*, as you put it, gets preferential treatment but my husband won't mind if I take a samosa off his plate, to add to the one and a half that I've been left with."

"Acha!" Mum huffs and spreads out the remaining five samosas on M's saucer to make it look full.

To tell or not to tell? This is probably the best chance I've got to share my pregnancy news with mum. It is the only time since I've got home that we've been alone. Everyone else is... well... everywhere else.

"Can you take samosas through?" mum hands me the plate, which also has a round dollop of ketchup to make up for the samosa I stole.

I take the plate and place it back on the counter.

"I will do but, mum, I need to tell you something. I'm -"

"*Eh-heh*, when you come here?"

Bloody hell, there goes my chance.

"Dad, I've been here for over an hour. Where have you been?"

"He be where he always be. Upstairs. In room. Could you tell your father that staying upstairs all time will only lead to depression? Need to go out. Fresh air. Walk. Go to shop." Mum nudges me, eager for my input.

"You should go out more, dad. It's not healthy to stay indoors all the time."

Dad shakes his head. "I know, I know. But where to go? What to do? Nothing." He looks down.

How long has dad been feeling like that? Granted, he's never had much of a social life. I don't remember any friends of his coming round. I don't really remember him having friends. But dad did stuff. He'd walk to the shop to get some milk. He'd get the bus to the mosque. Mum and him would occasionally go out for romantic walks in the park. I say romantic but dad would walk briskly about a metre ahead of her. But still, they walked. In more recent years, after he developed a taste for takeaway, dad would nip out for a cheeky burger, only to face the wrath of mum when he'd return home, not hungry for her freshly made curry. When did dad stop wanting to do this? And how come I've only noticed now? That makes me sad. Sad for him, for feeling like he has nothing to do. Nothing to give.

Mum, however, is less sympathetic.

"What to do? What to do? There be plenty to do! Food need buying. Hoover need to be pushed around carpet! Can't have all these jobs on my head!"

Now, I feel bad for mum, too. Dad's reluctance to do things means everything is on mum. She has to step up where dad has seemingly stepped down. His reluctance to go out means she has to do it for him. It's not fair. Being a second-generation immigrant with ageing parents is not fair. I'm not around enough for them. I can't ferry them from here to there. It's likely I'll do even less in the future, given my impending motherhood. Even if I were free, I have a life. I can't be there at the beck and call of my parents. I wish they had the forethought to think about this. To be aware that the house would be empty eventually. That their kids would grow up and have their own friends and own life and not be able or willing to constantly be in their orbit. I wish they made hobbies, lifelong friendships, relationships with family members that they actually like. But then, when could they? Their life was us. Getting by, domesticity, work and prayer. Now look at them. It's an impossible situation.

"Maybe we'll go for a walk tomorrow, dad," I say.

Dad looks up with hopeful eyes. "But, you go to your in-laws, no?"

"I will be. But not until the afternoon. Let's do a morning walk round the park. You should come, too, mum."

"*Nah, nah,* not me." Mum wiggles her finger. "I got too many jobs to do. Need to pray, then do the washing as it be sunny day tomorrow. Also, your sister here with children. I can't leave them. And they can't all go. Not enough space in the car."

"We could walk there?" I suggest.

Mum chuckles. "You expect your sister to walk? You crazy? She always be driven. That's why she getting big." Mum looks down at my belly. "Also, you be getting *lit-ool* tummy as well. You must control that. You not been married too long. Don't let yourself go like your older sisters. What will your husband say? I know he be big, but you must make more effort. Wife always have to make more effort."

There are so many things to unpack with her statement but now is not the time.

Dad shuffles out without saying another word. Hopefully he'll go into the front room to chat with M. Not that they have much to talk about. It's a shame I don't have brothers. Whenever M comes over, he ends up sitting on his own in the front room. If he's lucky, he'll get a nephew or niece for company. Otherwise, he'll sit playing on his phone. He's recently developed a fondness for retro games like Lemmings. I can't say I love it.

I hear the unmistakable sound of dad treading upstairs. I guess M's alone for a little longer. I suppose it also means that dad's done for the evening. Oh well, I'll have a special bonding time with him tomorrow at the park. As for mum...

"I'm getting a tummy for a reason," I say. "I'm pregnant."

"Really?" Mum stops.

"Yes."

"*Hassa?*"

"Mum, you just asked me the same thing in Bangla. But yes, really. I really am pregnant."

"*Mashallah*. Good girl. That's good news." Mum rubs the side of my arm. "Okay, you take those samosas to your husband." She hands me the flowery saucer again. "They getting cold."

Now, I wasn't expecting a standing ovation and a bouquet upon delivering my news but I expected maybe a little more ceremony than that.

I open the front room door to find M draped across the sofa. I can't decide if his position is slovenly or seductive, or whether I should tell him to sit up or paint his portrait. However, given that he's playing on his phone and his tummy has escaped from underneath his pink polo shirt, I'm going with slovenly.

"What are you doing?" I ask.

"Just watching the highlights of the Liverpool game." M peels his eyes away from the screen for a second to see that I come bearing gifts. "Ooh, is that a samosa restock?"

I lay the plate down in front of him.

"Your mum is on it today! We had semolina and cake a bit ago." M grabs a crispy triangle and dips the corner in ketchup. "I'll just have one. It would be rude not to."

I take a samosa, too.

"Hands off!" says M, in mock shock. "What would your mum say if she found out that you're taking the *damand's* portion."

"I'm sure she'll say it's fine for the groom to have one less, as there are extenuating circumstances." I rub my belly.

"You spilled the beans?" asks M. "How did she take it?"

"Pretty much how a Bengali mum would." I don't have to say anymore. M gets it.

"You've got to tell my mum tomorrow," says M.

"I know. I'm looking forward to it. I think she'll be delighted."

"OH, CONGRATS!" MIDDLE sis offers a warmer response with a tight hug. "How far gone are you?"

"I can never quite remember. About five weeks, I think."

"I could never remember, either. One minute, you're in your first trimester, complaining of morning sickness. The next, you're howling like a wolf, trying to get the damn thing out." Middle sis ignores my wincing and quickly passes the TV remote to her youngest daughter. "There you go. You can watch Tiny Pop. Extra loud."

My youngest niece squeals with delight at being able to watch TV at night.

"Does she know how to operate a remote control?" I ask, unable to fathom that this pigtail wearing preschooler is so tech savvy.

Middle sis rolls her eyes. "This one knows more than me. Let me tell you, the first time round, you try to do everything by the book. You hand-blend purees, cook from scratch and shield them from screens as much as possible. By the time this one rolled out, I was practically handing her the tablet. You'll be the same."

I only offer a "hmm", in response. My kids will be screen free, playing with wooden toys and eating organic, homemade food. And there is no way in hell that they're going to be munching on those starchy tomato crisps my niece is currently having. I doubt that packet has ever seen a potato.

"Have you downloaded a pregnancy app yet?"

"An app?"

"Yeah, to tell you what size your baby is every week."

"Not yet. I was just going to check on Google, to be honest. I don't fancy another app taking up my phone storage space. I need space for photos and things as I'm doing the blog."

"And how's that going? Any new freebies?"

I look down at my barely there belly. "No."

"Well, it's not worth holding off for photos for your blog then, is it? Also, you might get good stuff that's pregnancy related, like a breast pump or something if you blog about your journey. The app won't take up much space. Just get one. It's quite nice to watch, especially as it's your first time. Like I said, by the third, the baby will just fall out and you won't even remember being pregnant."

"I'm sure I will. I remember you whingeing third time round."

"Was I?" Middle sis looks blankly.

"Yeah, you were complaining about how heavy you were. And bloated and gassy."

Middle sis stares in disbelief. "I don't remember. That's the thing, once you become a mum, you don't remember much at all. It's Allah's plan. Take away the memory of pregnancy and forget the pain to keep us procreating. While we're talking about pain, obviously it's gonna be bloody awful, so I'll give you my Tens machine."

"A what-y what?"

"It's a machine you hook up to your back and it kind of gives you like an electric shock."

"That sounds awful. Why would I want to electrocute myself if I'm already dying from labour pains?"

"It's to distract you from the labour pains. Kind of like having a little pain so you can ignore the bigger pain."

"Like if I got slapped in the face then punched in the stomach, I'd forget the slap?"

"Sort of like that. But let's not try that on you now."

"Nope, best not."

Middle sis rubs my back. "But seriously girl, I'm really happy for you. You'll make a great mum." She strokes my hair, unaware that she just delivered words that are like music to my ears.

LITTLE SIS' REACTION is less enthusiastic. I corner her upstairs en route to the bathroom.

"Oh, no!" She looks horrified.

"It's okay! It's good news," I reassure her, despite the fact that she should probably be the one reassuring me. After all, I'm the pregnant one here, fluctuating hormones and all.

Little sis grips the off-white banisters as if she's scared of falling. "Are you sure? Is it what you want?" Her face spells more concern than I can comprehend.

"Of course. I've been married long enough."

"Does that mean you'll have to move back up north?"

"What? No!"

"But will you be able to do it on your own over there, without family?" Little sis asks the question that's been tip-toeing around the periphery of my mind. It's one that I know I have to answer but I truly can't say with confidence.

I shrug. "I'll be fine in London. Loads of people bring up babies by themselves. How hard can it be?" I'm trying to convince myself more than anyone else.

Little sis exhales loudly. "Alright then, I wasn't sure. I just wanted to check. But..." she leans closer, looking sheepish. "I kind of need the bathroom. So could you..."

I jump to the side, realising I've been unwittingly blocking her entry.

"There you go. And don't shout about it yet until I've had my scan and I know for sure."

"It's alright," says little sis, already closing the door on me. "I can't think of anyone who would want to know."

That's a bit harsh.

AFTER DINNER, THE LADIES of the household and I congregate in the living room over a cup of tea. Dad is upstairs praying and M crosses over the threshold to enter the women's quarters. This is something he only does when absolutely necessary.

"So, I'll be off home, then," he says, by which he means his parents' home in Droylsden. "I'll pick you up tomorrow?"

"That's fine," I reply, dipping a chocolate biscuit into my decaf tea.

"You go now? Stay for a bit longer. Have some..." mum grasps at straws for a culinary option she hasn't already offered tonight. "Juice! Have some juice."

Since he's been at my parents' house, M's had dinner, snacks and tea and biscuits. The diluted cordial is the last resort.

He puts his palm to his chest. "There is no need. I'll get going."

Mum and my sisters slowly follow M out into the hallway to say goodbye. They exchange obvious, readable smiles that are reserved for when there's plenty to say, but they don't want to say it.

I'm not offended that neither my mum, nor my sisters, offer any congratulations to M. Of course they won't. If they did, that would be a huge breach of Bengali family code. It would involve acknowledging the brutal, ugly truth that my husband and I have done the deed.

11th august, A brisk walk

"Slow down, dad!" I shout, barely able to keep pace with my 70-something father.

I forgot how fast dad walks. He's breezing ahead of me, one arm swinging back and forth like a pendulum, while the other is resting in his trouser pocket. It's a walk I grew up seeing. On the school run when mum was looking after little sis, going to the local corner shop, and in later years, these walks in the park. Dad always swings one arm as if to propel himself forwards. The only thing missing on today's walk is mum, though she's not far from the topic of conversation.

"You can hurry up. You young lady," says dad. "Don't be like your mum, all slow walking. She could step on an ant and it will be okay. That be how lightly she walks."

I can't tell if this is a compliment or a complaint. As it's said in dad's usual, gentle voice, it's hard to tell.

"I'm not as fast as I normally am," I say between gulps of breath.

"Why? You ill?"

I guess dad hasn't heard my news.

"No, not ill. It's just..."

Dad takes a deep breath. "Oh, okay... Yes... Understand."

Or maybe he does know I'm pregnant?

"You got any *faracetamol*?" asks dad. "Or I get from shop?"

I look around. The country park, which sits behind our house, stretches for miles. There are plenty of overgrown blackberry bushes, long grass, and cascading trees creating shadows on this sunny day. But not a shop in sight.

"I'm okay, dad. Why would I need paracetamol?"

Dad looks away. "For... *eh-heh*, you know."

Does dad know something about pregnancy that I don't? Perhaps, having had four kids, he has some crucial intel about paracetamol helping with endurance during brisk walks.

"I'm not sure... I don't think I need it?"

"You sure? Your mum said help with..." Dad's face darkens as he looks across to the overgrown, seed-sprouting grass... "*Fee-riod.*"

"Feeri-?"

Oh my God. Oh my life. Dad is talking about periods! He can't! Isn't he breaking an unwritten dad rule? How I wish mum was here to scold him. I can't do it. He's too cute, wearing his smart blue shirt, stainless steel watch and work shoes even though he doesn't work.

"Shall we go home?" asks dad, speaking for our collective mortification.

We've only been here about 10 minutes. I can't let the word period get in the way.

"No, it's fine. Let's keep walking," I reply.

I never get any alone time with dad. He's not one to talk much and most of my life our relationship has been functional. He gave me pocket change when I needed it. He walked me to the train station when I went to university. He was a constant presence around the dining table and when it was time for tea. But often, that's exactly what dad is...a presence. A warm body at the table. An impatient dinner guest. A patriarch that exerted very little authority.

I'd like to have more conversations with dad. From a very distant memory, I recall him telling stories. Little parables from Bangladesh. I'd listen with open ears. They were sometimes tales of ghosts, sometimes about family, and there'd always, always be a moral at the end of the story about how children should be good to their parents. I wonder if I can incite some conversation now.

"Dad, did you have trees like that in Bangladesh?" I point towards a tall overhanging tree with a white and green trunk that looks mouldy.

"Eh... I no remember. Shall we get going? My leg starting to hurt."

I sigh and reluctantly follow dad out of the park and down to our quiet cul-de-sac.

On the way home, we bump into Mrs Barker from across the road. I haven't seen her in years. My visits to and from my parents' house these days are usually by car and fleeting at best, so the chances of bumping into neighbours are slim. Looking at Mrs Barker, frail, small, and with a vacant expression, it looks like she doesn't get out much, either. She's clutching a teddy at her front door, perhaps waiting for someone.

"How are you, Mrs Barker," I ask.

She looks at me, puzzled. "*Ooh* are you?"

"It's me, from across the road?" I point to our UPVC front door.

She looks at the front door, and looks at me, still unsure. "No, you're alright. My son's coming to collect me," she says.

We stand still for a second, before dad says: "Come, let's go." He then waves to Mrs Barker, even though she is a foot away. "She got dementia," he whispers.

"Dad, I think she can still hear us."

"No chance," says dad, striding away with confidence. "She too old to hear."

I think it's only my dad that can be ageist and old at the same time.

It's not quite the bonding session I was hoping for but when dad climbs up the stairs as soon as we go through the door, I realise he's given me everything he has.

"She got dementia for while now," confirms mum, when I tell her about my encounter with Mrs Barker. "Poor lady. Son and daughter visit once a day. That's it. I bet house is so dusty inside. Probably no central heating, either. I'm sure son and daughter will fix it up nicely when she die, so they can inherit good money."

"Alright, mum," I attempt to avoid getting her on her soapbox.

"It not alright. Not right at all. So sad the way people treat their parents in this country."

"Not everyone can live with their parents, mum. It's not that simple these days. I wouldn't want to live with my in-laws."

"Okay, don't live but at least take care of them properly. Make sure house warm. That they got food. You regularly visit."

I'm not sure mum is venting or preparing me for years to come. Either way, it's duly noted. When mum and dad get older, we must step up, both emotionally and financially. Luckily, I've got a good career and so has M, so they'll be okay.

OF ALL THE PEOPLE I'M sharing my news with, I'm most anxious about my mother-in-law. It's not that I'm worried about what she's going to say. It's just that with my people-pleasing ways, I'm ashamed to admit I have this real desire to win daughter-in-law brownie points. I'm certainly not going to be praised for any culinary endeavours, so it might as well be because I'm pregnant. After all, the gift of a grandchild is much greater than a well-cooked curry, right?

Having arrived an hour ago, I have come to find that all the dishes of the day have been cooked. My mother-in-law has whipped up a chicken curry, a meat dish with bitter *shatkora*, some fried fish and sautéed vegetables.

However, if you think a full spread of lunch options is enough to stop my mother-in-law whipping up another unnecessary dish, you'd be mistaken. It's like you don't know her at all.

"Have you tried this before?" she asks, mixing together a batter of date molasses, flour, and some egg.

I'm not entirely sure what "this" is, so the only thing to do is shake my head.

"Your mum no make it?"

"I don't think so."

My mother-in-law smiles, safe in the knowledge that she has won this round of *who is the better mum?* "I will teach you lots of things you haven't had at home."

I shift on my feet, uncomfortably. My mum is not that bad, is she? She just doesn't have the same desire to cook around the clock that my mother-in-law does.

The TV is on, with the dramatic chorus of the Bangla news. That means my father-in-law has popped into the living room. I peer round the kitchen door to see him facing the TV screen, sat up straight in his armchair, wearing a chunky knit cardigan. I don't know how my in-laws do it. It's August. They have the fireplace blasting, yet still feel cold. It's like they've got their own microclimate.

"Do you want tea, *abba*?" I ask.

"No," he replies. Then he looks up and says: "Are you having one?"

I smile at him. "I can do."

"Then... I take one, too." My father-in-law nods his head from side to side. "Only half cup. Or two fingers full. And put one teaspoon of honey instead of sugar."

That's a new order. It's nice to see M's dad mixing it up a bit.

"Do you want a cup of tea, mum?" I ask as I put the kettle on boil.

"Should I have one?" My mother-in-law muses, looking into the distance as if I've asked a philosophical question. "Maybe... yes but make it strong. Use two teabags. It will go well with what I'm making."

And what exactly are you making? I think to myself.

M pops his head around. "What's cooking?"

"Apparently everything," I reply, pouring boiling water up to the brim for my mother-in-law's double teabag mug and carefully attempting to measure up two fingers' worth of tea for my father-in-law. I don't think I'll ever get used to their quirks. "I'm not quite sure what that is, though." I nod towards the light brown batter my mother-in-law is pouring into the pan.

M's eyes light up. "You making pancakes, mum?"

"Is that what they are?" I ask.

"Pretty much. But slightly Bangla-fied, with date molasses instead of sugar."

I learn something new every day.

Instead of flipping over the pancake, my mother-in-law folds it into itself. I'm offered the first one but it feels like something that would be best had after lunch, not before.

"Try it. It be different." M's mum pushes the plate towards me.

I tentatively take a bite from the hot, floppy, greasy pretend pancake. I try my best to hide my dislike. I much prefer the fluffy pancakes I'm used to eating.

"It's okay, a bit greasy."

My mother-in-law laughs. "A bit greasy! You no know good food. Bit of grease kill no one."

It would be rude not to finish the rest of it but I couldn't take another bite. I feel so heavy. I'm not sure if it's the pancake or the pregnancy but my appetite is slightly off.

"I'll break my news," I mumble to M.

"What news?" M asks, before the penny drops. "In that case, I'll take my pancake to the other room. The footy is about to start."

This is my chance. This is my chance to explain why I didn't want the pancake and hopefully elevate my status to the next level by gifting her a grandchild. M's brother and sister are nowhere to be seen, which isn't unusual. I'm glad for their absence.

"Err... mum, I have some news." I begin with so much caution.

"What is it? Everything okay?" My mother-in-law doesn't make eye contact, as she is laser-focused on her pancake duties. "Could you get one more piece of kitchen tissue? This one getting oily."

There is no amount of paper that could absorb the grease dripping off these pancakes but I bring a tissue over.

"The thing is... I'm not well."

My mother-in-law continues pouring. "I was ill last week, too. Change in weather making everybody ill. It no seem like August."

"No, it's not that." I lament the confusing terminology us Bengalis adopt to say anything but the word pregnancy. "It's... it's just that... It's my time." I don't really know the Bengali word for expecting. "I'm coming."

My mother-in-law carries on dropping little dollops of batter into the pan, thankfully oblivious to my unfortunate choice of words.

"Can you take this through to your father-in-law?" She points at the plate of fried pancakes. "And can you call your brother and sister? I don't know what they're doing."

"Are they at home?"

"I think your brother be at home, your sister may be out with friends. For study."

I'm pretty sure she's graduated but I say nothing.

I take the plate of pancakes to my father-in-law, who looks at them, confused. "Why this now? Lunch no ready?"

Why does my mother-in-law do any of the things she does? "Lunch is coming. Maybe have this for now?" I suggest.

My father-in-law chuckles. "I no be able to eat all this! Take some. Share with me."

"It's okay. I've had some, *abba*."

"You sure?" he asks, though his face suggests he's not too put out by having to have his pancakes by himself.

"I'm sure," I say.

"*Acha*, okay." And with that, my father-in-law carefully lifts up the pancake as a puddle of oil drips from its bottom.

I'm not going to call down M's brother yet. I need to get this news off my chest while I've got my mother-in-law to myself.

I return to the kitchen.

"They coming?" she asks.

"Who?"

"Your younger brother and sister!" My mother-in-law exhales with exaggeration, clearly exasperated by my idiocy.

"It's just, the thing is, mum."

My mother-in-law folds up the final pancake in the pan.

"I'm pregnant."

Without looking at me, she simply asks: *"Hassa?"*

"Yes, it's true." The doctor who doesn't know me is more trusting than my own mum and mother-in-law. "I really am pregnant."

I'm bracing myself for a slightly awkward hug and perhaps a rub on the back.

Instead I get: "About time! I was saying to your big sister-in-law, what on earth are you two playing at? You getting older and older! I don't know what this business is. So good if you be finally pregnant!"

After that response, I have only one thing to conclude–Bengali mums are weird.

20th August, A pea in a pod

"Have you ordered your Tube badge yet?" asks M.

"No."

"Why not? I thought that would be the first thing you'd do."

I look away from him. "I don't want to jinx it. Let's get the scan out of the way first."

M throws his head back. "You and your worrying!"

"What do you mean? Of all things to worry about, this is a big one, right?"

He shrugs. "If you say so. I just think it might be a good idea to have the badge for when you're getting the bus or Tube, so people know to give you a seat. Anyway, it's up to you." M yawns as he leans into our faux leather sofa. "Speaking of letting people know, who else do you need to tell?"

"I haven't told big sis yet. Then it's just my friends but I'm definitely telling them after the scan."

"Have you told my sister-in-law?" M asks.

"I haven't. Should I? I was hoping the information would filter down from your mum. Wouldn't it be a bit weird to announce it?"

"I don't know. Would it?"

"Well, considering that both our mums only ever whisper the word 'pregnant' like it's some dirty little secret, I'm assuming I should let your mum tell her."

Another shrug from M. "If you say so. I don't get you women and your rules, to be honest with ya."

"To be honest with *you*, I don't make the rules. I just follow them."

M shifts his attention to the TV, flicking through the channels to find something decent, before settling on a police procedural programme. "Can I watch this, babe? You know I love a bit of cops and cars?"

"Go for it," I reply. "I need to call my big sister anyway to share the news."

A high-speed chase ensues on the TV screen, leaving M hypnotised. Given that he didn't hear what I said, I think it's my cue to leave.

I head to the bedroom to call big sis. The phone rings endlessly before going to voicemail. Bloody big sis, always busy doing something. Probably cooking a fish curry, no doubt.

I have to tell one other person tonight. This is exciting news. Seriously exciting. Over a year in the making, no less. I'm bursting to share this. And in general, I'm feeling like I'm about to burst. I don't even have a pregnancy belly yet but my body feels bloated.

Maybe I could call my cousin, Naila? After all, she happily rubbed her pregnant bump in my face last year.

Actually, she didn't, really. She just documented it on social media while I devoured all her content like a stalker. Perhaps she's not the best person to share it with, on second thoughts. She always manages to ruin the moment by stirring the pot or outdoing me somehow. Who knows, she may be pregnant with her second baby, or have some other life event she can use for one-upmanship.

Let's have a nosey at what Naila's up to. Don't judge me. I open up TikTok. Her latest video shows her doing a hair flip in slow motion. She now has an ombre mane, with blonde ends and dark roots. Is it a wig or her real hair? I can never tell with her as she changes it up so much.

Most of her recent videos don't give much away, apart from one with a teasing caption of: *Watch this space.*

Oh, don't worry, Naila, I will.

With Naila off the table, who else can I tell? There's my cousin Hassna, from my dad's side. I've never had the busybody vibe from her. Plus, when I last saw her, over a year ago, she was busy enough with a baby of her own. Then again, if I tell her, she'll likely tell her mum. Auntie Jusna is that last person I want knowing right now. She'll have an opinion one way or another. And it will be a bad one.

There's only one thing for it... I'm going to have to go downstairs and tell whoever is on night duty at the concierge that I am pregnant. Or, go to Sainsbury's and casually mention it to the lady at the checkout. Someone needs to know this.

I'm seriously considering putting my coat on over my pyjamas and heading out when my phone rings. Oh good, it's big sis.

"Hello lady. Did you call? I was reading namaz. Have you done yours yet?"

I look outside to see that our busy London road is lit up with street lights, headlights, and many an apartment spotlight. It's time for Maghrib prayers. "I haven't yet," I reply.

"Hmm," says big sis, possibly judging, possibly indifferent.

"I just called to share a bit of news. I don't know if mum's told you yet... but I'm pregnant."

"Oh, that's good news, isn't it, lady?" Even though we're speaking on the phone, I can picture my big sis clasping her hands in glee right now. "Mum's not said a word. I spoke to her this morning and she was telling me about her tummy troubles and how she's been eating figs but they're not working so I suggested she try chia seeds. So, how are you feeling?"

Big sis disarms me with a pivot towards mum's constipation. "Erm... I'm the same but a bit more tired. And bloated."

"I did wonder if you were expecting, come to think of it. When you posted that photo on Instagram from your friend's party. Was it a hen do or something? You were wearing bunny ears and looking rather silly and I do remember looking at your face, thinking it was puffy so I thought you might have some news."

I think back to that photo. "Hang on! That hen-do was ages ago. We're talking months back. I wasn't even pregnant then. It was probably just weight gain." Big sis' ability to offend me without even trying is rather skilful.

"Right." Big sis clears her throat. "How come you only posted it a couple of weeks ago?"

"Because I'm really slow with social media."

"Hmm. You might want to fix that and be more consistent. Remember you showed me Naila's Instagram feed? She's posting regularly and that's why she's got a lot more followers than you. She's big on TikTok now, too. You probably want to do a bit more now that you've got a blog to maintain."

I sigh. "Yeah, I should but I've been so busy with work and then not feeling great– hold on! We're completely missing the point here. I told you I'm pregnant!"

Big sis laughs. "Sorry, lady. That is great news. I'm delighted. I'm glad you finally got a move on. I just want to check, is this a proper pregnancy? Have you been to the doctor, or is it like last time when it was a late period?"

"This is a proper one. As proper as can be, at least. I've been to the doctor. They referred me to the local hospital and I'll be getting booked in for a scan."

"I'm glad to hear it. I just thought I'd ask, as I didn't want you getting ahead of yourself." Big sis' voice fades as though she's moved the phone away from her face, or perhaps laid it down somewhere. "It's exciting, isn't it?"

"It is. And also a bit scary."

"You'll be fine. Just remember, keep walking slowly when you're out and about and don't bother going on the Tube if you can avoid it. They're too overcrowded and busy. Plus, the good thing about being your own boss, it's not like you need to be anywhere, is it?"

Yet again, another person thinks that my own PR consultancy is make believe, and I sit in my pyjamas all day doing nothing.

"I do have to be some places. I rent office space and I have clients to meet-" I stop myself from running into defensive mode. It's just not worth it with big sis.

"Fair enough. Now..." big sis pauses, "I've forgotten most things as my pregnancies were such a long time ago but you need to take folic acid and prenatal vitamins. I can't remember if the doctor prescribes them for you, or you have to buy them. You'll probably get them for free, as you're in the inner city."

"Maybe."

"You know, it's like a deprived area, so you get better facilities."

"Got it."

"Because it's a bit scummy where you are, isn't it? So you'll get more for free."

I scoff. "Okay, you've made your point. I'll get my free vitamins from my scummy GP."

"Blimey lady, I'm not saying that! You know what I mean. You are in the poorest borough in London, aren't you? It's not a secret. There is more support there because most people can't afford it. It's a good thing."

I want to remind big sis that I live in an apartment with a concierge and a lift that doesn't stink of pee. I want to tell her that we pay a princely sum every month to live here. I would also like to inform her that we are in zone one, the most central-est of central London. And while we are in a metropolitan melting pot, with many Bengalis around us, my end is not scummy.

Then I remember, this is big sis. There's no point.

"BABE..." M INCHES TOWARDS me tentatively in bed. "I want to see how big our baby is."

He has puppy dog eyes that are hard to refuse, so despite my reluctancy to download a pregnancy app, I go online to find my fetus measurements.

"Right, how many weeks am I? God, I should be better at this." I shake my head as if to gain some clarity.

"You're about seven weeks, aren't you?"

"Check you out, knowing stuff!" I lightly punch M's arm. "You could be my baby nurse."

"I'd rather be your oncologist." M raises a suggestive eyebrow.

"That's a bit dark! Why do you want to be my oncologist?"

"Err... to check out your lady parts?" M huffs as though he's stated the obvious.

"Why would an oncolog- wait, do you mean a gynaecologist?"

M throws his hands in the air. "I don't know, whichever one is the fanny doctor."

"Yeah, that's a gynaecologist." I burst out laughing. "*Fanny*. You're so childish."

M tickles my belly. "I bet you didn't expect that from the boy you met on the internet all those years ago."

"I didn't expect a lot of things. Least of all a husband," I say, recalling how hopeless the whole finding a husband process seemed.

"And I came in and swept you off your feet."

"It was you or the pizza boy from Bangladesh but I guess you could say you swept me off my feet." I turn back to my phone screen. "Right... seven weeks... seven weeks. How big is the baby at seven weeks?"

I scan down the list on a pregnancy website and land upon a picture of sweet peas.

M looks confused. "Are they saying the baby is the size of a pea, or the pod?"

"Good question." I look at the other weeks. "The week before, it was supposedly the size of a sesame seed. The week after, it will be the size of a blueberry. I'm going with it being pea-sized."

"Hello, little pea," M whispers gently into my belly. "I'm your daddy."

As he talks in his cute baby voice, the one he reserves only for my ears, it dawns on me that this is truly happening. There is a pea in my belly.

30th August, A strawberry

My baby is officially the size of a strawberry. According to the NHS website, it has formed eyes, protected by eyelids, a mouth and even a tongue with tiny tastebuds. Though I imagine the gastronomic offering in my belly isn't much to shout about.

It's my office day today. I'm in two minds about whether to walk there or get the bus. It's a nice day for a 25-minute walk. I'd get to admire the tall Sushi Samba tower, gaze up at Saint Mary's Axe and then head to the bustling, suited thoroughfare that is Cheapside. Today, however, I'm thinking I should bus it to preserve my energy for the toll of pregnancy, as big sis warned.

At the bus stand, there's a lady in a green hijab and matching abaya. She has a toddler in tow and the little boy keeps balancing along the edge of the pavement, much to his mum's horror.

"Hamza, be careful! Get away from there."

He ignores her and instead holds his arms out like an aeroplane for extra balance.

"How old is he?" I ask, despite knowing full well that I'm breaking public transport etiquette by talking to a stranger.

She looks at me, almost startled. Then she smiles. "He's three. But it feels like we're not past the terrible twos."

The toddler wobbles on the edge of the pavement and just about manages to stumble back to safety as a black cab roars past, beeping angrily.

His mum pulls out a secret weapon. "Hamza... lollipop... it's yours if you come here." He takes the bait, climbing onto his mum's knees, dirtying her abaya in the process. "Do you have any children?"

Now it's my turn to be startled. I've never been asked that before. I've always put it down to my youthful appearance but, looking at this woman, I can see that she's about my age. Plus, I'm in my 30s now, so totally age-appropriate to be asked if I've got children.

Should I share my pregnancy news? After all, it's not like she's a friend. She's a total stranger who I'll never see again. What would it matter if I shared the news?

"No kids yet," I decide is my answer. Best wait until the scan before telling strangers at bus stops.

She unwraps the lollipop for her boy, not taking her eyes off him the entire time. "Enjoy being kid free. Once you're a mum, everything changes."

"That's what I keep hearing."

The bus says it's four minutes away, which is an unusually long wait for such a usually frequent bus.

While Hamza sucks on his lollipop, I ask his mum: "Are you getting the number 25?"

"We are. It's Hamza's day out. But we're only going as far as Saint Paul's."

"Oh, that's where my office is."

The lady raises her eyebrows in approval. "That's a really nice part of town. What do you do?"

Well, stranger at the bus stop, I thought you'd never ask.

I tell her about my PR consultancy and how I manage a steady portfolio of clients. I try to avoid too much marketing jargon and sound overly sales-y, as she's not a prospect. I don't mean that in a judgemental, unconscious bias sort of way. It's just she's a mum with a toddler that's sucking on a lollipop. Therefore, if it turns out she runs an SME that's in dire need of publicity, I'll be surprised. Yes, alright, there's a lot of unconscious bias there.

She smiles politely, cooing at Hamza in between, as he tries to get her attention by grabbing at her chin and tugging at her abaya. All the while, I can't help thinking I recognise her. Just as the bus is about to arrive, I dare ask: "Have we met before?"

She adjusts her scarf after it's been shifted by Hamza. "We've not met but I've seen you around. Do you live at Tower Plaza?"

"I do," I say, thinking to myself that she doesn't live there, too, surely?

"We're neighbours, then. I've spotted you near the lift and at the bus stop before. I'm usually lugging around this one, or my older two, so never get a chance to say anything."

How come I've never noticed her, while she's seen me? I would've definitely realised if we had a Bengali neighbour in the flat. After all, there's hardly any of us. Despite being on the border between Aldgate and Whitechapel, the most Bengali populated area in London, our apartment houses very few fellow Bangladeshis. There aren't many people of colour, in general. There are a few different accents but it's largely gentrified. Also, with its steep price tag, it's the reserve of young, child-free working professionals who don't want to settle in the suburbs. I'm surprised that she lives there, especially with children. There it is again, my unconscious bias.

The bus rolls up to our stop, making a hissing sound as it lowers itself to kick out a ramp for Hamza's buggy.

"I don't know why I bother with this. Half the time he wants to walk," she says, expertly pushing the pram onto the ramp and holding on to her son's hand. "Well, it was nice to meet you. Next time I'll say hi, if I spot you by the lift."

As she settles down at the standing side of the bus with a space dedicated for buggies, I decide that now is not the time to ask her name, or solicit further conversation. I have to check myself. It is London after all and this will get borderline weird. Instead, I move along to the back of the bus, only to find that there aren't any more seats available. Bloody packed out London.

I have to stand between the seats, holding on to the headrest either side of me. The bus occasionally sways and, as per usual, nobody makes eye contact, let alone offers their seat. Then, why would they? As far as it seems, I'm a healthy, non-pregnant young woman.

I think I need to order a Baby on Board badge.

TECHNICALLY, I DIDN'T need to come into the office today as I have no meetings but I wanted to. I need a distraction from some thoughts that are meandering in my head. Little thoughts that were always there but have become more prominent since little sis asked me what I'm going to do. I could see what she was getting at. She's thinking this whole having a baby while working and living in London without family is a crazy idea. Is it really that nuts?

However, if I thought that going into my co-working space would be the distraction I needed, I was wrong. It's a reminder of all I currently have and all that may change drastically.

I hear Loren in my left ear, delivering the same sales spiel, yet again: "My name is Loren and I work for QuickTime Solutions. I'm calling to tell you about our services. We've been featured in the Financial Times, the Guardian and the Daily Express. Have you seen us in any of those?"

"Fancy a brew?" Benedict asks.

It's a welcome diversion. "Yes, please. Actually, I'll come with you. I could do with a break."

Benedict gives a lopsided smile. I've only been here half an hour, so I'm hardly due a break.

I follow Benedict across the scuffed carpet to find there are no clean cups in the kitchen.

"Do you want to check the dishwasher?" he asks.

"We have a dishwasher?"

Another lopsided smile. "To the left of the sink."

I feel sheepish, having never noticed the big white appliance next to the fridge. To be fair, I'd pardoned this place from having any mod cons when I learned that they didn't have a water filter.

Wait, am I supposed to avoid caffeine? I'm sure I heard that somewhere.

"Do they have decaf here?" I ask, already knowing the answer.

"Unlikely. I think you'd have to bring your own teabags for that," Benedict replies, pouring boiling water from the limescale-laden kettle into his bright red mug that says *World's Best Boyfriend*. "There is a mug here. You might want to rinse it under the tap." He holds up a black tin mug with a white interior, rotating it in his hand as if to highlight the dark tea stains inside.

"I'll skip the tea." I reach for a mucky glass instead.

Note to self: bring my own teabags and mug.

Jasdeep walks in. He looks like he was about to head in our direction to make a brew but instead turns on his heel and goes straight out of the door. My female intuition senses he was embarrassed for having approached me on the Muslim dating site back when I was single and looking, despite being married himself. I must say, I'm not hating seeing him squirm.

I return to my desk, decaffeinated, to find a missed call from Joy. I take a few deep breaths before I call her back.

"Hi, I called earlier. Were you out?"

"No, Joy, I was just away from my desk, making a cup of tea. That's why I'm calling you back."

"Right, yes, well that's fine," Joy says, as though she's granting me permission to not be tethered to my phone. She only pays me £400 a month for one and a half days' work. I heard once that the lowest paying clients are the most demanding. Joy is no exception.

"Okay, I'm calling because I thought I'd have another pop at the national magazines. It was such a lovely spread we got last time and I thought we could try again."

"I'm glad you like the coverage, Joy." Now I'm warming to her. Maybe she's not that demanding after all.

"It was great. It looks really good but I have to say, I didn't get much business from it. Maybe we need a bigger splash next time."

And she's got me feeling cold again.

"Sure, though I do have to warn you, national media is hard to come by. We did really well with what we got. However, it's not to say we can't secure a nice piece again. Do you have another story or angle in mind?"

"Not really. I thought that's something you could come up with as my PR expert."

My stomach twists. Is that because of the baby or Joy? "Yes, of course. I could work up some ideas with you. I just thought you might have had something if you wanted more national coverage."

Joy makes a weird sound, like she's sucking in her lips. "That's what I've hired you for, isn't it?"

I take a deep breath as quietly as I can. Expectation management. Glass half full. Think positive thoughts. £400 a month. £400 a month. Only bloody £400 a month! Right... back to taking deep breaths. I cradle my stomach, which is now turning.

"We can certainly brainstorm some ideas if you like. Do you have five minutes?"

"Now?" Joy sounds exasperated. "I won't be able to do that now. I'm far too busy. I've got a client lunch in town shortly. How about you come up with a list of bullet points of what could work for my business and we'll take it from there?"

My inner thoughts go: *It doesn't work like that, Joy. We are in a partnership here. You have to tell me about your business as you are the expert. You know what's going on. It's my job to extract from these facts some newsworthy stories. I can't magic things out of thin air. I mean, yes, I am a PR person and I have polished many a turd in my time. But they need to be turds to start with. So at least give me your turds!*

Deep breath, deep breath. Remember, a calm mum equals a calm and happy baby. I put back on my figurative PR hat and say: "Not a problem, Joy. I'll work something up and get back to you in the next few days or so."

As I hang up, I have mixed feelings. How am I going to manage this? How will I deal with demanding clients? What will I do when I go on maternity leave? How long will I be on maternity leave? Who will I recruit in my place? Or do I shut up shop for nine months? And what about after the nine months? Could I get a nanny? But, a bigger question is popping up in my mind and clouding all the others... Would it be so bad if I chucked all this in?

6th September, Shopping

"CAN WE GET THIS?" M bats his eyelashes at me, whilst stroking a tiny, collared white outfit.

"I told you, I don't want to buy anything yet. It's way too soon." I glare at him. We weren't even meant to be in this baby section today. This is our usual browsing Saturday, where we check out the Ralph Lauren store in search of any clearance items.

"I know but... surely buying one thing is okay? I'm excited. And imagine how cute our baby would look." M shows me the outfit as though he's a salesman on commission. I must admit, it is adorable. Crisp and white, it's like a tiny shirt. I can't imagine the baby being small enough to wear it. "This could be the outfit the baby wears when leaving the hospital. It's good to have a smart coming home outfit."

"I'm sure it will still be there in a few months. If not, we'll find plenty more cute baby clothes. Let's shop properly once I've had the first scan."

"Come on." M nudges me. "We don't even need to look at it once we've bought it. I'll buy it and put it away. It's just really cute. And we have to kind of celebrate a bit, don't we? We're having a baby!"

Another expectant mum, who is much further along than I am, stops examining a pair of baby socks to smile at us. "That is lovely," she says, as though it's any of her business.

I glare at M again and reluctantly agree. I don't know what it is. Do all pregnant women feel like this? It seems so early to start talking about the baby, shopping for the baby or planning for the baby. My glass half empty nature has reared its ugly head big time. The thought of there being any problems with the baby, with so many months to go... it's overwhelming. It's not like I want to wish the pregnancy away. I really don't. I should enjoy these nine months. It's just that, as each week passes, I say a little prayer and feel slightly better that I'm further along. I'm closer to meeting the little one.

M has now turned his attention to a tiny pair of socks. "These are cute, aren't they?"

Gosh, I can barely slide my thumb into them. How would a baby foot fit inside? I stroke the ribbed cotton. They're like socks for elves. Or pixies. Not a human being I'm carrying inside me. M's doing his salesman look again, complete with eager eyes and a cheeky smile.

"Alright, you can get them. But that's all, okay?"

M grins, happy with his victory. "They do have a buy one, get the second cheapest item for free offer going."

"No!"

M holds his hands up, admitting defeat. "Fine, we'll just get these. Let's hurry to the till before we see anything else."

En route, we pass many women at various stages of expectancy. There's a lady with a bump bigger than mine, dressed in a maroon jumper that's struggling over her belly.

She's rifling through a rack of baby vests. There's another woman with a small bump, pushing a pram with a tan leather trim. Since I found out I was pregnant, I've noticed these prams everywhere. That leather trim looks like it would be lovely on the hands. Soft and luxurious.

We spot a couple. The lady has long, straight blonde hair and is dressed in what looks like cashmere, paired with riding boots. Her husband's auburn hair sits in waves and he looks dressed for the office, in chinos and a pale pink shirt. I can smell the money. He has his arm around her, while they both admire some ostentatious baby feeding chairs that come in brushed gold and shiny silver.

"Check out those high chairs," says M. "They're more like little thrones."

"Fit for a prince or princess." I smile.

"Shall we?"

"Let's not," I tell M, halting another impulse buy. "But, when all is good, we could look at them. I imagine they cost a bomb."

M muses. "It would be nice, wouldn't it? To give our baby stuff we never had. My feeding chair was a hand-me-down from my brother. And it was given to him by an old neighbour!"

"Lucky you, I never even had a feeding chair," I say.

I look at the chair. It's gaudy, blingy and totally unnecessary. M is right. After a lifetime of struggling, it would be nice to give our baby the best. A way of acknowledging how far we've come, despite the disadvantages we both faced. Being second-generation immigrant children, we didn't have parents who could provide us with much. After-school clubs were non-existent. Extra tuition was unthinkable. Growing up, we got by. We didn't have a lot, but we got by. For our baby, I want to do more than just get by. I want to be doing great. I want us to give this baby the best we can afford. It's not just for our baby, it's to show the world. It's a big eff you to society. It's to say, haven't we done great? Despite it all, haven't we done great? And what bigger eff you is there, than buying a ridiculous gold throne with our eff you money.

21st September, Today is the day...

This is the part of pregnancy that's extra exciting. It's the bit that mums-to-be gush about on Instagram. It's the time when they leave hospital with an undecipherable photo of a growing baby.

In recent weeks, I've been scanning many a photo of a fetus. I've poured over the captions of multiple pregnant women, and like the true psychopath I am, I've even looked back at my cousin Naila's feed from when she was expecting. I also browse her new material, obviously. She recently posted about her gold and diamond pendant with her baby's initials at the centre. She got that for free. Lucky cow.

Okay, enough about that. Today is not a day for negativity. Today is a day to fill that glass right up. For today is my turn. I'm sat in my local hospital's prenatal waiting room, ready for my scan. Thankfully, M left work in the nick of time. Though he did take umbrage with his boss' attempts at keeping him in the office for longer, again.

"She's a proper pain in the arse," says M. "I should seriously consider going to Kamran's firm. He's always telling me about it. They need someone in Pensions."

"You should," I say, not fully engaged in the conversation. I have bigger fish to fry today.

"Are you nervous?" asks M.

"No," I reply, though my uncontrollable foot tapping suggests otherwise. "Maybe a little excited, that's all."

M puts his hand on my knee, settling me. "I'm excited, too."

Just like my doctor's surgery, this place appears locked in time. Despite being a busy city hospital that got a big chunk of government funding for some state-of-the-art facilities, it looks no different to some of the community hospitals I've visited for my work. The light blue chairs have hard seats. There are bulletin boards with various pamphlets about breastfeeding and how to anonymously report domestic abuse. The wooden corner reception desk has multiple seats, though currently there's only one receptionist sat there, trying her best to ignore everyone waiting to be seen. I'm not sure if that call she's taking is real or fake. Then, in the far corner, is a toy station, with a winding beads maze taking centre stage. There are two children playing there, simultaneously working together and competing to get their beads across the rollercoaster-like metal wire. They're not siblings as they're of different ethnicities. It's amazing how children, unlike adults, just play with anyone and everyone. They don't have that filter we have, which stops us from interacting wholeheartedly with strangers. They don't have years of etiquette drilled into them, teaching them how to live and how to behave around other people. They don't understand the concept of keeping themselves to themselves and living in isolation. They're free to play with whomever they want. It's as democratic a relationship as can be. I wonder when that changes? I wonder at what age children realise they have to play with certain children based on location, friendship circles, ethnicities, religions, social or economic status. When do those barriers, which we like to pretend don't exist, become apparent to small children?

There's a little kerfuffle, followed by a tug-of-war over the beads, which is funny as it's a stationary unit. Those wooden balls aren't going anywhere.

"Come on, Peter. You need to share," a lady in dungarees and a white T-shirt with a big baby bump, tells her golden-haired child.

I look around to see who the other boy belongs to. Then he runs over shouting: *"Mama, mama!"* to a tall lady wearing a niqab. While speaking on her phone in Arabic, she lifts the little boy onto her lap and carries on chatting.

The other boy, Peter, is now sat next to his mum, staring at a small pad as he swings his legs to the tune of the cartoon he is watching. The mum is on her phone, scrolling.

I guess there won't be any small talk on this ward.

"How do they see the baby?" M asks.

Okay, I suppose there will be some small talk. Bless my reliable M.

"I think they put a probe across my belly. At least I'm hoping it's my belly."

"Why? Where else would they probe you?" M looks worried.

"On some American reality shows, it shows ladies being probed internally."

M grimaces. "You mean through the-"

"Is that Helena?" A nurse tentatively walks over, interrupting both M and my speculative thoughts.

I look up and smile, hoping and praying that she will scan over my belly, rather than inside my lady parts. I wince enough when it comes to having a cervical smear. That's just a speculum.

"I'm Esme and I'll be helping do your scan today. Would you like to follow me?"

M and I dutifully follow Esme, whose small shoulders are hunched as though she's struggling under the strain of a 12-hour shift. Her hairband is so loosely wrapped around her red hair, it is in danger of falling off into the corridor. Her accent is indecipherable, except to say that she's not from the UK.

Esme leads us to a consultation room where another nurse is sat waiting for us. She checks my height and weight, offers me a pack of prenatal vitamins (big sis was right about this scummy area), and talks me through the timetable of appointments I am to have before the baby is born. By the sounds of it, I am going to see more health professionals over the next nine months than I have in my entire life.

"And, what do you do, dad?" the nurse asks M.

Having zoned out for much of this preamble, M suddenly springs to attention. "Uh... I just work in finance."

My M, so modest. He sells himself short by saying he 'just' works in finance. When I'm asked about my profession, I stop myself from waxing lyrical about my PR career, as it doesn't seem appropriate given the setting. However, I don't use the word 'just'. There is no space for that in my line of work.

"And does this apply to you?" The nurse points at a section on the form where it asks if I suffer from domestic abuse.

I glance over at M, who wasn't paying attention to begin with and reply: "No," though perhaps my pause made things seem more suspicious than necessary.

"Good." The nurse puts a cross in the box. "You don't have to worry about this just yet as you've got a while to go but, nearer the time, it would be good for you to think about how you'd like to give birth. For example, if both you and baby are healthy, you could opt for a home birth. A lot of evidence shows that women are more relaxed at home rather than a clinical hospital and the birth time can be shorter as a result."

She notices my face before continuing: "Of course, it's your choice and that's not for everyone. Another thing you might want to consider is that we've got a new birthing unit. It's basically halfway between giving birth at home and being in hospital. So there will be midwifery support there but it will feel like a home-from-home setting. However, if you do have any complications, you're only an eight-minute ambulance ride away to get you to the hospital."

I say nothing, as I am perhaps unlike most women and feel I'd be much more comfortable in hospital.

"But anyway," the nurse continues, "you don't have to think of any of that until later on."

Our talk continues for what feels like the longest consultation ever. My answers are populating a form that is so exhaustive, it's like a magazine. I'm told it will become my antenatal document which I will need to keep with me at all times.

M is doing his best not to yawn. I'm not sure if it's out of fatigue or boredom. Perhaps it's both?

Once it's over, Esme returns to collect M and I, like we're the prize in a game of pass the parcel.

"Have you drunk some water?" Esme asks.

"I haven't but I'm okay, thanks."

"No, I mean, did you drink water before you came here?"

I furrow my brow. "I didn't realise I was supposed to. Nobody told me."

"It helps us get a better look at the baby," says Esme, holding open the door to the scanning room.

I suddenly feel like a schoolgirl that has forgotten her homework. Did I miss something on the appointment letter?

M looks unsure, like he's heading to detention with me. Surely I won't get told off during my own scan?

"She hasn't drunk any water," Esme mumbles to a colleague.

"No worries." Her colleague smiles, putting me at ease. "I'm Abigail, your sonographer today. So you haven't drunk any water before you came?"

I shuffle from one foot to another. "I didn't realise I had to," I say, my voice lowered. "Should I drink some now? I did pass a water cooler on the way in here."

Abigail shakes her head, her severe bun barely shifting. "No, it won't make much of a difference drinking water now as it won't fill your bladder in time. You need to have it about an hour beforehand. But let's see how we go. Hopefully we'll see something," she says this as though we're going to a supermarket just before closing time, when everything has run out.

I follow their instructions and lie on the examination bed. I unbutton my jeans and peel them down, grateful that I'm being seen by an all-female team. I lift up my top, revealing what now looks like a very small bump. Or it could be mistaken for a food baby. Or premenstrual bloating. I wonder if anyone else has noticed that doesn't know yet. Like M's best mate, Jam, or my best friend, Julia. I need to tell Julia soon, only I'm not sure how.

Abigail, the sonographer, squeezes some cold gel across my stomach, startling me from any thoughts about Julia. She spreads it around with a handheld device, not dissimilar to a wand. I guess she will be performing some magic tricks today. Across to my left is a screen, which M is glued to, even though it's not showing anything yet. His hand is resting on the bed, next to my thigh.

After swishing the wand around my stomach repeatedly, Abigail says: "Could you lower your jeans some more?"

"Sure." I tug at either side of my jeans, pulling them down further.

"And your underwear? Just a little, so we can get a good look."

I wish I'd groomed myself this morning. I've been very lax in my lady landscaping recently, on account of being tired and pregnant.

I'm wondering why Esme is here. She's just sitting and watching the screen like M. Meanwhile, Abigail is thrashing the probe around my belly, pressing uncomfortably hard at some points.

"Right, here we are." Abigail exhales and so do I.

Here comes the magic.

A fuzzy little creature appears on the screen. It's hard to make out exactly what I'm looking at. M squeezes my hand. His eyes crinkle with joy. This is it. Our baby. There she is. Wait. Did I just say *she*?

While M and I are in awe, Abigail and Esme look less enthused.

"The baby is in a bad position." Abigail frowns.

Wait, what?

Esme shakes her head.

Abigail presses the wand into my pelvis. It hurts. "Could you jump up and down for us?" she asks.

For a second, I think she's joking, so I laugh. When my giggles are met with a serious face, I have to ask: "Me? Really?"

"Yes," says Abigail. "Sometimes it helps move the baby into a better position."

M looks at me in disbelief. I am not believing this either. I'm not sure if I'm being pranked and someone's going jump out from behind the curtains and tell me it's a joke, I'm not even pregnant and those pregnancy tests aren't accurate and I should've got a blood test from the doctor. Because the reality...this... sounds insane.

Given that Abigail and Esme have straight faces, I have no choice but to slide off the examination table and start jumping up and down.

"That's it. Jump a little more," Abigail says, as though I'm a performing seal. I feel like I should clap for them. "Let's really get some movement, so we can have a better scan."

This is tiring work. And I'm still not 100% sure that this isn't one big joke. My sisters, having had numerous children between them, not to mention my own mum, have never, ever told me that they've had to jump up and down when pregnant, at the request of a medical professional. Then again, they don't tell me much when it comes to pregnancy, or periods, or intimate care, or anything else they deem inappropriate.

"Okay, I think that's enough." Abigail raises her hand and gestures for me to get back on the examination bed, signifying the end of my performance.

She squirts some extra gel to my stomach, though I'm surprised she needs any more. My underwear is soaked with the strange lubricant.

"Did you apply oil today?" Abigail asks.

I think for a second. Did I? "Oh, yes, I did. I used body oil after my shower this morning."

Esme tuts, while Abigail tells me that I shouldn't use body oil on the day of a scan as it affects the visual. This is surreal. I shouldn't wear body oil? I wore it especially for them! It's perfumed! Plus, haven't they heard of a thing called stretch marks? I've been doubling up on oil since the day I found out I was pregnant.

After another attempt, Abigail sighs. "Come on, baby. Come on, little baby. Let's see the head."

Now I'm worried. Very worried. What is wrong? Why is the baby in a bad position? I've heard about stuff like this before when the baby is upside down and it affects pregnancy. I think it's quite dangerous. Shit. Is that what's happening?

M notices my worried face. He squeezes my hand tighter and whispers that it will be okay.

"I have an idea," Abigail exclaims. "Do you want to go to the toilet? Empty your bladder."

"I thought I was supposed to have a full bladder."

"In general, it is best to have a full bladder but sometimes having a wee can help. We'll try it all. Plus, walking to the bathroom might help generate some movement."

Because hopping up and down on the spot wasn't enough?

"I can show you where the toilets are," Esme finally speaks.

I roll off the examination bed for the second time, my legs like jelly and my belly and underwear covered in the stuff. For the first time in my pregnancy, I'm worried. Not the usual low-level worry I carry around where I always find something to fret about. Real worry. Is my baby okay? Have I been too happy and glass half full about it?

With trembling fingers, I press down on the handle of the bathroom door. "You really scared me," I say with a smile that hides my true feelings.

Esme's face softens. "Oh no! Why?"

"Because you said the baby was in a bad position. Will it be okay?" I'm scared of the response.

"No! We mean the baby is in a bad position for us to see. Everything is fine, that's totally normal. It just means you got a bit of a cheeky one that won't stay still. It makes it harder for us to scan."

"Right, okay. I didn't realise. I'll just go wee now." I quickly close the door behind me.

As I collapse onto the toilet seat, I feel a weight lifted from my shoulders and my tightly wound body starts to loosen as I exhale.

The baby is okay. The baby is okay. The baby is okay, I think to myself.

However, here is a bigger thought: Why the hell didn't they say that? Why did they make me worry, thinking the baby is in a bad position? They know it's my first pregnancy.

I take a deep breath to calm my nerves.

After emptying my bladder on the sonographer's orders, I wash my hands and splash my face with cold water. I look in the mirror and see how stiff my shoulders are. It's as if I'm carrying all the tension there. I take a further three long, slow, deep breaths. Everything is okay.

Second time around, I lie on the bed with ease, squeezing M's hand and telling him I'm okay. We're okay.

"Much better!" Abigail exclaims as the screen becomes less fuzzy and shows the unmistakable appearance of a large head. "You have a naughty one! Come on, keep still, baby. It's a little acrobat!"

It's amazing. In front of our very eyes, I can see my baby doing somersaults in my belly. Sheer magic.

The rest of the examination is a game of cat and mouse. The sonographer slides the device across to get a better look and the baby moves out of the way. Both Esme and Abigail laugh. M does too. I try my best to joke along, tossing away the worries from a moment ago.

I look at the screen in disbelief. There's a little acrobat there, swimming around in my belly. My baby is there. My baby is *there*.

17th October, Baby on Board

I've only gone and done it. I've only gone and ordered myself a Baby on Board badge, which should afford me priority seating on public transport.

Shit's getting real.

Now that I've unboxed my badge (I totally should've recorded myself doing that so I could share it on social media a few weeks after the event, as I'm too scared to announce things yet) I feel like I've entered a new club. The mums' club.

I finally downloaded the pregnancy app, which tells me week-by-week how big my baby is and what to expect. It's particularly exciting to see what size fruit I'm carrying in my belly. I'm currently at apple and in latter stages, I'll be hefting a watermelon. That still feels so surreal. Even though I am officially pregnant, I've seen the scan, I've got the badge and the app, everything in my day-to-day is normal. I'm going into work, I'm attending networking meetings. M and I still have date nights and dinners. Nothing has really changed. I do have to think about the future, though. When things do change. But, for now, I'm enjoying the semi-surreal phase of my life.

I'm currently sitting in our apartment, in the middle of the afternoon. The luxury of working for myself. I'm pondering over a press release for Joy, based on the very vague brief she gave me when we last spoke. Honestly, when I was working for the big PR agencies, earning big bucks, she would not be on retainer. Now, however, needs must. There are bills to pay and a baby on the way.

My procrastination over Joy's story is interrupted by a knock on the door. Oh yeah, I forgot to mention, we've hired a cleaner. It's something that M wanted to do for ages but I've been resistant as I felt... well... a bit silly. We live in a two-bed apartment! How much cleaning could it possibly need? I don't know if it's my northern pride, or my stingy nature but having someone clean such small quarters seemed excessive. However, now that I'm pregnant, I'm fully on board with this idea, much to M's delight.

I open the door to see Ana for the first time. She was recommended by Julia (along with a nudge about tennis) as she is someone she and Miles have been using for years. They commission Ana every fortnight to clean their plush pad. I'm thinking of using her once a month, or maybe every three weeks at a push when I can no longer touch my toes. Stingy and all that.

"Oh yes, it's very dirty," Ana says, whizzing through my flat to survey my worktops, windowsills, and bath. Offensive, much? I'm hoping it's just lost in translation from Polish, and she means my flat just needs a good sprucing. "I start in bathroom?"

"Yes, please do."

"You have Viakol?"

I've never heard of that before. "No, but I have some antibacterial spray."

Ana shakes her head and her short, bleached fringe flaps in agreement. "Okay, I try with that. But it won't be good. You need something stronger. It's too dirty."

I'm offended again.

"Next time I come, you buy Viakol, yes?"

I'm now forgetting who the client is, as she's too forthright to argue with.

I leave Ana to tackle my dirty bathroom but then, what's that lurching feeling? Oh no! I need to run back in and use it.

"Sorry, could you give me a minute?" I say between gasps.

"You not go to toilet before?" Ana puts a yellow-gloved hand on her hip.

"It's not for that. I feel sick."

Ana leaves with a tut. I don't even have time to shut the door. I lean over the sink, wretch, and release some watery stomach acid. Is that morning sickness? No, it can't be. It's the afternoon! I've been lucky to have escaped it so far. Maybe that's my comeuppance. A breezy first trimester and sickness in the second, when, according to my app, symptoms should ease.

As I turn on the tap, Ana peers round the door. "Next time, be sick in the toilet. Not sink. Now the bathroom's even more dirty."

19th October, Mum's the word

I decide that the bumpy bus isn't the best mode of transport at the moment. While I can't complain of full-on morning sickness, I have found myself gagging and retching more often of late. Brushing my teeth, leaning over to reach the TV remote or doing pregnancy yoga are no longer safe activities.

So, I'm doing something different today. I'm getting the Tube to my office. There's only one downside. I'll have to do more walking than usual. While the number 25 bus drops me minutes from my office, the underground isn't so straightforward. I'll have to either get off at Monument and walk an extra five minutes (ten in my current condition) or, I'll need to change Tubes and take the Central line to Bank, which is not only grossly overcrowded but it feels like you're travelling to the centre of the earth as it's so damn hot.

I'm getting off at Monument.

Despite going at 11am, there are so many people waiting on the platform that it might as well be rush hour. Most are men in suits, with some younger women more casually dressed, which suggests a job that might be creative. I pin my Baby on Board badge onto my blazer.

The Tube arrives and people shuffle indiscriminately to get in. I'm shoved from both sides. I can't move as quickly as the expensively dressed, not pregnant men. People are packed into the aisles, leaning against the glass walls and clinging onto the poles. There is zero chance of getting a seat here. Damn my Tube badge. It's way too small. A big belly would be more of an indication than this tiny circle on my jacket.

A lady, who is also holding onto the green pole, peers down at my badge. She then looks up at me and smiles. That's all she can offer. She doesn't have a seat to give up. Aren't there designated seats for pregnant women? I've never thought to look.

The carriage pulls away. My stomach does a somersault. That'll be my acrobatic baby. I instinctively stroke my belly. It's softer now but still in the indecipherable stage of pregnancy where it could be mistaken for bloating.

The Tube grinds to a halt, causing some people to tumble forward. I'm holding onto the pole for dear life, hoping that my occasional swaying doesn't make me look like the world's least sexiest stripper.

A few people get off but more get on. The seats that become vacant are quickly seized upon by the passenger standing nearby. Nobody looks. Nobody looks around at anyone. Nobody looks out for anyone. I bloody hate Tubes. Everyone is locked in their own world and not paying attention to their surroundings. I guess they don't want to. If they did look up, they might see a pregnant person, or an old person and have to either give up their seat or risk being exposed as an uncaring git.

I close my eyes to settle the sickness in my stomach.

"Excuse me, would you like to sit down?"

I open my eyes to see who the good Samaritan is. It's a woman with shoulder-length brown hair and hazel eyes. She smiles at me as she stands up from her seat, which has a pram in front of it. Wait a minute, she's a mum! Judging by the pram, she's a new mum! She is the last person who should be giving up her seat.

"No, it's fine. Only a few stops now," I say.

The woman sighs. "Honestly, sit down. I've been there."

Like I said, there's a secret mums club I'm now part of.

I wobble over to take my seat, while the Tube is still chugging away.

"Thank you," I say.

"You're alright." The lady smiles, holding onto her pram for support.

I am so grateful. I'm so grateful that someone gave me a seat. But I'm so annoyed it was the one person who shouldn't have to.

I look around. The man next to me has his eyes closed. To my other side, an older woman is looking straight ahead as if she has tunnel vision. On the opposite side, a younger girl has her AirPods in. Some are reading books. Most are on their phones. Nobody is paying attention.

Bloody London.

As I leave the carriage, the lady who gave up her seat pushes ahead and waits at the bottom of the stairs. A man, who I'm guessing is her partner, comes over and helps her lift her buggy up the steep steps to the exit. I didn't even notice she had a partner with her. Why didn't he give me his seat, instead? Rude.

I follow closely behind as she gets to the summit. I want to offer a very unorthodox, non-London, additional thank you and maybe even a 'have a nice day'. Then, she turns to the man and says: "Thanks so much."

He replies: "No worries," and they both walk off in different directions.

He's not her partner! First, I'm glad for the chivalry and that politeness isn't dead. However, that presents another dilemma. When I have a baby, I'll have to get the Tube by myself. Will I have to rely on the kindness of strangers? What would I do if there isn't a nice person to help with the pram? How could I scale all the steps with one of those huge, four-wheeled contraptions? I've never really noticed mums with pushchairs on the Tube before. I don't see them often, at least not the times I travel. It never occurred to me that there aren't many lifts at the London Underground. Most stations don't have any, yet they have hundreds of steps to negotiate. Why is it so child unfriendly? How are mums supposed to get around? Or should they just stay at home?

All of this is presenting lots of questions with answers I'm not so comfortable with. There's more to this motherhood business that I've never thought of before because, frankly, it wasn't my problem.

Right, I'm in need of something nourishing. All the steps, all the anxiety around the underground, it's rendered me ravenous. On the plus side, it's nearing lunchtime, which means Neetu will be on the picnic bench, selling her curries.

I unpin my Baby on Board badge and drop it into my handbag, as I don't want to share the news with my co-workers so soon. I must remember to put it on for the journey back.

I sidle over to the picnic bench as the first order of business. I can't do any work on an empty stomach. Neetu looks at me, delighted. It must be a slow day for her. She gets up and greets me with a hug.

"Congratulations!" she whispers in my ear.

"Oh, right, thanks." I'm caught off guard.

She puts her hand on my belly. "I could tell as soon as you walked in."

Do I really look that pregnant? I'm wearing a loose fitting tunic.

She leans in again. "I'll tell you a secret. I'm pregnant, too."

I check out Neetu's midriff. I can't believe I never noticed before. I guess it's because she's always seated when I see her.

"How far along are you?" I ask.

"13 weeks."

Upon seeing my surprised face, she says: "I know. I look more pregnant than that. What about you? 12?"

"16."

Neetu sighs. "Well, I'm a lot heavier than you to start with. So it makes sense that I'd look more pregnant sooner. But anyway, I'm keeping it on the down low as I'm hoping to secure some funding for my business. So, mum's the word."

I smile in agreement. "Mum's the word."

"I know it's Ramadan but I take it you're not fasting?" asks Neetu.

"Nope. One of the perks of pregnancy. It's just as well, as your chicken bhuna is calling me."

I abandon the idea of having a curry at my desk, which I'm sure will be to the relief of my co-workers and join Neetu instead. In between serving the odd customer, we share our pregnancy journeys. She tells me about her weird craving for soil. I never knew that was such a thing. I've been hankering for sour, salty snacks. Poor Neetu was also floored with morning sickness during the first six weeks but has come out with renewed vigour and an appetite to, as she puts it, get shit done. I tell her about my scary scan involving me bouncing up and down and she shares her more poignant moment where her husband sang to her belly in Hindi, and she swears she felt her first kick, even though it's way too early.

I didn't even know she was married. Apart from our initial conversation, where we talked PR (or rather, she slagged it off), Neetu and my relationship has been strictly transactional. She sells curry. I buy it. But today, we are really talking. I have had many moments in my life where I felt left out. These have occasionally been punctuated by real feelings of belonging. Right now, I feel like I belong. I've joined a sisterhood, a pregnant ladies' club, and it feels good. I feel like I'm a part of something. Part of a journey many of us make. That's what I've been missing so far. Keeping a secret from everyone except my family means I've had nobody to share it with who's going through the same thing. The excitement, the worry, the jumbled thoughts that come from having heightened emotions. I realise I need more of this.

"It's a bit early now," says Neetu, "but you should consider joining an NCT group later on."

"What's that?"

"It's short for National Childbirth Trust and basically is a bunch of classes which prepare you for labour and mum life. You'll get to meet women who are expecting at the same time which, to my understanding, is the main reason people join."

I lean forward, listening intently as Neetu imparts some further secrets of the pregnant ladies' club.

3rd November, A bell pepper

I think the pregnancy app is the best thing on my phone right now. Forget social media. There's no need to monitor the lives of others when I've got a life growing inside me. The app gives me weekly updates on the baby's size, on what to expect in terms of growth and development, and what changes I will see and feel in my body. I can't figure out if the latter is more of a placebo and I'm feeling those things because I've read about them, as opposed to experiencing them for real but, whatever. I'm rolling with it.

My baby is officially the size of a bell pepper. It's crazy to think that I've got a pepper inside me, aside from the copious amount I consume through eating curries.

Luckily, with the help of my app, very little is ruffling me. My pre-pregnant self would've been freaked out by some of the body changes (hello constipation and wooziness) but, with one tap of the app, I can confirm that everything is normal. It's also comforting that every week I am inching closer to being able to share my news with the world. I've been dying to tell people but at the same time, I'm scared for fear of... you know. Me and my superstitious ways.

I have decided, however, that with a slightly more protruding belly, I am going to share my news with the ladies at my monthly networking event. That seems like safe territory as it's on a strictly business basis. At 20 weeks, once I've had my second scan, I will share with my friends.

Speaking of which, I'm meeting Reena after my networking event, so I'll have to wear something looser to hide my burgeoning bump.

That reminds me.

"Have you told Jam about the news?" I shout over my shoulder to the kitchen, where M is making tea.

"What news?"

"Erm... hello?" I stroke my bump.

He scratches his head. "Oh yeah. We should at some point. He could be visiting London any time soon. We were lucky that last time he just wanted to meet for food outside."

"If you want to tell him, I'm fine with that."

M comes over with two steaming mugs and places the yellow one in front of me. "To be honest with ya, while I hadn't said anything outright, because I wouldn't unless you are ready for us to tell people, he kind of sussed it out."

I put my phone down and sit up. "How? He's not seen me for weeks?"

"When I met him last, he was asking where you were and how come you didn't come out. I kind of said you're not feeling too well and then he read into that the way Bengali women do. They're always banging on about being ill when they're actually pregnant, aren't they? So, once he figure it out, I felt I couldn't say no." M looks at me with fear in his eyes. "Is that okay? It's not like I just came out with it."

I roll my eyes. "Of course it is. It's Jam, after all."

M exhales. "And another thing, you know I was telling you about that contracting position?"

"Contracting position?" I furrow my brow, as this is something that's clearly gone over my head.

"Yeah, you know the one at Kamran's new place?"

I still have no idea and my face makes it obvious.

"We were talking about it when we were waiting for your scan?"

"We were?"

M sighs. "I've been telling you how shit work has been recently with the new boss. I've been there years and they're not promoting me as they should. Anyway, I said I'd applied for the position."

Some vague words come back to me. "Sorry, I know you mentioned something about Kamran moving but I was a bit distracted because of the scan."

"That's understandable." M dips a cookie in his tea. "I'm thinking I might go for it. The money is good. I'll be better off than I am now." His eyes are bright with enthusiasm and he's waiting for me to drum up the same interest.

"Sure, apply if you want. I guess there's not as much security though, a bit like my gig."

"True." M looks down, the light fading from his eyes.

I think back to how M remained so calm when I was made redundant. How he hid his concern when I wasn't getting anywhere with the recruiters. How he has been my best cheerleader as I've embarked on this solo-preneur career, which has resulted in a drop in income and bouts of financial instability. He's had my back through all of it.

I feel bad not being as excited about him going contracting. It's just... there is a risk with both of us having unstable jobs. Plus, there's a real deep-seated belief that goes right down to my core, that men should be the providers. It's been passed on to me from generations. It's become filtered by modernity as I am currently paying half of the rent but M and I are acutely aware that when baby comes, the lion's share of the financial burden will land on his lap.

Despite all this, I don't want to stand in his way.

"Go for it," I conclude. "Contracting is big money, which we could do with right now. Just don't turn into one of those investment wankers, okay?"

"I won't. I'm not an investment banker, anyway. I work in Pensions."

I shrug my shoulders and say: "To-may-to, tom-ah-to."

DESPITE BEING IN CENTRAL London, the old pub where my networking meeting is held could be anywhere in the country. It's as far from cosmopolitan as you can get. It's musty. The pale pink curtains and velvet seat cushions are dusty and all the pale pink faced punters are ruddy. Before I got married, I used to occasionally go for after work drinks with colleagues, just to fit in. I never particularly enjoyed it and I felt that having moved to the capital, those days were behind me. However, once a month, I traipse through this old man pub, quickly walking past the drinkers who raise an eyebrow at my brown-ness and head straight up the creaky stairs to the meeting room.

I'm not the only minority at the meeting. There are two Indian women. I wonder if they feel the same coming here, when they go through the pub that could easily be in a small village in the 18th century? Or is that just my self-conscious hang up?

The meeting follows its familiar format. Sitting around the huge table, we all take turns to stand up and plug our business for a minute. This event has every type of personality. There's Chelsea, the copywriter, who works from home and is happy to forego a higher retainer fee for more time with the kids and being able to do the school run. Elena, the photographer, covers weddings and bar mitzvahs, and shuts up shop during the school holidays.

Then, there are the uber ambitious. Anita has bought the franchise of a fabric business. Dressed to the nines in her golden yellow shift dress and blowdried hair, Anita is not the person I want to be sat next to in my current state of bloating.

"I am Anita and I own House of Fabric, which is located just round the corner from here. We've recently been commissioned to provide some bespoke materials for a very high-profile celebrity client."

This is followed by many 'oohs' and 'aahs', much to the delight of Anita. She goes on: "We're going from strength to strength and people particularly like the fact that we offer something you can't get anywhere else."

Apart from all the other House of Fabric franchises, I think to myself. Sorry, pregnancy has made me snarkier than usual.

Anita runs her jewel-adorned fingers through her hair. "And this season, I'm pleased to launch a new range of exquisite designs, inspired by my recent trip to Rajasthan. It's ethnic wear at its best." She holds up a small square of fabric no bigger than a handkerchief. It has green paisleys, on a red backdrop. "Despite being a British-born Indian, I have never seen anything like this." Anita nods in the direction of Sunita, the other Indian woman at the networking event. She then offers a smile towards me, which I return. The fabric isn't too dissimilar to the stuff I've seen at Longsight market but then what do I know about high-end design?

After Anita, it's the turn of Joy. She stands up and flattens out the creases on her salmon coloured tunic and begins her pitch. "I'm Joy. Of course, you will know me as the slimming lady. Well, business has been booming, especially since I've been showing off my amazing weight loss."

This is greeted by rapturous applause, while Joy basks in the glory, hands on her hips, shimmying from side to side. "I've decided to practice what I preach and not only talk to people about the slimming mindset but also provide the tools for them. That's why I'm starting a new venture, called Joy's Culinary Delights. I'll be making my very own range of healthy meals and delivering in the SW19 area, initially. That's before I go global, of course."

Some giggles come from the enchanted audience.

"And I've no doubt this business is going to take off because I've got my fantastic PR guru by my side!"

There are cheers and big whoops, while Bethany, who's sat to the side of me, rubs my shoulder. It's the first I've heard of Joy's business plan. There was me tapping her for stories and she was delivering nothing.

Joy clasps her hands together. "I'll get to the point, as I know my seconds are running out." She hesitates, running down her time even further.

Mavis, the group chair, holds her spoon near her wine glass, ready to tap vigorously.

"Right, okay..." Joy rubs her temples in a bid to release more words. "I'm Joy and as you all know I've been coming here for years. I can get you slimmer. I can get you eating better. And even better, I can make dinner for you. And if you don't believe me, keep your eyes peeled on the news because I will be everywhere."

She smiles at me, as everyone offers another round of applause. All I can think is, when are we going to find the time to get Joy everywhere, as she says? More to the point, does she even have the budget? I'm doubtful. A lot of this networking game is about bluster.

It goes on like this. Cheryl talks about her baking business. Joan plugs some multilevel marketing company (I don't know why she doesn't just call it a pyramid scheme). Then Jade, the makeup artist, name-drops a celebrity wedding she was recently commissioned for. I don't recognise the celebrity's name.

Then, it's my turn. I've been paying to come here every month, without fail, for 18 months. It is all ladies, most of whom are much older than me and have a plethora of different businesses and budgets. I plug my business every month in a bid to get client work from someone around the table, or somebody they know. So I have to make every word in my one minute pitch count. Luckily, I know a thing or two about PR.

Here I go: "I recently scored a great national PR win for Joy, as you know."

This is met with a few half-hearted cheers.

"But I'm not stopping there. My PR course is still available to everybody and I promise you, it will turn you into your own media relations guru."

I look at Joy and pause for a second as I remember that she took the course and promptly wanted her money back. I shake off that memory. It doesn't matter. It's all about bluster. Put your best face forward. Fake it till you make it.

"Anyway..." I must say something funny and memorable that they ponder long after this meeting is finished. I'm a PR person. This is my thing. Words should roll off the tongue. Where are these words now? Why can't I be witty? Come on... think... *think*.

"I nearly fell off my chair this morning when a national journalist wanted to follow up on a client story with a tight deadline. It threw me off and not just because I am pregnant with my first child."

I receive the loudest cheers yet. Everyone is clapping heartily. I feel like a low-grade rockstar. There have been a few moments in my life where I've been the centre of it all. My hen do, when Julia and Reena organised a lovely meal, complete with penis straws. My mehendi party, where I very much felt like the main character. Plus, of course, my wedding. This is one such moment. It is the moment I've seen so many others experience. I've been witness to colleagues, friends, and strangers on social media making amazing pregnancy announcements. This is my announcement. And I have to say, it feels great.

Over a rather unappealing lunch of pulses and grains (I always get a raw deal with the pescatarian option), Joy corners me.

"Lovely news!" She offers half a hug.

"Thank you, it's very exciting!"

"It is. Have you thought about what you're doing business-wise?"

Bloody hell! She could let me bask in this moment for one meeting, at least.

"Well, I certainly want it to be business as usual for my clients and I'm planning to hire somebody in my absence." That was a lie completely off the top of my head.

"Oh great. With any luck, you won't be off for long at all."

"Really?" I wrestle with a piece of couscous that is stuck in my teeth.

"Yes, quite a few of my clients went straight back into work after having their baby. And of course, one of the first things they did was hire me to get them back on track, you know, weight-wise. All being well, who's to say you can't come back a couple of weeks after giving birth?"

"That was certainly the case for me," says Debbie, a recruitment consultant who looks to be in her 50s. "I had five weeks off between having my two boys. I couldn't wait to get back into work and it's the best decision I have made. They're both in uni now, so it didn't work out so badly."

I have questions for Debbie. What did she do? Did she put them in nursery? Hire a nanny? Or was her husband a stay at home dad? Before I have a chance, she is pulled away by Anita to talk about fabrics. That's the thing with networking events. You only have a few minutes to talk to people before everyone moves onto the next potential client. Speaking of which, Elena, the resident photographer, comes and hugs me from behind.

"Congratulations! We'll need to talk about a pregnancy photo shoot." She beams down at me, a little too keenly.

"Sure, sounds good," I say, before turning back to Joy. "I never thought women could go back to work that quickly. It's good to know."

"Us women can do it all if we put our minds to it. Anyway, I'll leave you to it. There's some braised beef calling me."

As Joy saunters off, I wonder whether it'd be that easy for me to spring back into work within a few weeks. Technically, I could. I don't have to go into an office. I won't have a regular commute. I can work around nap times and evenings. Yeah. *Yeah*, I can do this. I can make this work. Anyway, if my pregnancy is an indication of how motherhood will be, I should be fine.

WELL, THAT WAS A MISCALCULATION. In what parallel universe did I think it would make sense to have a networking meeting in Holborn, then go home, only to have to trek to Covent Garden later to meet Reena for dinner? I am wiped, and the aches and pains are not letting up. I literally got to lie on my bed for about 20 minutes, staring at the ceiling, before it was time to go back out again.

As I leave the Tube station, I know I'm late but my pregnant legs will only go so fast. I spy Reena near the market stalls in Covent Garden. She looks at me peculiarly, probably because I'd usually hotfoot towards her. Instead, I'm dragging one foot in front of the other as my heartbeat quickens. Why did I agree to meet her? Oh yeah, she's getting married soon. As she's rarely in London, it made sense to see her. But, right now, it's painfully awkward as she's stood watching me make my way towards her in slow motion.

"You look so tired." Reena makes the understatement of the century.

"It's been a long day." I give her a half-baked hug, hoping she doesn't feel the softness of my stomach. "I'm starving. What do you fancy? You get to choose as you're the visitor."

Reena scratches the back of her neck. "Well, since it is my choice, there are two places here I've been wanting to try for ages."

"Go on..."

"They're the ones you featured on your blog recently, the lobster and burger place, and the dim sum house."

Damn, why did I give her a choice? I love the lobster and burger place, but I'm meant to avoid seafood and the burgers aren't halal. The dim sum place is loaded with fish, too.

Reena is waiting for my response. I can't exactly say I don't fancy either, as I recommended them on my blog. I'm just going to have to suck it up.

"I'm fine with either. The dim sum place is closer."

Reena throws her arm around my shoulders. "Let's do that. You look way too tired to walk any further."

As we sit down at the restaurant, I take off my chunky, berry-coloured coat.

"Your boobs look huge," Reena declares.

Crap. Have they grown that much already? I glance down at my cowl neck dress. I wish I'd worn something more discreet. "It's just the bra. You know me and my padded bras."

"I could do with some help myself." Reena adjusts her orange woolly jumper. "Though I can't be gaining weight anywhere. Wedding diet and all that."

"Speaking of which, how's the planning going? You haven't turned into a bridezilla, have you?"

Reena clicks her tongue. "Not quite but we are going all out at the wedding reception. Are you gonna stay for that?"

"I'll try to." I'm yawning already at the thought of having a late night dancing away at Reena's big fat Gujarati wedding.

As we eat our tiny steamed dumplings, Reena tells me all about her plans.

"It's gonna be mega. We'll be having a string quartet, a 365-degrees camera, Photo Booth and a live DJ. Not that my mother-in-law's keen on any of it."

"Really? Why is that?" I ask.

"They're more religious and traditional. She's all about keeping it simple and doesn't believe the wedding should be showy. I told her, if she doesn't want a show, she's got the wrong girl. I waited my whole life to get married and she expects a few prayers, a quick walk around the fire and then we go home?" Reena tuts. "As if!"

"Did you actually say that to her?" I know Reena's bolshy but that sounds brave, even for her.

"No man, obviously, I didn't say it. But I gave her a dirty enough look so she got the hint. Mum says I ought to keep my trap shut until I'm married. Wait until I've got my feet under the table and all that. Believe you me, I intend to. His mum and me have disagreed and stuff but I've held back as much as I can. Once we're married, she'll know about it." Reena snaps her fingers. "Don't be showy. Yeah, right."

I remember requesting a chocolate fountain for my wedding. Even then, mum said it wasn't worth it because all the kids would make a mess, resulting in a huge cleaning charge at the end. I resented her at the time. Hearing Reena talking about her clashes with her in-laws over her reception outfit, the menu and everything else in between, I want to tell her that none of it matters. It's just one day. What's more important is her and her husband spending the rest of their lives together in harmony. I don't say anything, though. I know full well, having been there myself, that when a girl is in bridezilla mode, you need to let them have their moment. Any reasoning will fall on deaf ears. The truth is, every bride-to-be wants to have her day as she would like it. Of course, she won't be sweating the small stuff afterwards but she needs to go through this herself. She has to live through this crazy phase. She needs to be a mad bitch with everyone. Her husband, her in-laws, her own family. Only then will she realise just how unimportant it all is.

"Do you know they're expecting me to live with them?" she says.

"Really?" I feel like Reena has mentioned this to me, perhaps at her hen do, or over the phone? Honestly, my mind has been fried lately so I don't remember.

"Yeah, it's their pride talking. They want their eldest son to stay at home for at least a couple of years. I don't know how I'll survive it, man. I don't even like living with my own family half the time. How would I live with someone else's?"

"I wouldn't know. I didn't do it." I take a bite out of my crispy spring roll, sad that it's my last one.

"You're lucky." Reena looks down at her crumb-coated plate.

It's ironic, all the time I've known Reena, I thought she's the lucky one. Being a Gujarati Hindu, she seemingly had more freedom. She could go out late while I was at home. She found it so much easier to bond with white friends and colleagues as she drinks and goes to bars and clubs. Her mum wears English clothes. As an eternal outsider, with a saree-wearing mum, I envied her ability to blend in, when that's all I wanted to do. Now, however, I can see that despite this, we are not so different.

Mum says you never really know what someone's life is like until you're sitting eating rice with them, or something like that. It's true. From the outset, some people seem to have it all but we don't know their reality. It's a shame it took me 32 years to realise this.

As the bill arrives, I am decidedly unsatisfied. Dim sum is not the dish of choice when you're eating for two. However, it was that or having nothing but fries at a burger and lobster place.

I guess I'll be having a second dinner with M when I get home.

15th November, Another scan

Today will be a good day. Today will be a good day. I am happy, healthy and strong. My baby is happy, healthy and strong. The scan will be fine. The baby will be fine.

I thought going for a scan would be an exciting event. I've seen enough movies and TV shows to believe that the experience of seeing your unborn baby on camera is nothing short of magical. My last experience wasn't magical. There was nothing enchanting about bouncing around, belly hanging out, and then being told that my baby was in a bad position. I wish they'd worded it better. I'm now scared of what today will bring.

Deep breath. Deep breath. I interlace my fingers on my belly, breathing slowly. Four seconds in. Eight seconds out. It's what I learnt in yoga. M is not one for mindfulness. He also thinks manifestation is a load of hippie mumbo-jumbo. Luckily, M is not here to see me mouthing affirmations to myself. His last text message, 10 minutes ago, informed me that he was leaving Tottenham Court Road. I hope his interview went well.

Sadly for M, there is no room in my affirmations for him today. It's all about the baby. He or she (though probably she), is monopolising my prayers and focus. Once I get the scan out of the way, I will be able to tell the world that I am with child. No more avoiding Julia. No more hiding under loose clothing.

The hospital is just the same as I last left it. Staff come and go. Ladies, with bumps of various sizes, sit with their knees apart, as they can no longer close their legs. My app tells me that my baby should start kicking but I haven't noticed any movement yet. It says that if I don't feel any kicking, I shouldn't be worried, as that's totally normal and some babies start moving later. Of course I'm worried.

"Hey babe, sorry I'm late." M sits down next to me, placing his jacket, laptop and backpack on the next chair. "I thought they'd have called you in by now."

"They must be running late," I say. "How did the interview go?"

"I think it went good but we'll see." M pulls off his green jumper. "I'm proper sweaty now. It's disgusting."

I hold my nose in jest. "I can tell by the smell. Did you see Kamran?"

"I did. We grabbed a quick coffee after the interview, to be honest with ya. That's why I took a bit longer. I figured it's worth chatting to him to get more info. He basically said the day rate is negotiable and they need someone ASAP."

I continue stroking my belly, manifesting good thoughts and brushing away my worries, though they keep coming back. "You won't get paternity leave if you're contracting, right?"

"I won't. But Kamran says they pay so well that it wouldn't matter if I took three weeks off. Basically, the pay is so good that I could take care of the three of us and you won't have to work, unless you wanted to." M sits up tall in his chair. "I was thinking about this. Say I got the job, I could use all my holidays to finish at my current place early.

Or they'll probably let me leave before my notice period, to be honest with ya. Especially as I'm going to a competitor. Then, I could get a few months in before the baby comes. And if the rate's as good as Kamran says, I'll save enough to take a few weeks off when the baby is born and–"

"Hold on! You've not even got the job yet, nor have I had the baby. Let's not get too ahead of ourselves."

M smiles. "I know I'm getting ahead of myself but it's exciting." He rests his palm on my belly. "Everything is coming together. Plus, with your worrying ways, someone has to be positive. Between us, we're the perfect combination."

A toy car hits M's foot and a little boy scurries across the floor to retrieve it. M picks up the car and hands it to the boy, who promptly runs back to his mum. She has a bump that's about as big as mine, so I'm guessing she's waiting for her 20 week scan, too.

"Do you want to find out the gender?" I ask.

"Dunno. It'll be good, if you want to. What do you think?"

I clasp M's hand. "I think we should. I already have a feeling, do you?"

M shrugs. "What's your feeling?"

"I think we're having a girl."

M smiles. He'd make a great girl dad. "There's only one way to find out," he says as we are summoned from the waiting room.

As we head over, M mumbles: "Did you drink some water before you came here?"

"Yeah. Bucketloads."

I'm glad to see someone different in charge of today's scan. Her name is Beth and she's warm and reassuring.

"Okay, so there are quite a few things we're going to look at today, as the fetus will be more developed. If I go quiet, it doesn't mean there's anything wrong. It's just that I'm concentrating to make sure we check everything properly. It's not always easy to make things out."

Within moments, I've bared my midriff and am basted like a Christmas turkey.

"Right, here we go." Beth sloshes around the scanner and then my baby appears on the monitor. "I can see there are the four heart valves. Let's look at each one to check it's all as should be."

She counts down each individual valve, while I wait with bated breath. She then looks at the brain, the spinal cord and the kidneys.

As she examines my baby's vital organs, I give thanks under my breath. There are so many moving parts and so many things that could potentially not work as intended. It's scary.

Glass half full. Glass half full. Glass half full.

"Oh, that's quite rare. Your baby is sucking its thumb."

M and I look at the scan and we can see the tiny skull hunched over towards its tiny hand.

Amazing!

"In the scan, we can determine the sex of the baby, so I want to check if you'd like to know?" Beth looks like she's dying to tell us, so we put her out of her misery.

"It's a girl!" she exclaims, as excited as we are about the news.

That must be the best part of her job.

As Beth returns to looking at her scan, M shakes his fists in excitement. It's like his favourite football team has won the championship.

"Let's call her H2," he whispers.

"Yes, let's," I agree. "It's the perfect name for her, until we come up with her actual name."

We have a girl. We have a baby girl. It's what I wanted.

Beth then goes silent. "There's just one thing... is it okay if I bring my colleague in? I'd like to check something, to be sure."

Check something? What is it now?

As she leaves the room, M puts his arm around me. "We're having a girl!"

"Yes." I try to smile, but my nerves have kicked in. Why does she need another colleague?

Beth returns with an older, more serious looking lady. The lady asks if she can take another look. I agree, as I'm already lubed up. She runs the device around my stomach, looks closely at the scan, pressing harder near my pelvis. I wince. That's the bit nobody tells you, scans bloody hurt.

She removes the device and takes off her glasses. "Right, so everything looks great but we would like to call you in for another scan in a few weeks, as the baby's head looks slightly small. And it might just be how she is. You've got quite a small head, too."

I stroke my hair. Is my head small? I never realised.

"It's worth bringing you back later on, to be sure. In a few weeks for a double check. Does that sound alright?"

The baby's head is small? I have to wait weeks to check everything is okay? The NHS wouldn't do unnecessary scans. There must be a real reason. They must have genuine concerns to call me in again. Oh God. Oh no. Bad thoughts spin around in my head but, of course, my PR politeness, which is never too far away, kicks in.

"Yes, that's fine."

16th November, Confusion

The baby's head is small? What does that even mean? Call me naive but when I first found out I was pregnant, it never occurred to me that there could be an issue. Health is the one thing that we take for granted the most.

When I've had a toothache, I couldn't think beyond that pain that clouded my thoughts, preoccupied my mind, and impacted my decisions. The pain was suspending. It stopped me in my tracks. I remember praying for the pain to go away. I vowed to be good and stop eating cakes and drinking fizzy drinks. I felt repentant. And, true enough, the pain went away. My prayers were answered. Did I ditch cakes and fizzy drinks? No. You see, a human memory is fickle. Once the pain has subsided, I'd forgotten it was ever there. I'd forgotten the suffering, the hardship. I carried on as usual, taking my health, or at least oral health, for granted. When everything is good, you don't appreciate it. When something is bad, you long for it to be better.

The baby's head is too small? Is that a thing? I don't know how worried I should be. Having to go back for another one of those dreaded scans is the last thing I want to do.

"It's good news," says M.

He's sitting next to me in bed, running his finger across my knuckles. It's tickling and annoying me. "Our baby is fine.

Just think, we're gonna have a little girl. Don't think about the other thing. They're just being thorough."

I wish they weren't so thorough. I wish I could fast forward 40 weeks, have my baby and know that everything is okay. That she is okay. I haven't even met her yet but the thought of her not being okay is too much to bear.

There is some good news. Shortly after the scan, M received a call about the contracting gig. He's got it. Therefore, perhaps his overspilling positivity wasn't completely unfounded.

M hugs me and leaves for work, muttering something about how he's going to hand in his notice with glee. I'm not sure what else he said. Something about dinner, maybe? Don't bother cooking, or something like that? It was all white noise.

Must silence these thoughts. Mustn't worry.

I examine my head in the full-length mirror. I have a regular sized head, don't I? If it is small, as the sonographer implied, it hasn't affected my brain capacity.

My phone pings. It's Julia:

Hey, how you doing? I haven't seen you in ages. I'm sorry I've not been in touch much. It's been crazy busy at work. Lots of divorces. Just to say I've not forgotten about tennis. The courts near you are available next month if you fancy it?

I wish she'd bloody shut up with her tennis. Nobody cares for tennis. I know I suggested it but that was before I found out I was pregnant with a baby that may have a small head.

I turn to write in my journal. It's given me comfort so far.

Grateful...

What am I grateful for today?

I'm grateful that I've had my 20 week scan.

I'm grateful that my husband has a new job that should hopefully make him happier and earn more money.

I can't think of a third thing. Come on. Come on now... There's plenty to be grateful for.

I'm grateful that I've not lost control of my bladder yet.

I'm grateful that I haven't farted in a meeting.

I'm grateful that my baby was sucking her thumb so peacefully in my belly.

I close my journal and lay it carefully on the bedside table, as though it's a precious tome that holds the key to happiness.

I've got work to do today. Calls to make. However, I just want to curl up and sleep. Could I have a cheeky nap? It feels like the only way to push out thoughts that keep coming at me, thick and fast.

When big sis was having her youngest, I asked her whether she wanted a boy or a girl. She replied: "Oh, I don't mind, lady. As long as the baby is healthy."

I remember thinking: *Well, of course the baby is going to be healthy. That's a given!* I was so young. So naive. Never, ever, did it occur to me that health is not promised.

18th November, Spilling the beans

I've been giving it some thought. The sonographer said I've got a small head. So it must be genetic. Better than a big head, right?

A bit of mummy reassurance will help.

"Oh, it be nothing, InshaAllah, all be fine. They just need to check," says mum.

"That's what I think, too," I reply, though it's a lie. I've been worrying non-stop.

Despite being in my thirties, I still turn to my mum for everything. She gives soothing words of comfort, when she's not doing my head in. Yes, as time has gone on, she relies on me for more things. Driving around, looking at letters, making official calls. However, mum has something nobody else can replace. Not even M. It's the comfort that only your mother can provide.

Dinnertime at my parents' house is always nourishing. It's eaten without the aid of screens, unlike my life in London, where M and I always sit in front of the telly. It's as though not having something to watch will force us into conversation. We can't have that.

I'd like to do things differently when our baby is born. Bring things back to basics, like how I grew up. Eating lunch and dinner at the table without any distractions.

"Have you told your clients yet?" asks big sis.

"I've told the ones that see me as there's no denying it now." I have to sit further away from the dining table these days as the belly gets in the way. "The rest can find out when they absolutely have to. I only need to give a month's notice and it's the same for them, so there's no rush."

Big sis helps herself to some sautéed cabbage. "You do what works for you, little lady. If your fella can support you, then why not take a break? You worked so hard all these years."

"Maybe," is all I can say. "I suppose we should be okay now, as he'll be starting his new contracting job, which is better money."

"That's good. I always assumed you earned more than him," says big sis.

"Really? Why?"

Big sis gulps hard, as though she's tackled a long piece of cabbage. "You're quite the high flyer, aren't you? I never really understood what he does. Plus, what with you ranting about having to work so hard." Big sis shakes her head.

"I've never ranted! Besides, has it occurred to you that I enjoy working? Not everyone wants to be a kept woman."

Big sis holds her hands up in the air. "Alright, lady. I'm just saying. Good for you if you want to make mega bucks. You won't be able to do it forever, though. Especially after kids." She returns to her rice and vegetables.

She isn't *just saying*. She's always planting seeds. This time I will not rise to it. She can say all she likes, it's just words. She doesn't mean it, though I can't always tell.

"Well, he'll be on really good money."

Big sis looks up. Now I've got her interest. And everyone else's, it seems, as mum and little sis temporarily stop eating.

"Why? How much is he on?" little sis asks.

"Is it like £600 a day?" big sis interjects. "I've heard men working for those investment banks earn that much. I should call my kids to come in here so you can tell them. It might be a good career route for when they're older."

Big sis shouts for her three children, demanding they come back to the dining room. I hear the volume of the TV show they're watching increase.

I shrink back in my chair as my shoulders deflate. "No, he's on £350. But that's still very good!"

Big sis hesitates. "Oh well. It's not bad, I guess."

"I imagine he's making more than what your hubby gets at the restaurant," I say with a snarl.

Damn me, taking the bait. Big sis constantly says stuff and I always rise to it.

She rolls her eyes.

Mum chimes in. "Anyway, no worries. If you no need more money, you can have rest."

"Why is everyone thinking I'm going to rest? I've actually got a plan. I'm going to get a nanny."

"A *nani*?" Mum looks dumbfounded. "I'm the *nani*!"

I'm not sure if she's joking or not, but I don't mean nani in the Bangladeshi sense, as in maternal grandma.

"I've been looking into it. I could hire someone to come and look after the baby for a few hours while I work."

Mum's eyes narrow. "You mean you leave baby with stranger?"

"I won't leave the baby," I say, though I haven't really thought this bit through. "I'll be working in the next room. I've got a two-bedroom flat, after all. I can do my work, while the nanny looks after the baby. Anyway, this isn't for ages. I don't need to worry about it yet. I'll be on maternity leave for about a year. In that time, I'll get a freelancer to pick up my clients."

It sounds like a foolproof plan in my head, at least.

"Okay, but don't leave baby with stranger. You can't do that, you don't know what they're like. I saw this programme-"

"Mum, just because you saw something bad on TV doesn't mean it's going to happen. Anyway, what choice do I have? It's not like you'll be able to come down to London and help me. Nor will my mother-in-law. Even if we move back up north, you still wouldn't be much use. So, unless you're able to help, your opinion doesn't really matter."

I can see from big sis' smirks and mum's grimace that they don't approve. Deep down, neither do I. I'd rather it not be this way. Mum was always at home. Her life was us kids. I got to eat home-cooked curry every day. I was picked up and dropped off at school by my parents. I never had strangers raising me. I'm conflicted. I'm caught between two worlds, the one I knew growing up, where women would stay at home and the one of the modern world, where I get to have my children and my freedom.

"At least you're getting maternity pay from the government. I didn't think you would, what with being your own boss."

Bless big sis, she's always glad when we get to take from the system.

She rests her palm near my plate, not quite touching my hand. She's about to say something deep. "As you say, you don't need to worry about it yet. You can't predict how you'll feel when you have children. Perhaps you won't even want to go back to work."

I don't say anything as it's a debate not worth having. I know full well that I absolutely, 100%, will want to keep working.

There is a rumbling in my stomach. That's strange. I shouldn't be gassy. I've eaten plenty. It's not hunger. What is that? It's like when you go on a rollercoaster and your stomach does somersaults. Hold on, it's not my stomach doing somersaults, it's my baby! My acrobatic baby! H2 is kicking me! By the feel of it, kicking and elbowing.

"What is it, lady?" asks big sis, upon seeing me grinning like a Cheshire cat.

"It's the baby."

"Ooh, let's have a go," says sis, placing her hand on my stomach. And just like that, the kicking stops. "I can't feel anything. Perhaps little one wants to have a rest. By the way, do you know what you're having yet?"

"No, we wanted a surprise," I lie, as I won't be able to keep up the facade of letting people know I know.

Big sis slips her hand away.

"Eww, that's really weird." Little sis winces.

"It's not weird, it's actually really nice."

I'm playing down my feelings. It's not just nice. It's bloody fantastic! It's amazing. It's unbelievable. Despite being a wordsmith, I've never been one for big, flowery words, but it's beautiful. There's no other way to describe it. My baby's kicks are amazing. It's also given me the reassurance that I needed. It's filled my glass all the way to the brim. She is okay. It is okay. Everything will be okay. I've got to wait weeks until the dreaded scan to be sure but those kicks, even more than M's words, even more than my mum's, have put my mind at ease that all is okay. I can tell my friends. I can tell the world.

19th November, Telling the world

Okay, I've put it off long enough. I've dragged out this secret for as long as I could and it's come to a point that it's silly. I need to break my news to the world. I should be excited about this but there is that hovering worry about H2's little head. However, I won't really get any closure on that for a few weeks. I can't keep this pregnancy under wraps for that long.

I'm currently at my mother-in-law's, so I won't be making any lengthy phone calls. That would eat into my sous chef time and not look very good. In fact, I shouldn't be holed upstairs at all and really ought to be in the kitchen, helping with whatever dish she'll decide to make. That said, there is one person I have to call as she wouldn't allow any other way.

"You're pregnant!" squeals Sophia. "My Gosh, it only feels like the other day that we met at the charity event when you were single. I feel like I've been on this journey with you. How far along? How are you feeling? I want to hear it all!"

"I'm fine. Symptoms haven't been too bad but I'm 21 weeks now, so I'm guessing things are meant to get easier?"

"21 weeks! You blimmin' kept that quiet."

I guessed that would be Sophia's reaction. I don't blame her.

"I wasn't sure whether to say anything until everything was okay, you know? Especially with this being my first time, It seems like so much could go wrong."

"Hon, I get it. I was a lot less nervous second time around than I was when I was pregnant with Imran. The reality is, something could go wrong right up until when you give birth, which is why I decided there's no point keeping it to myself."

I say nothing.

"Oh God! I don't mean to worry you. When I say something can go wrong up until the end, that's true, but unlikely. It's just one of those things. Anything can happen. Sorry hon, you'll have to forgive me. Dealing with a newborn is exhausting. I forgot how bad it was. Plus, I've got another unhappy side-effect..."

"Oh no, what is it?" I am so focused on my pregnancy that the post-partum world is a mystery to me. "It it the sleepless nights?"

"No. Chafed nipples."

"Ouch." I recoil on my temporary bed. Sophia hasn't lost her ability to make a deadpan statement.

"You don't know the half of it, though I expect you will soon."

Again, I say nothing.

"Sorry hon. Again. Can I blame the hormones? I'm still breastfeeding round-the-clock."

"I'll let you off, then. Plus, I can't speak for long. I'm at my mother-in-law's, so better go down and show face."

"That's fine, hon. Reach out if you need any advice or anything. As you know, I've got all the books to see you through the bubba's first year of life. Also, have you put together a birth plan?"

"A birth plan? I plan to give birth. Isn't that enough?"

Sophia giggles. "There's a bit more to it than that. It's where you want to give birth and how you'd like it to be. For example, if you want any interventions."

"Oh, the midwife mentioned it to me briefly at the 12 week scan. It's not something I need to really think about now, is it?"

Sophia gasps. "You are more than halfway. It is definitely worth thinking about. You might want to go round the hospital and look at the ward. Or you could have a water birth, which was my preferred choice. It really helps with the pain. I even got to play music during labour."

"Really?"

"Yes, I played some classical music with a mix of Bollywood. It was a compilation Adnan helped me put together. You must have a birth song. Something meaningful. No gangster rap."

I couldn't imagine playing Bollywood music whilst giving birth. It's so unapologetically Asian. What would the midwives think?

"I'll add it to the list," I say, making a mental note to research some classical music. "I must ask, are sleepless nights really a thing? As in, can you literally be awake all night some nights?" I still can't believe this is quite true.

Sophia exhales sharply. "I'm not going to sugar coat it, hon. The sleepless nights are like nothing I've ever experienced. I now understand why they're used as a form of torture. But there are strategies you can adopt to make it easier. I've got all the baby books on how to sleep train and get all that stuff sorted."

I can't help but smirk. "Of course you have, Sophia."

Once we say goodbye, I open up a blank message on my phone. I'll first inform Reena.

Hey, how are you? I hope all the wedding planning is going well. I just wanted to let you know I've got news of my own, I'm pregnant! X

I don't think I need to say much more than that. I'll let her initiate the questions and be excited on my behalf.

I copy and paste the same message to send to Bushra. Just in the nick of time, I remember to omit the point about the wedding planning. That reminds me, I must check in where she is with her love life. Last I heard, she was seeing Ahmed. I'm not sure if that's still the case.

Then I remember Sonali, my old uni friend I reconnected with at Reena's hen do. I ping her the exact same message as Reena, as she's in the throes of wedding planning, too. Lazy, I know. However, as a pregnant woman who is about to head into the trenches, a.k.a. my mother-in-law's kitchen, I need to reserve all the energy I can.

While I'm at it, I'll also message Bryony, my old colleague. We are barely in touch these days, but it's a nice excuse to reach out.

My finger hovers over Julia's number. Shall I tell her like this? Doesn't she deserve a call? It's a difficult one for me to share, as I don't know how she'll feel about it. Then again, she should be happy for me, right? I don't know. I haven't got time to call her and if I meet her, with my very obvious bump, wouldn't she feel ambushed?

I start typing...

Hey, how's it going? Sorry I haven't got back to you about tennis but there's a good reason. I'm pregnant!

I delete this as the exclamation mark seems insensitive. I need to say something more. Should I include something like: *I hope you're okay with this?* No, that's stupid. Why wouldn't she be? Oh, I don't know. I don't know whether by telling her, I'm rubbing it in, whereas if I don't tell her, she'll feel kept in the dark.

That's it. No more dillydallying. I reuse Reena's message (Julia should be wedding planning, too, though her engagement will be longer) but omit the exclamation mark at the end as I don't want to sound too happy. I add another sentence:

I didn't want to say too much, as you know how superstitious I am. Plus, the scan hasn't been smooth sailing, so I want to make sure everything is okay first. However, I didn't want to keep you out of the loop any longer.

As I'm about to hit send, I wonder why I have to play down my happy news and filter my feelings to soften the blow for Julia. Is that right? Am I not tempting fate by sharing the bad news and the worry?

My finger hovers over the send button. Then I move it away.

I don't hit send. I am a wimp.

I'm not expecting a reply from any ladies, so I head downstairs. And yes, I do have more than these friends. However, everyone else falls into the random bucket of acquaintances collected over the years, so they can find out with the masses through a social media update.

I'VE COME TO DISCOVER in my five years of marriage that my mother-in-law and I don't actually have a lot to talk about. Once we've covered the scope of what to make for lunch or dinner and how the general health of my parents is, there's not much left.

My sister-in-law, perhaps courtesy of being born and raised in Bangladesh, has so much more chat about her. She talks about the food she misses from back home. She'll regale M's mum with tales of what Bengali vegetables she found at a local market. She can drop random anecdotes about people who I've likely met but don't recognise their names. She's confident in conversing in mother tongue and has plenty of material to work with. I don't have that. I can talk for England in the Queen's English, but Bangla gets me tongue tied.

As we are sat having a post-lunch cup of tea, my sister-in-law is discussing school options.

"I don't agree with all-girls schools. It doesn't feel natural. Boys and girls need to mix freely. Otherwise, and I've seen this happen in Bangladesh, the girls go crazy when they see boys."

My mother-in-law giggles girlishly, covering her mouth with her scarf. "*Nah, nah*. Mix school be better. I don't want my granddaughter going mad for boys."

I always thought that kind of conversation was off the table.

"Did you go to a mixed school?" M's sister-in-law asks me.

"Yes. I don't think they did single gender schools where I lived. That might be something more in Asian areas," I reply, unconscious bias coming to the fore.

M's sister-in-law shakes her head. "No, they have them in lots of private schools as well as the good grammar schools around where we live. Maybe they think children work better without distractions. I think it backfires. Luckily, you don't have to worry about that for a while. Anyway, how is everything with the baby?"

I receive a kick to the stomach. H2 must know we're talking about her. "She's fine."

My sister-in-law gasps. "You're having a girl?"

She's caught me off guard. "What? No! Did I say that? I mean, we don't know what gender baby we're having. We want a surprise. But the baby is fine."

My sister-in-law raises an eyebrow, knowingly. Damn, she doesn't miss a trick. Or a slip of the tongue. Mum always said people from back home are crafty. Must deflect somehow.

"To be honest, I didn't even think about asking about the gender, especially as the sonographer got me all worried."

"Why are you worried?" My mother-in-law sits up.

My father-in-law, who has been mute all this time, staring at the TV screen, turns to look at me. "Everything be okay?"

Damn. I've done it now. What did I say about struggling to rustle up conversation? I'd have done better to stay quiet.

"I'm sure it's not anything, except when they did the scan, they said the baby's head looked a bit small."

"Yalla!" My mother-in-law grips the armrest in shock, which seems a little over dramatic.

"What you say?" asks my father-in-law.

M's sister-in-law grabs my mother-in-law's hand as though she's about to fall. "Ignore them!" she shouts. "Ignore them with all this silliness. They just say stuff, unnecessary things that make you worry. For my pregnancies, both times, they told me my babies were small."

I suddenly feel better. "And they didn't turn out small, did they?"

M's sister-in-law bites her lip. "They were a bit small but it wasn't a worry or a bad thing like they were making out. They just do these things to scare you. I don't know why. Silly sonographers."

My mother-in-law grabs at her chest as if she's having palpitations. I think she may have been watching too many Asian TV serials, where the matriarchs are nothing if not theatrical. "What is this small head business? What could it mean?"

My sister-in-law continues to stroke her hand, saying: "It's nothing. It's silly. Don't worry."

Meanwhile, I'm sitting here with the baby in my belly that might have a small head. A little bit of hand stroking my way wouldn't go amiss.

My father-in-law returns his gaze to the Bangla news. "Just pray," he says. "Just pray it will be all okay. You need to read namaz and he needs to read namaz, too. It make everything better. Everything is part of a bigger plan."

That's the most words I've heard from my father-in-law in a while. Like my dad, he doesn't say much, but when he does, he makes it count.

"Did you keep any fasts this Ramadan?" my mother-in-law asks me.

"No, I'm exempt, aren't I?"

"You can still do some fasting when you're pregnant. Extra reward."

My sister-in-law rolls her eyes. "You don't need to fast," she mumbles.

Of course I don't, I think to myself. It's just M's mum being extra.

In the nick of time, M comes in to witness the hysterics.

"What's going on?"

"What she saying?" His mum points at me, index finger trembling. "Your baby have small head?"

M looks ambushed, understandably. "Oh, that. It's nothing. We're going to get her re-checked as we're having a scan in a couple of weeks."

"Her?" my sister-in-law asks, with another raised eyebrow.

M looks nervous.

"A couple of weeks? How I will I sleep for two weeks? Get them to see you sooner," says M's mum, blissfully unaware that the NHS is on its knees.

"I can't believe you'll be a dad soon. I still remember you cradling my girl for hours on end."

M grins. "I'd sit on the front doorstep in the summer and hold her all day."

"It was great for me. Free babysitting." M's sister-in-law laughs in my direction. "He was so good with my girl, so you can be confident he'll be great with yours."

"I worry how you'll cope over there by yourself," says M's mum, adding another stress to her already distressed self.

M's sister-in-law, who's now taken to kneading our mother-in-law's arm in a sort of massage, adds: "It is hard on your own. I'm glad I had my first here, as you need family around."

Hold up, what's she getting at? Why is she hinting, in front of my in-laws, no less, that we're better off up north once the baby arrives? That's the last thing I want. Moving back up north might mean more hands to hold the baby but it doesn't mean I'll be hands free. I'll have to do my fair share of helping around the kitchen to earn my keep. After all, there is no such thing as a free lunch. Or free childcare.

That's got me really annoyed. How dare M's sister-in-law imply something she wouldn't want for herself? She is miles away from her in-laws with her own freedom. Would she really want to give that up to make samosas on tap at my mother-in-law's? I doubt it. So why suggest it for me? We'll be just fine down south after having baby H2, thank you very much.

Right, we need a change of subject. Something that will rouse my mother-in-law from her Shakespearean, wrist-wringing melancholy, deflect from any unintended gender reveals or suggestions of relocation. It's a tall order.

"Shall we make soy fita?" is the first thing that pops out of my mouth.

Now it's M's sister-in-law's turn to look nervous. She knows full well that she'll get lumbered with most of the work. I see her eyes dart around for a diversion.

"*Maa*, I love your *khombol*. I wish I had it," she says in haste.

I beg your pardon? Did M's sister-in-law just compliment my mother-in-law's bum? I mean, I know she's a bit of an arse kisser but surely that's taking things a bit far? She reaches over to a thick floral handcrafted blanket folded up on the sofa headrest. "Such a nice *khombol*."

I stifle a laugh as best as I can. What is happening? Am I delirious? Is it mum brain? Why does she keep complimenting M's mum's derriere?

M comes over to me and whispers: "*Khombol* is also blanket in Bengali, not just bum."

So, being ill can be code for being on your period, or pregnant, or literally unwell. And apparently the word khombol has dual meaning.

I hear the door slam, then M's big brother, little brother and sister stroll in.

Since when do they have outings together? I look to M for signs of jealousy.

"Where did you all go?" M asks, eyes twitching.

Yep, he's jealous.

"We went to the Trafford Centre. I needed some new work shoes." M's big brother puts down a couple of paper shopping bags.

"And some more things, I see," his wife teases. "I hope there's something for me in there."

M's big brother looks guilty as he puts his hands in his pockets. He's likely forgotten to buy her anything.

"I tagged along as I needed some new trousers. Casual ones for the weekend," says M's little brother.

"And I just went to escape the smell of *shutki sheera*," M's little sister adds, wrinkling up her nose at the smell of smoked fish, which has made its way into the living room. She then looks around the room, wide-eyed. She knows something's gone down but doesn't want to ask. I don't blame her.

"What's happened?" The question is left to M's little brother.

My mother-in-law's face contorts. "She – she said the baby's head be small!"

"Which baby?" he asks.

"*Dooro!* Who else baby? Their baby. Your nephew or niece. Why would head be small? Will that mean small brain?"

"Ah..." M's big brother looks down as he heads into the kitchen, clearly as awkward as my family are about discussing my pregnancy, as this would acknowledge that M and I are having sexual relations. "It'll be okay," he says, based on no intelligence whatsoever. He then uncovers the various pots and pans, releasing yet more pungent aromas into the atmosphere.

Despite her clear upset, M's mother doesn't stop mothering. "Make sure you eat everything!" she shouts towards the kitchen. "I made fish and beef curry."

It's like the scene from a play. My mother-in-law is still wound up with worry, my sister-in-law is kneading away like a massage therapist, while M's little sister is trying to tiptoe out of the room unnoticed.

The men, however, are carrying on with business as usual. M's dad is watching the telly, his big brother has loaded his plate with rice and curry, and his younger brother is holding up a pair of khaki cargo pants against his waist.

"Do you like these?" he asks anyone who'll listen. "They were in the sale, innit?"

M's family... they are a funny bunch.

WHILE M SNORES AWAY, I'm finding it difficult to get into a comfortable position. I try sleeping on my side but that doesn't work. When I try to sleep on my back, it feels like all the weight of the baby and her surrounding water is pressing into my spine. Obviously, sleeping on my front is out of the question now.

My phone pings. It's Reena:

Oh my days, that's amazing news. I had a feeling you were up the duff. Your boobs were huge the last time I saw you. P.S. The wedding invite is on its way to you. Not long now!

Damn, I'll be heavily pregnant at Reena's wedding. I've no idea if I'll find an outfit that fits. Can you even get desi maternity wear?

25th November, Work woes

M is late home from work today. Later than he's ever been. Though he whined about his previous job, he always got home before eight. He's barely started his contracting gig and is already working overtime.

"I was about to start eating without you," I say, as he comes through the door and drops his laptop bag on the floor.

"Sorry babe, it was the new boss, Karen. She's a bit of a ball buster."

"More than the last one?"

M huffs. "A different kind of ball buster. Lucinda was more of a micromanaging type. Always on my back, always bringing me things last minute. She was proper flustered all the time. Karen leaves me to it but decides to check on my work at the end of the day and always finds fault. She did the same thing today as I was about to leave."

"That's not good. Is she like that with everyone?"

"She used to be. One of the girls I work with, Becca, said that she gave her grief at the beginning but now she's been there a while so she's earned Karen's respect." M sighs. "It looks like I've got to tough it out for a bit."

He reaches into the kitchen cupboard and retrieves some biscuits. I'm not sure why. Dinner is about to be served. Then I remember, it's chickpea curry. His least favourite of my dishes.

M plonks himself down on the sofa next to me.

"Are you okay?" I say, reaching for his hand.

"I'm fine. It's just... harder than expected. They want me to go to Bradford soon."

"Oh." I sit up. "You could go and see my sister while you're at it!"

M looks at me, dumbfounded.

"I'm joking! Obviously, you can't visit my sister without me. That would be well weird. Like if I hung out with your older brother, how random would that be?"

M suddenly sits up, too, like a man with a plan. "I was actually thinking that. Not me going to see your sister, obviously. Or you hanging out with my brother. But the meeting's on a Friday, so technically you could come up to your sister's while I'm there."

I love how M's always enthusiastic about making things happen but he needn't take my flippant suggestion seriously. "I was kidding. How would I even get to Bradford? I don't fancy the train journey with this belly."

"I could speak to Jam because, rather conveniently, he started seeing a girl near there. I think she's from Keighley. That's near Bradford. He can run you up after work and I can meet you at your sister's."

I hesitate so M fills the silence, for a change. "I'm just thinking it might make the best of a crap situation. Also, your days going up north in general will be numbered, won't they?"

"True, but is it a bit inappropriate if I travel up without you, just with Jam?"

"Why? It's better than getting on a train with a bunch of strangers."

I turn very Bengali. "It's just... I don't know how my family would feel about me travelling alone with another man."

M smirks. "It's not another man. It's Jam! And to be honest with ya, if I don't have a problem and I'm your husband, why would anyone else? When it comes to safety, especially in your condition, I'd rather you travelled with him in a car, than sit in cattle class on the train."

M does have a point, though it's at odds with the notion deeply ingrained in me, that you cannot, and should not, travel alone with a man. I'll need to give it some thought.

"Let me know what you think." M reads my mind. "Then I can tell Jam in advance. He'd love an excuse to see that girl. He's talking like she's the one. Though he has had many ones."

"Are you sure he won't mind? It is a big ask."

"He'll be fine. The number of things I've done for him... he owes me. Anyway, it's a win-win. He gets to see his girl, you get to see your sister. Then, maybe if we're not too knackered, we can go to your mum's and mine. I might catch up with some of the other guys. Bilal has been asking for ages to meet up. I think it's 'cause he wants to get in the contracting game, too, and wants to pick my brains. Though I'm not sure I'd recommend it." M sits back into the sofa, or, should I say, it's swallowed him up.

He's given me a lot to unpack. Firstly, he does a lot more for his friends than I would ever do. Julia and I never make long distance trips for each other. M says that guys do more for their mates than girls do. I don't think it's as simple as that. I think guys have more freedom from the outset. He and Jam can make cross-country trips willy-nilly in the middle of the night. There's less accountability for them. For us girls? We have mothers, fathers, in-laws and every other family member wanting to know our whereabouts. And, truthfully, while I like to see myself as a modern British-Bengali woman, the reality is a lot of these feelings that have been passed down from mum are also deeply entrenched in me. I don't want to do a late night drive from the south to the north of the country. I feel best when I'm at home. My reasoning could also be to do with coming from a white area and living by the rule that good girls don't go out when it's dark. How my parents hoodwinked me with that one for years. It's only when I moved away to university that I realised that Asian girls don't turn into pumpkins if they're out after hours. I also realised that many girls have the freedoms that were curtailed for me.

The second thing is easier to unpack.

"The work thing, it will get easier," I say.

M throws his head back, resting his neck on the back of the sofa. His eyes are closed. "I hope so."

It has to, I think to myself. *Now more than ever, you need to suck it up and endure your work, as mine is going to be coming to a pause very soon.*

27th November, Dinner with Julia

"You won't bloody believe it, mate!" Reena shouts down the phone.

"Believe what?" I ask, whilst adding a spoon of mango pickle to the sautéed onions.

"Bloody Sonali's wedding is on the same day as mine! What are the odds? I sent my card to her -" she pauses, "on that note, did you get my invite?"

Did I get Reena's invite? I recall seeing a blood red card with various inserts and pictures of men on horseback, flanked by elephants. Oh crap, that was Sonali's invite! And I RSVP'd to say I would attend. Crap. Crap. Crap. Mustn't mention this to Reena while she's spiralling.

"I'll have to double check with M, sorry. Mum brain, or pregnant brain, has got the better of me."

"Well, I'll let you know now... it's on the 28th December. Are you free then?"

"Erm... I..."

"Come on, man. I know you're not that busy. It's not like you celebrate Christmas so will be attending lots of parties." Reena laughs, though there's a hint of nervous anticipation.

"I'm sure I am free. You know me, I never plan my weekends that far in advance."

"Fine. Just check and let me know ASAP, yeah? His mum's already giving me grief about finalising numbers. I'm like, what the fuck can I do when every man and his dog from India wants to come but hasn't confirmed? And how come she's still waiting on her side's numbers? The old hag..."

Oh dear.

"Anyway, I sent the invite to Sonali and she told me she won't be able to attend because it's her wedding the same day. Next thing, she sends me an invite to hers! Like I'm gonna skip my own big day to go to her wedding! Is she mad?"

"Maybe her card was also in the post before you spoke?"

"Yeah but she never brought up her wedding day once. Even when I was messaging her about makeup artists and whatnot. She never said a word."

"Did you?"

"Did I what?" Reena doesn't sound like she's in the mood for reasoning.

"Look, if Gujarati weddings are like Bengali affairs, the bride rarely has a say in the matter of setting the date."

"Hmm," says Reena. "Well, make sure you come to mine, yeah? It's not like you knew her that well."

Now it's my turn to say: "Hmm."

I say goodbye as M comes into the flat, having returned from the shops. "Right, I got everything you asked for but they didn't have pre-fried onions in the supermarket, so I had to go the Asian shop on Brick Lane for that." He lays the bags down on the floor, before realising that I'm too pregnant to bend down and reach them. He then lifts them onto the counter and starts taking the groceries out. "I had to check in three different shops. That's why I'm a bit late."

"Aww, what a mission. Anyway, we got bigger fish to fry."

"Don't tell me you're making a fish curry, as well? Your morphing into my mum," M teases.

"Not literal fish, thankfully. Julia would not like the smell. I've double booked myself. Reena and Sonali are getting married on the same day. I've already RSVP'd to Sonali but I obviously can't miss Reena's wedding. So I don't know what to do. Would it be truly awful if I retracted my RSVP to Sonali? I feel bad even thinking it but Reena wouldn't forgive me if I missed her wedding to attend someone else's who I'm barely in touch with."

"It would be a bit rubbish to cancel on her. Where are the weddings?"

"They're both in London. I'm not sure exactly where," I reply, as I tend to leave the logistics and driving to my husband.

M rests his hand on my shoulder. "Don't worry. We'll figure it out. We might be able to attend both."

"What? How?" I stroke my belly. "That would be way too much, wouldn't it?"

"Maybe, but we've done crazier things before. Leave it with me, I'll make it happen. Anyway, before that, you've got another friend situation to deal with, haven't you?"

M KEEPS SNIGGERING to himself.

"Sorry, babe. I can't help it. It's like you're hosting the prospective in-laws of your unborn child, with the amount of effort you're making. I don't even think your mum did as much for me when I first came round to yours."

"I'll have you know, mum was rolling samosas for days before your arrival. She even introduced spring rolls to the menu." I take the towel off his shoulder. "Anyway, less sniggering, more cooking. Did you stir the roast?"

"I did, though I didn't have anyone to talk about. I guess I should've just stirred the pot about Julia and Miles making my pregnant wife cook a feast." M peers into the deep pot of Bengali roast chicken. "Will Miles even be able to handle this amount of spice? It's not a lot for us, but for him..."

"Don't worry, I've got some yoghurt on standby if things get too hot."

Another smirk from M. "You really have thought of everything, haven't you? Pulling out all the stops for our royal guests."

As I reach for a tin can to scoop out the rice, my stomach brushes against M's back.

"You won't even need to announce that you're pregnant. She will be able to see for herself."

I look down. My growing baby is apparently the size of a mango, according to my trusty app. M is right, I won't need to announce it at all. I couldn't look more pregnant if I tried. I hope Julia won't be annoyed at how long I've left it. I hope she understands my reasons.

As I spread out the coasters on the coffee table, I get another look from M. Okay, maybe I'm making a little extra effort than usual. But these days I don't host much (unless you count Jam), so it's nice to create a fuss. Also, I am hoping that delicious food softens any ill feeling Julia may have.

The doorbell rings. My heartbeat quickens. Why am I so worried about this? I'm being ridiculous. I know I am. Julia will be thrilled for me. Any friend would. Just as I would've been for her if it were the other way round.

M opens the door and ushers Julia and Miles through our tiny hallway into our open plan, kitchen/living room/dining room situation. I keep my body turned away from them. I now realise that it is going to be a huge reveal, which is exactly what I didn't want. I lift the heavy tagine pot, in which I transferred the roast chicken, and hold it in front of my midriff. I carefully carry the pot over to the table, keeping it in front of my stomach for as long as possible.

"Hello you," says Julia with an intrigued smile.

This is it. This is it. I'll have to put the pot down and she is going to discover my secret. As I lower the terracotta tagine down on the coffee table, all eyes are on my belly. Even M's, which doesn't make sense as he should know I'm pregnant by now. He had a hand in the matter.

Julia's eyebrows rise.

I can't tell if the look of shock is laced with happiness or jealousy. Stop it! I must stop reading into everything. Of course she's not jealous. Of course she'll be happy for me. These bloody hormones are driving me potty! Making me think the worst. I need to get a grip.

"Congratulations?" says Miles with enough of an upward inflection at the end to suggest it's more of a question than a declaration.

Julia blinks as if waking from a daze. "God, yes. That's amazing! Oh, come on, let me give you a hug."

This time, Julia can only just about get her arms around my shoulders for an embrace, as there is a baby mango between us.

I WISH I HADN'T MADE curry. Miles keeps reaching for his glass of water, his face getting pinker with each mouthful. Worse still, M is eating with his hands. That's right, eating with his hands, the proper Bangladeshi way. He's scooping up little mounds of rice mixed with curry. Miles can't stop staring at the spectacle, as though he's observing feeding time at the zoo.

I'm sticking to a tablespoon, though I'm sure M will call me out on that later. I admire his comfort in his own skin. It's something I've never possessed. However, a little restraint would be nice.

"How's the new job going?" Julia asks M.

"It's alright," he replies. "Though it's hard work." He reaches for some Mr Naga chilli pickle. "Want to try some?" M offers the spoon to Miles.

"I wouldn't." I say, lowering M's arm. "Not unless you want to spend the night on the toilet."

Julia grimaces.

"I'll pass for now," says Miles. "However, I would like to confirm that I can take my heat. I had an arrabbiata the other night and it didn't blow my head off." He guffaws.

M and I smile, knowing full well that a spicy arrabbiata and a pickle made entirely of scotch bonnet chill are two very different things.

"Anyway," M continues, "they get their pound of flesh with contracting. You're dropped in at the deep end without any induction. They just expect you to know it all."

"It's a bit like that with freelancing," I say. "Because they're paying you by the hour, they don't want you learning on the job. They expect you to know."

I'm not sure why I said that. Looking at Julia and Miles as they give each other side glances, they're not sure, either. I realise I sounded more combative than I needed to. I forget that M was previously with the same company for years. I however, am used to change. I've had to sink or swim and I've learnt to adapt accordingly. Therefore, M's gripes don't mean much to me.

"A few of my colleagues are contractors and, frankly, we're all jealous, as they get paid twice as much as us. Come to think of it, there are always contracting opportunities where we are. So, if ever you fancied a change..."

M looks up from his hot and fiery plate. "Yeah, I'll let you know. It's always good to keep options open."

It bloody isn't, I think. *Not when you've already moved jobs during your wife's pregnancy. We need stability, not change.* I force a smile as I struggle to separate the chicken from its bone. This isn't really the job for a tablespoon.

"Do you want a hand?" M reaches over and dismantles the roast leg. "It looks like I'll have two children to look after." He laughs.

"That's an art in itself." Julia marvels as M leaves no flesh attached to the bone, before pushing my plate back to me.

M rolls his shoulders back, proud. "You should see me in Nando's. I don't leave any chicken behind. I even managed to pull off the veins and cartilage."

Miles looks with a mix of awe and disgust, Julia winces, while I say nothing.

I note that Julia and Miles' plates are far more populated than M's and mine. Oh well, at least the salad is a hit. Julia reaches for the bowl a second time. "This tastes amazing. Are they heirloom tomatoes?"

M shrugs. "Dunno, to be honest with ya. I got the good ones that are darker and still attached to the vine. They're always much nicer in salad. Plus, they were reduced as the sell by date was today, so I thought, why not?"

"Hmm." Julia looks down at her salad as though she's lost her appetite, prodding at the cut-price tomatoes.

Has M always been this embarrassing? Or are my senses heightened with pregnancy? I'll have to have a word with him later.

"What are you going to do when you go off on maternity leave? Regarding your clients?" asks Julia.

"I've started putting the feelers out for freelancers, to see if someone can cover my work. A couple of people have got back to me so I'm going to interview them to see if they could be a good fit."

"Amazing!" Julia exclaims with genuine surprise. "It's like you're your own little agency."

"That's the dream," I say, not sure if her statement was flattering or condescending. Never mind, it's probably my hormones again, making me overthink.

I serve up Julia's cheesecake for dessert, while M takes one for the team by foregoing his beloved football to watch a game of golf on the TV with Miles.

"Now I see why you didn't want to play tennis," says Julia, prodding my side gently.

"I'm sorry about that. When you brought it up, it was way too early for me to tell anyone. And then, as time progressed, I've been a bit superstitious about the whole thing. I was nervous to tell people because you know how much of a worrier I am. Also, I didn't want to upset you, as I know how it's been for you. What with the..." I hesitate.

"Miscarriage?" Julia fills in the blanks.

I look down at my stomach. "I'm so sorry about that. I just wasn't sure whether you'd feel... I didn't know how you'd feel about my news. I didn't want to rub it in."

Julia offers a wry smile. "I was thinking the other day, how we've known each other for nearly 30 years."

I gasp. "Has it been that long?"

"A couple of years off, but yeah. I'm 33 now. We met each other when we were five. Basically, it's a lifetime." She strokes my arm. "Don't mistake my sad feelings for anything other than that. They're just sad feelings. I'm allowed to be sad for myself but happy for you at the same time."

I grasp Julia's hand, glad and relieved I've been able to tell her. I don't mention the scan scare. I don't tell her about my baby's head. I think the more voice I give to these concerns, the more real they may become.

I CAN'T HELP IT.

I can't stop refreshing my Facebook feed to see all the messages coming in thick and fast from friends, acquaintances and randoms congratulating me on my pregnancy. There was even a comment from my old classmate, Jim. I'm pretty sure he was racist in school.

He's put: *Congratulations! That's lovely news x*

I didn't know 'lovely' was a word in his vocabulary. He was more grunting and thuggish from what I remember. I'm sure he got expelled in our final year. Regardless, it seems that baby news melts the most menacing of hearts.

Now that I've told Julia, I've been emboldened to share with the world. And it feels great. All these people, who I've known through various parts of my life, are all basking in my good news. I've never felt so popular. It's scary that I am taking so much enjoyment from praise via social media. I know it only takes people a second to congratulate and I know that shouldn't be the barometer of happiness. But by God, it's like a shot of sunshine. I guess this is what makes social media so addictive. We want more. We need more. We are fed and satiated through the acknowledgement of others. While I deride it at the best of times, tonight, I'm happily complying.

10th December, A new friend

"We're actual neighbours! I never realised," I say to the Bengali lady I saw at the bus stop with her toddler.

It's all a lie. I had discovered that she lived on the same floor as me, a while back. I saw her leaving her flat and going into the lift but I was so far behind, my pregnant arse couldn't get to her in time.

"Oh." She looks at me in surprise. "Which number are you?"

"I'm at 45," I reply. "Further back that way."

"That's probably why I never see you," she says. "I'm right by the lift and usually hotfooting in and out with my kids. Though today it's just me and this little guy." She smiles down at Hamza, who looks ready for the outdoors in his fur-lined parka. "The older two are at school."

She has three kids? In these tiny apartments? I have so many questions. How do they make it work? Who shares rooms with whom? How do they survive in such close quarters without getting on each other's nerves?

As she presses the lift button, she looks down at my bump. "Can I say congratulations? How far along are you?"

I momentarily forgot I'm pregnant. I've been carrying H2 round for so long it feels like my permanent state of being.

"Oh, yes... thank you. I'm about six months." I've decided that it's too complicated to keep track of the weeks now.

"Gosh, I remember those days. How are you feeling? Any symptoms?"

"Nothing major, though I have been craving tamarind lately. I'm not sure if it's a full-on craving as I like tamarind, anyway. It has to be in block form, extra salty and sour."

She closes her eyes and licks her lips. "Throughout my three pregnancies, I was craving sour fruit. I didn't care what it was. Grapefruit, gooseberries... the more sour the better. If you want tamarind, the grocery store in Whitechapel is your best bet."

"That's where I'm headed now. I need my fix."

"Same," she says, pushing her pram through the lift before the door closes. "I'm going to Barking to see my in-laws but I'll be getting the Tube from Whitechapel."

"How do you manage with a pram?"

She looks at me, confused.

"As in, how do you manage those stairs? Most Tube stations don't have lifts."

She adjusts her hijab in the mirror. "Honestly, if I wait long enough, someone will help me take the pram down the stairs." She lets her boy press the button for the ground floor. "That's his job now. If I press it, there's hell to pay. I'm Taslima, by the way."

That's it. I've made my first Bengali friend.

As we walk down to Whitechapel High Street, Taslima shares her pregnancy nightmares. She had morning sickness so severe that she had to be hospitalised. She also had prenatal diabetes, which meant she couldn't indulge in comforting foods like chocolate and cream cakes. Once again, I feel grateful that my symptoms have been relatively mild. Apart from the odd aches and pains and sudden feelings of nausea, I can't complain.

She tells me how she trained as a teacher but then fell pregnant and decided to swap work for motherhood. She seems happy with her lot, content.

I tell her our families are up north and I'm worried about how we will raise the baby without their support. She offers reassurances, reminding me that she lives on the same floor so can be called upon if I need anything. That's a huge comfort. Not just because we live in an anonymous apartment block where you rarely see the same face twice but because she's been through it. She's a Bengali woman who knows the ins and outs of our community and culture, whilst also understanding the challenges of being a modern mum.

We also discuss Ramadan. She says she cooked for at least two hours most nights, satisfying her husband and children's samosa and pakora cravings. I count my blessings once again, as M is so easy-going when it comes to food. He was happy to have spiced chickpeas and kisuri, which he mostly made himself. When he had a samosa craving, he'd go to the shop and get it. Speaking to Taslima, I can't tell whether it's a tradition she has carried on from her mum or mother-in-law, or a job she has created off her own back. I don't know if most men expect it. I wonder whether it's a given that she will do more cooking because she's not working. Is that how it is? Is there a scale, with work on one side and housework on the other, and if one empties, the other one fills? I imagine that's what it is.

We say our goodbyes and Taslima walks towards the Tube station, standing at the bottom of the stairs. I watch as a rush of commuters stream past. One guy, dressed casually in jeans and a bomber jacket, helps her lift the pram up the short flight of stairs to platform level. Perhaps she's right, you wait long enough and someone will help you. Maybe getting the Tube with the pram won't be so bad. I mean, every mum in London does it.

I head to my next stop, the Bengali food store, which has everything from meat, to yoghurts, crisps, and an array of herbs and spices. Nestled between the various dried goods and canned foods is the pregnancy snack of dreams– a block of tamarind. Sticky, sweet, sour, and salty, it's like a flavour explosion in my mouth and I need it right now. I grab two packs because, you know, cravings. While I'm there, I queue up to get some chicken for tonight's dinner. The queue in front of me is long, with many shoppers, young, old, male, female, and all Bengali. They have baskets full of coriander, fresh ginger, garlic, tomatoes, and jars of pickles.

I go to this store quite regularly and always have the same thought. I never quite fit in with the rest of the clientele. Everyone speaks mother tongue and most women look like housewives, hurrying home to make the night's dinner. The men are often dressed in a panjabi and speaking with an accent that suggests they are from back home. It's funny that the shop is about eight minutes' walk from my flat, yet it seems like another world.

Whenever I come here, or browse the wares at Whitechapel market, and a non-Bengali person walks past, I find myself speaking loudly, confidently in the Queen's English. It's like, subconsciously, I want to separate myself from the masses. I want the random white person who walks past to know that I am British-born, fluent in English and educated. I don't know why I do that. I think there is a major, down-low issue of displacement that I should tackle at some point.

My phone rings. It's Bushra.

"Well hello there, stranger," I say. "It's nice to hear from you after the two-word reply you sent in response to my pregnancy announcement."

"I'll have you know, it wasn't a two-word reply. I said 'I'm so happy for you' and included an 'x', so that's five words. Or six, if you count the 'x'."

"Which you shouldn't, it's not a word," I tease.

"Whatever, it's an expression. Or is it a statement? Sod it. I don't know. You're the PR person. Anyway, I'm sorry I've been rubbish. I was meaning to call you. So here I am, ringing to say congratulations on getting up the duff."

I stifle a giggle. The lady in front of me, dressed in a grey burka and holding a basket full of cake rusks, looks back at me to see what was so funny.

"Thank you, that's the nicest thing I've heard."

"When are you due?"

"April and, yes, I know the date off by heart. I know exactly how far along I am and how big my baby is. It's nearly the size of an aubergine. Its eyelids should be opening right now for the first time."

"Okay, okay. I don't need a life story. Seriously though, man, that's well exciting. I can't imagine having an aubergine inside me. Actually, I can imagine *something* like that."

Bushra laughs. She is so childish.

"Spare me the details. Speaking of aubergines, are you still speaking to Ahmed?"

Yes, I can be childish, too.

Bushra hesitates. "Yeah, we've been speaking and sort of seeing each other. Don't judge!"

"Why would I judge? I told you, if you like Ahmed, it doesn't matter what anybody else thinks."

"I know but I still wonder whether I'm seeing him for the right reasons, or if it's because I just want to meet a nice Pakistani boy."

Despite my pregnancy brain, I do have some pearls of wisdom to impart. "The two don't have to be mutually exclusive. When I was looking to get married, I wanted to meet a nice Bengali boy. There's nothing wrong with it. You just have to make sure you like him enough to make it work."

"That's the thing. I was out the other night. I don't know why I bothered. I didn't even enjoy it. Emma and the other girls got hammered, as always. Anyway, I bumped into this guy I was seeing. Actually, you probably wouldn't even call it seeing. You know me, we met up a few times. So I'm there in the club, slightly out of it but nothing happened, just so you know. But I caught myself watching him. I was having a good old perv. It made me think, if I'm still looking at other blokes, is that fair on Ahmed? Does that mean he won't be enough for me?"

"Bushra, everybody looks. They just don't admit it."

"Do you?"

"Okay, well everybody except me. But I am heavily pregnant so these days I don't even look at my own husband. It's too much effort."

"Right, I guess you fall into the category of not admitting it. I was thinking of you, though. I remember you told me you didn't fancy M in the beginning. Then your mate talked some sense into you about how you shouldn't be just looking at looks. Give it time to fancy the pants off him. Do you fancy him now?"

"Bushra, if I've not mentioned before, I'll say it again. I'm pregnant. It wasn't an immaculate conception. So yeah, I do like my husband a bit, for the most part. Look, if Ahmed is the one for you, you'll know soon enough. Also, it's a good sign that you didn't do anything with the guy. Did he try it on?"

Bushra huffs. "No, he didn't see me. If he did, he'd obviously be all over me. That's the other thing. In all the times I've met up with Ahmed, he's not tried anything. Not even a cheeky feel via a hug. I feel really... What's the word?"

"Respected?"

"That's the one. No guys I've been with have been that patient with me before. But I still wonder if it's a compromise. I also... and don't judge me... worry what people will think."

I can empathise with her. I was concerned what my family would think about M's lack of hair. It seems ridiculous now but it worried me at the time. "Bushra, don't pass him up because of other people. Have you told anyone, like Emma or your family?"

"I've mentioned him to my mum. Obviously, she's super excited and wants to meet his family but I'd rather take it slow and really be sure. And also make sure I do fancy him and I'm not just like super horny because it's been a while."

"Yes, if it's just horny-ness, that won't do," I say.

"Sorry sister?" The man behind the meat counter looks up at me, confused.

I hadn't even realised I'd reached the front of the queue.

"Oh, sorry, I mean can I get one baby chicken, cut into small pieces, please?"

IT'S DARK WHEN I STEP back out onto Whitechapel High Street. The market sellers are packing away their wares. Men are loading vans up with boxes of fruit, vegetables, and yards of fabric. A bunch of people walk past me dressed as elves, fairies and sexy santas. It's a bit early for Christmas celebrations, isn't it? They stand out from everyone else in this predominantly Bengali area, who are dressed in civilian clothes.

The East London Mosque delivers its rousing call to prayer. The group of festive revellers head to the nearby pub. Unwilling to wait until I get home, I unwrap the plastic, free the tamarind and take a bite. A piece of shell is nestled within the smooth, silky brown flesh. I don't mind, this is bliss. Tangy enough for my cravings and sour enough to almost lacerate my tongue. Again, I don't mind. I don't mind at all.

H2 gives me the gentlest of kicks in my stomach. Some mums have told me they found their baby's kicking painful.

That they've been whacked right on their bladder. I enjoy the little movements from my tiny acrobat. My rotating aubergine is dancing like a synchronised swimmer in my womb. I stroke her gently. Another kick, or is it an elbow? It's something. It's a tiny protruding limb pressing against my palm.

There's the call to prayer in one ear, the sound of clinking glasses in the other, the stampede from commuters bursting out from the Tube station and my baby dancing to the beat of it all. Right now, on this cold day, my tastebuds are satiated, my belly is full. I feel truly content.

12th December, Dinner with middle sis

"What's the most embarrassing thing that's ever happened to you when you were younger?" asks Jam, interrupting the few minutes of awkward silence as we begin our journey from London to Bradford, minus my husband.

It doesn't take me long to think of my answer. "A few school friends, who were all white, obviously, used to knock on to see if I wanted to go to the park. I would never be allowed out as mum and dad didn't like it. Anyway, one day I was chatting with them at my front door, when my dad comes out of a taxi with a 20kg sack of Tolly Boy long grain rice on his shoulder. He plonks it down on our doorstep, and shouts: "What do you want?" to my friends. They were trying not to piss themselves laughing, while I was mortified. Story of my life, really. Always embarrassed, always different in one way or another."

Oops. I hadn't anticipated being that vulnerable with Jam.

"What about you?" I'm hoping the deflection helps.

Jam shakes his hair from his eyes, keeping his gaze fixed on the road ahead. "I didn't have any issues around being a minority. Where I'm from, everyone is Bengali. My thing was usually around money. Having loads of brothers and sisters, money was spread more thinly. We never had the best trainers or bikes but then everyone was skint."

"I always thought you guys were quite comfortable, from what M's said. Your dad had a business, right?"

"He did but he wasn't the best at spending on us. Most of it went back home. I think M says we're comfy because we had a slightly bigger house than most people. My dad made sure of that, so people could see we'd done well in that sense. It mattered what people thought. But yeah, I guess some people were worse off. From the outside, we probably looked like we were okay. I suppose M just saw what he wanted to see."

I think about that for a minute. Isn't that something we all do? We see what we want to see? Or what we've been conditioned to? We always think someone else is better off, more attractive, has a better life. The grass is always greener. Yet, we only see a snippet and never the full picture.

"Are you hungry, by the way?" Jam asks.

That's nice of him. Especially given that he won't be eating. To my surprise, Jam is doing an additional, voluntary fast in honour of the Hajj pilgrimage currently taking place. I never thought Jam was that religious. There I go again, unconscious biasing but I can't help myself. I certainly didn't expect it to occur to him to ask whether I needed food.

I say no, as I'd feel awful eating in front of him. He's not M. Though I wish I was with my husband right now and he wasn't already in Bradford for work. I'm absolutely starving and I would happily stop off at a service station for some chips.

Instead, Jam puts his foot down, weaving through the motorway traffic a little quicker than I would like. I wish I'd sat in the back. I did contemplate it for a second, being a married Bengali lady taking a journey with my husband's single Bengali friend. Then I shook off my mum's thoughts and reminded myself that M insisted on this little jaunt. Plus, Jam would think it odd if I sat in the back of the car, while there is an empty passenger seat in the front.

H2 is doing another somersault in my belly. She's pressing down on my bladder now. Bloody hell! That came out of nowhere. The urge to pee comes thick and fast. God, what can I do?

"Do you know how far off the next service station is?"

Jam looks at the signs we whizz past. "The next one isn't for a couple of miles. Is that okay? Are you alright?"

"Yeah, I'm fine. I could just use the bathroom. Pregnancy makes you... never mind."

I don't really want to share too much information with Jam. He's got all this to come, therefore I'd rather not sully his opinion on women by revealing that we have weak bladders when expecting. I cross my legs and squeeze my pelvic floor, which I don't think is the wisest thing to do as it may cause a urinary tract infection but needs must.

Sitting for a long time in a car isn't comfortable, either. Not least because Jam's bashed up BMW isn't much younger than me. The threadbare fabric seats are worn down from the weight of too many bums. The recliner is stiff. The headrest is way too high and it doesn't go down anymore because it's knackered, apparently. I don't get how someone who earns so much money as a contractor doesn't get a nicer vehicle. Speaking of which...

"I think M's having a hard time with his new contracting gig," says Jam.

"It seems so." I nod, unsure of how much to divulge, as I don't know what's been shared with Jam. Then I remember, it's Jam. M has obviously shared everything. Perhaps more intel than he's given me.

"I've told him he's got to show his worth. M is more of a quiet, get your head down and get it done, type. When you're contracting, it's a dog's game. You have to blatantly demonstrate what you've done. Send emails and copy everyone in. Don't do things quietly, as someone else will take the credit for it." Jam looks at me for my reaction but I give away nothing. "It can be like that, you know. You need to get in with the right people early on. A lot of times, people aren't hired or kept on because of their work. It's about making sure they fit in."

"He's certainly been trying. And putting in the hours."

"It's not even about that. You can come in at 7am and leave at 7pm but if nobody knows what you're doing in that time, it means nothing. At my place, I've seen people rock up in the morning, log on and then go straight online to do some shopping or read the news. They'll get their work done quickly but won't send it until the end of the day so it looks like they've been working on it for ages. As much as I hate to say it, you have to be like that. Play the game."

As much as *I* hate to say it, Jam has some rather sage advice. Who'd have thought it?

I know I shouldn't but sometimes I wish M had a more go-getting streak about him. Don't get me wrong, I love my lovable snail. His relaxed nature means he's relaxed with me. He calms me down, brings out my glass half full nature and nips my worrywart ways in the bud. Yet sometimes, just sometimes, I wish he was more ambitious. I've always been a hard worker, a hustler. I've prided myself on my work. I am almost always the only ethnic minority in the team and I need to work harder because of it. Getting praise and getting a promotion gives me a dopamine fix. Even now, when signing a new client, I get the same rush. For M, his work is just a job. It never bothered me before. It didn't matter. He earns well enough. Yet, now that we have a baby on the way and I'm thinking of taking a step back from my work, I want him to step up. I *need* him to step up.

A change of subject would be nice to distract from my urge to pee. "I hear you've got an ulterior motive in coming up to Bradford. Who is this girl? Do I need to buy a new saree?"

Jam smirks. "No, I wouldn't bother yet. Wait until you've had the baby as you don't know if you'll get back to your pre-pregnancy shape."

I glare at him and he raises his hand to his mouth. "Oops, sorry. I didn't mean that. And that is why I am single. But yeah, she's alright, this girl. I won't say too much yet. Wait until there's something to tell."

Jam not saying too much? Then this girl must mean more to him than his usual dates. To have him withholding words is a rarity.

AS WE TURN THE CORNER off the main road to get to middle sis' house, I'm hoping I can make a speedy exit from Jam's car before anyone notices him. Especially given that mum and dad, upon hearing that I am coming, decided to make the trip to my sister's to see me as they felt it would be too much for me to go to Manchester. Little sis has driven them, which is a novelty in itself. Maybe, now that I'm finally pregnant, I can delegate some carpooling duties.

Unfortunately, as we pull up outside, mum, dad and middle sis are all standing at the door, waiting for my arrival. So much for being covert. I know there's nothing wrong with me travelling with Jam. Of course there isn't. M insisted. It's safer and better for me to come with a known person than be in a packed train with strangers. Strange men, no less. Yet, the prim Bengali in me knows that it's a tad weird to be travelling with an unrelated man.

Dad's face spells it all. Bewilderment and confusion. "Eh heh, where is your husband?"

"He's coming later, dad."

"Who this man?" He looks at Jam, squinting.

"That's his friend."

"What you say? Your boyfriend?" dad shouts.

Is dad okay?

"No, it's *his* friend."

"Okay, okay. Who else with you?"

"No one, dad!"

Jam is smiling nervously from the driving seat of his car. He didn't come out. It's probably for the best.

My sister walks over to him. Actually, I'd call it a saunter. What's her game?

She leans into the window. "Do you want to come in? It will be time to open fast soon. You can eat here."

Wait, what? Is everyone doing this voluntary fast? Is it a common thing? Since when?

"No, it's okay," says Jam, with a shake of his floppy fringe. "I'll be meeting a... friend for dinner."

Dad turns to me. "Why your husband not come?"

Mercifully, mum intervenes. "*Dooro!* She already told you he has work. He coming later." With that, she holds him by his elbow and leads him back into the house to avoid further confusion.

"I didn't know your husband had such a nice looking fella for a friend." Middle sis elbows me as we walk in together. "It's ever so trusting of him to let you travel together."

Jam is good-looking? I can't see beyond the hair and eyebrows.

SIMILAR TO WHEN I'M on my period during Ramadan, feasting when you haven't fasted isn't quite the same. There isn't that sense of anticipation. Not least because I wolfed down a packet of crisps and a glass of milk when I got to my sister's house. A weird combination, I know, but when I'm hungry, I'll take anything.

There's two minutes to go before sunset. Now M is here, we can all sit down together. He messaged me before arriving, to say he was knackered and is hoping middle sis can put us up for the night. I must warn her to make up a spare bed. When I whispered to him about the day of fasting, he looked as confused as me. However, he is now dutifully playing along with the waiting game, as we all stare at the spread in front of us.

Middle sis knows how to throw down a meal. She's made samosas, spring rolls, tandoori roast chicken, kebabs, chicken pulao, meat curry, sautéed vegetables and a prawn jalfrezi. I'm going to try everything, apart from the seafood, of course.

I've not been to her house in ages. Before I was married, it would be at least an annual trip. Now, any gathering is at mum's. It's easier, being the default home for all of us. Sitting here today, I feel like I'm appraising the room for the first time. She has a huge open-plan kitchen, with a wooden pine coloured dining table. The kids are on the breakfast bar, sat on stools, apart from the youngest, who has a wooden expandable highchair. I must ask her about that. It looks fancy. Not quite on the scale of the golden egg M and I spotted in the department store but nice, nonetheless.

The bifold doors that spread across the back of the house are steamed up from all the cooking, while the giant clock tells us it's time to finally eat.

There is a silence around the table for a moment, as glasses of water are gulped down, date fruits are ripped open and de-seeded and a plate of samosas and spring rolls is picked at.

I always wondered how middle sis and her husband can live in this big house and cook these fancy meals on his teacher's salary. Though it sounds like I'm about to find out.

"How long have you been selling cars for?" M asks, resting his elbows on the table during a break between deep-fried snacking.

My brother-in-law leans back in his chair. "Years. Years and years. I wouldn't change it, either. I love it. More even than my day job."

"Would you ever quit teaching and do the car business full time?" M asks.

"I would, if it wasn't for the Mrs." My brother-in-law looks at middle sis, who snarls back at him. "What? I'm just saying. It's way more profitable. These days, you don't get respect from the kids or the parents in teaching. The pay is rubbish compared to the cost of living. It doesn't make sense."

"But it's stability," middle sis chimes in. "With the car business, you haven't got any guarantees."

"You say that but every month this past year I've made over 2K. Imagine what I could do if I did it full time. We could pay off the mortgage much quicker."

M listens, in awe. "I wouldn't mind jacking the day job in."

I look up from my plate. I hope M isn't getting ideas.

"It's not for the risk averse but my view is, if you don't take any risks, you don't get anywhere. Think of all the big entrepreneurs." My brother-in-law sits up in his chair, happy to hold court. "They had to throw all their chips in. They took out loans, worked full time on their business and it paid off. If you half go into it, you'll get half back. That's why they're billionaires and we're grafting away every single day."

I must intervene. "Those are the ones that have done well. Most businesses go bust. You only hear about the success stories. For the majority, they don't make it past the first year. I'm around entrepreneurs that come and go all the time."

"Yet, you did it," says my brother-in-law. "I think it's great. You took the plunge."

I lower my voice. "Mine was more circumstance than choice."

"Not a bad circumstance though, is it? I'd love to be made redundant. Then I could go full pelt on this gig."

"I wouldn't mind being given the boot either." M chuckles.

I don't like this. I don't like this at all. M is being indoctrinated into the idea of selling souped-up cars. Why would he want to? He's been to university, got the qualifications and has a lucrative career in finance. I don't get it.

"You boys," says middle sis. "Always wanting to be your own boss. Dad was the same."

"Heh?" Dad stops mid rice-gathering.

"Nothing," says middle sis.

She's right. Dad tried his hand at business and it was okay for a while. I thought it was successful. Until it wasn't. I never really understood what happened but I felt the repercussions. I felt the time that we signed on to benefits. I ended up having free dinners and feeling so different, having had to join another queue with my food voucher. I didn't see it as free food or free money. I saw it as failure. Even then, as a teenager, I felt that my family were other. And this was beyond skin deep. The way I saw it, instead of coming to the UK, seeing and conquering, dad came and failed. I know he tried his best. He just didn't have a head for business. He wasn't educated, he didn't have qualifications he could transfer over. So, he did what most Bangladeshi men do. He did what my older brother-in-law does. He went into the restaurant trade. While big sis' husband has been more successful, my dad wasn't. He didn't have options like us. It's what he had to do. We, with our free education, leg up the ladder and a chance to really get into the corporate world, why would anyone risk that? Why would you go back and do what our parents had to do? Surely, their suffering was to make things easier for us? Dad's experience of having tried his hand unsuccessfully at business formed an early opinion on money and life choices for me. It taught me to be risk averse, stingy. It taught me to be happy with a steady wage, rather than risk it all to make a fortune. So, when I hear M's ears pricking up at the prospect of setting up a business of any sort, I bristle. It makes me uncomfortable.

"It was a nightmare driving here," says little sis. "The roads are so steep."

This leads to a conversation about how hilly Bradford is compared to Manchester and I'm relieved for the change of subject.

AFTER EATING, THE MEN head to the mosque, the children watch a movie with little sis, and mum prays upstairs.

"Now that you're six months' pregnant, girly, you're going to have the baby, regardless. It has to be born," middle sis informs me. "Don't worry about the head thing. It will be nothing. Just pray and it will be fine."

"I'm finding praying quite difficult these days." I rub my stomach. "This bump is hard to negotiate when bowing and prostrating."

"Then do it sitting down. Did mum show you the sitting down prayer?"

"She did vaguely, once. I thought that was for old ladies."

Middle sis sighs. "You're pretty much in the old lady bracket now as everything will ache."

"Everything does ache. Even sleeping is hard work."

"Have you got a V-shaped pillow?"

"A what-y what?"

"It's a pregnancy pillow. You put it between your legs and under your stomach and it helps you sleep. Honestly, are you not looking into all this stuff? Have you even started buying things yet? Like a Moses basket, or baby clothes?"

"I bought a coming home outfit for the baby," I say, feeling silly. "And my friend's offered to give me a Moses basket, though I'm not sure what mum will say about that."

"What you talk about?" As if by magic, mum comes in to the kitchen diner.

"I was just saying, my friend Sophia asked if I wanted her Moses basket."

Mum grimaces. "You don't want that, do you? It's your first baby. They should have new things. Not second-hand furniture that a baby has sleeped on, pooed on, maybe been sick on."

I knew mum would say that.

"I'm sure it's clean, mum." Middle sis laughs. "But I did get everything new for my first one. All my kids, in fact. I gave the stuff to charity in between before I had a chance to use it again. I ended up buying three Moses baskets in all."

"That seems a little wasteful."

Middle sis and mum share knowing looks with each other. My eco-conscious comments are a bit too English for their liking.

"Now you listen to me, buy new things for first baby. It be nice. I can give you money for Moses basket if you want."

"I don't need money, mum. Anyway, I haven't done any shopping yet. It's too soon."

"Yes, yes. Wait until *lit-ool* bit later. When you sure everything okay before you buy too many things," mum says, providing a further reminder as to where I get my worrywart ways from. "You read namaz?" She turns to middle sis.

"No. Not praying today. I'm on my period," she replies.

"You should've told me. We could've had sneaky snacks together."

Middle sis sighs. "I thought I best not blow my cover. It's okay for you to eat in front of people. There's no denying you're pregnant but I think dad and your husband don't need to know that I'm on the rag."

There it is. Another reminder, yet again, that we are as Bengali as can be when it comes to the female body. We deny and hide our periods, even though it's a universal known that it comes every month and hangs around for a week.

17th December, Yet another scan

I have come to accept that scans are not my favourite part of this pregnancy. I love the little butterflies in my stomach, the somersaults. I have been blessed with a symptom-light pregnancy. However, everything is measured equal and I haven't got off scot-free. The lighter symptoms have been more than made up for with buckets of worry.

Today is the day when I get to see if all is okay with H2. As if to add to the anticipation, the appointment is delayed, as is M. It's his bloody work. Those damn contractors seem to think because it's a healthy day rate, they can stretch the day out for as long as possible. Over the week, I'm sure he's working 50% more hours than he should.

It's fine. It's fine. It's good that he's not here, because it means I can do my manifestations, deep breathing and mindfulness exercises that he finds weird.

Let'd do some breathing. Four breaths in... one, two, three, four. And... eight out. One, two, three, four, five, six... and I'm out of breath. It's hard to gather air down to the pit of my stomach these days, as the space is monopolised by a small human.

I'd prefer to close my eyes during this exercise but I don't want to go into full mindfulness mode, as there are people around me. Other mothers-to-be, who are not meditating. There is one lady in a black maxi dress, fanning herself. Now

I think of it, is this waiting room warmer than it need be? After all, there aren't any newborns here requiring heat.

Another lady, sat in the far corner of the waiting room, is dressed in leggings and a floral tunic dress. She has accessorized her bump with a laptop. She's punching at her keyboard at lightning speed. I'm the same when bashing out a press release, though there hasn't been much of that of late. Joy keeps hinting that she's running out of budget and asked if she could reduce her retainer to half a day. I mean, half a day per month? What could I even do for her with that? I can barely walk to the office in that time, let alone fire off a media statement.

Positive thoughts... Positive thoughts... Today, there is no room for negativity.

Maybe it's a blessing in disguise. God's will, if you will. Maybe the bigger plan is that clients fall away at the right time, when I'm too tired and, frankly, can't be bothered servicing them. I have actively worked since the age of 22. Actually, from when I was 16, if you count my part time jobs around college and university. The day I got my GCSE results was the same day I had an interview at a clothes store. I got the job and started working on Saturdays. I've never stopped since. Maybe it's my time to kick back and put my feet up like my older sisters. They've not done too badly from being kept women.

I wonder what the hold up is on the scan. After my second toilet break, I ask at the desk.

"The clinic is running late." The receptionist offers the most redundant information possible. "You'll be seen next."

M isn't quite so easy to get a straight answer from. His phone keeps going to voicemail. He must be on the Tube. Oh well, back to people watching... The lady in the black maxi-dress is summoned. She waddles across and looks way further along in pregnancy than me. Why are they scanning her now? This late? There must be something wrong. The NHS couldn't perform extra scans unless there's a real reason. That's why they've called me today. They're worried about something.

If she'd have sat near me, I would have talked to her and got a feel for the situation. She's come alone, as has the lady in the floral tunic. They're doing it by themselves. I'd have liked to have chatted to either of them. Speaking to someone who is also pregnant, sharing the same concerns, and swapping reassurances would have been very welcome but that's not what we do, is it? We keep away. When we go to the waiting room, we sit as far away from the next person as possible. We keep seats empty between us. Otherwise, God forbid, we might have to make small talk. Is that just a British thing, to avoid conversing at all costs?

Never mind, I'll make mum friends in the NCT group. That reminds me, I must see what's in my local area. Will there be one in Tower Hamlets? I'll have to find out.

Also, note to self, I must write down a list of things I need to do. For ages, it felt like time wasn't moving. Now it's ticking away at a scary pace. I need to document everything as my brain is slowly going to pot.

"Excuse me, mum," the receptionist calls, though I'm not sure who she's referring to.

Wait... Is she looking at me? I'm not a mum. Not yet, anyway.

"Yes you, mum. Are you able to provide a urine sample just before you go in?"

I head over to the receptionist to retrieve the small plastic pot, which I will no doubt miss as I wee on my hand.

She chuckles. "Sorry mum, I should've told you before you went to the loo."

"Don't worry," I say, feeling H2 sit on my bladder. "I've got an endless supply these days, inconveniently so."

Also, I'm not your mum, I think to myself. *I've only got a decade on you, tops.*

Providing a urine sample is such a familiar task these days. I've had to do one for every single doctor's appointment, even the ones where they haven't checked the baby. I recently had a blood sample taken and even then they wanted to extract my urine, as if I'd not expelled enough bodily fluid already.

I leave the bathroom, with the fresh, warm urine sample to find M, looking forlorn. Bless him, he doesn't like to show his worry but I know he feels it. I guess he has to act strong to overcompensate for my concerns.

I want to tiptoe over carefully and surprise him. You know, break the ice and soften the worry we're both going through ahead of today's scan. Except, I'm not exactly covert. With my heavy, laboured treading, he spots me as soon as I approach.

I park myself next to him and rest my head on his shoulder. He's about to reach my hand and then feels the warm piss sample and instead rests his palm on my knee.

"Don't worry, it will be fine," he utters the soothing words I really need to hear.

"Are you worried?" I ask.

M inhales. "I am a bit, to be honest with ya. But we needn't be. Everything will be okay." He squeezes my knee.

"Excuse me, mum?" the receptionist calls again. "Could you go over to room eight, please?"

M smiles, though the glee fails to reach his eyes. "You'll have to get used to that, mum."

It's a short walk from the dark blue waiting room into the white lights of the corridor. M is walking like a hangman, which is odd as we are about to see new life. As we approach room eight, my heart quickens. Here we go again. Another dreaded scan. I say a prayer under my breath as we cross the threshold.

"I'm Dr Hargreaves, the senior consultant radiologist on the ward. I believe you've been brought in to have another scan? Would you like to tell me more?"

Really? I have to explain? Isn't it in my medical notes? Maybe she's humouring me. I suppose I'll indulge.

"At the last scan, they said something about the baby's head being small." I deliberately sound vague, as though it's not something that's been on my mind for the last few weeks. "Then again, they did note that I've got a slightly small head."

This leads Dr Hargreaves and my own husband, who should be very familiar with my head, to stare at my mane. I'm glad I washed my hair yesterday with all this attention.

"Yes, that could be it. Let's have a peek, shall we?" Dr Hargreaves slides herself onto the chair next to the examination bed.

"Sorry, I forgot to wear trousers," I say, mortified at my mishap. "It's just that, most of my clothes don't fit and I only bought a couple of pairs of maternity trousers and they're both in the wash-" I raise my hand to my mouth to prevent myself from sputtering more word salad. I am sharing way too much information and outing myself as a stingy git that refuses to buy a full maternity wardrobe.

M looks down to the ground and shakes his head, laughing. Well, at least someone finds this amusing.

"Not to worry," says doctor Hargreaves. "You can just hitch your dress up."

I know that in a matter of months, I'm going to get it all out in front of midwives, consultants and anyone else who happens to be passing by on the maternity ward but, right now, I want to preserve what dignity I have. I thought I'd done it all. In previous scans, I'd had to lift my top right up, unbutton my jeans beyond what is decent and jump like a performing seal.

This is way more awkward.

I slide my stretchy red dress up past my big knickers (oh dear), over the dark brown line that has developed along the centre of my stomach and let it rest just under my chest. I have neglected my female landscaping of late as it's very hard to reach down there with a razor and even the big knickers can't cover this. This is bad. Really bad. The only saving grace is that in this busy central London hospital, it is likely I will never see Dr Hargreaves again.

"Okay. Shall we hear the heartbeat first?" Dr Hargreaves slides the dictaphone-type device across the bottom of my belly, as though she's scanning for gold. She stops and I hear my most favourite symphony, little H2's heartbeat. I will never, ever get bored of the thwacking, throbbing siren that emanates from my womb.

I look up at M and smile. He's lost in thought. Then he notices me and grabs my hand.

Dr Hargreaves goes quiet as she gets to work running a handheld device across my freshly lubed tummy. I don't like it. I don't like quiet. *Deep breath. Deep breath.* I remind myself how the previous sonographer warned me that when she goes quiet it's not because anything is bad. It's because she's focused.

"We'll just go through everything while we're here, if that's okay?"

I nod my head, though inside I'm thinking: *No, please, let's not do this again. Please, let's not check the fluid between the brain and the neck and the four valves of the heart and look at the lungs and all the tiny parts where potentially something could be wrong. We know that's okay. We checked it all at the 20 week scan. If it wasn't for the small head, we wouldn't be doing this again. We wouldn't need to check again so why are we checking this? Why do we have to be extra, extra sure? Can't we just go with the last results at 20 weeks and focus on what you think is the problem? Do we have to rehash this to find something else and make me worry more?*

M laces his fingers with mine, squeezing tightly. "It will be okay."

I breathe out, exhaling loudly as though I'm doing yoga. I'm okay. I've got my safety blanket with me. H2's heartbeat was so strong! Of course she'll be fine. She's doing somersaults every day now.

Dr Hargreaves goes quiet again.

Then she starts listing. "Okay, that's the first heart valve... the second one is looking good..."

She talks through everything with precision, while I tune her out, looking at the scan and occasionally glancing at M, who seems to be looking through the screen. Of all the times to be pessimistic... I need my glass half full husband now.

With some more sloshes across my stomach, rendering my granny pants soggy, Dr Hargreaves declares: "Right, everything looks fine to me. I'm just going to make a call to one of my colleagues to pass on the information but essentially, all is looking good. The head seems as it should be. It's actually quite nice to have a smaller head, isn't it?"

I laugh and so does M. What a relief! Now I think of it, most babies do have big heads, don't they? Perhaps disproportionately so. My baby will be just right. My tensed up shoulders soften. My whole body sinks into the examination bed. It's as though I've been carrying all this weight, all this worry, on every joint of my body since the last scan. I've tried to put my best face forward, carry on with business as usual but it's been there. That worry has been right there all along, like a little monkey on my shoulder, keeping me in check. Now it's gone. Now I can get back to enjoying my pregnancy.

"This baby is beautiful. I'm very happy with what I've seen," Dr Hargreaves says on the phone to a colleague.

I know she's just being polite, but wow, what a compliment! My baby is not only healthy and well with a good sized head but she's beautiful, too. And all that has been gauged from a scan. Maybe it is a good thing I got to have an extra scan later on in my pregnancy. It's like having VIP treatment, especially with the way the NHS is now.

As we walk back through the corridor and enter the waiting room, I notice the walls are brighter. The space isn't dark blue, as I initially thought. It's a rich indigo. There are colourful bulletin boards which I hadn't noticed before. One highlights an antenatal class held at the hospital. Must look at that. It's probably free of charge. There is another with a smiling chubby baby sat cross-legged in a nappy. That reminds me, I must get those pregnancy books from Sophia. In fact, scratch that. When will I see her again? I'll just order some baby books online.

And furniture! Must buy a cot and a Moses basket. Yes, H2 will need new things. No hand me downs. Mum is right. It's my first baby. She should only have the best. I will go back to that department store and get that ostentatious feeding chair that looks like a golden egg. I don't mind dropping some eff you money on that.

Must also check out the NCT. Oh, I need to speak to my midwife about the birth plan. I need to understand exactly what my options are and what's the best thing for me to do. From what I've heard so far, the birthing pool would be the best. It sounds amazing. Ooh, I need to pick birth music, too. God, this is so exciting!

As we leave the hospital, I am struck by how warm it is, given that it's December. I'm wearing just a dress, yet I don't feel the chill at all. Maybe it's because everything now seems brighter and lighter. Or maybe it's because I've got a little heater in my belly, in the form of H2, keeping me warm.

M is very quiet while I'm lost in my thoughts. Usually, he'd ask me what I want for dinner. He's not holding my hand either. Then again, we are walking through Whitechapel High Street, which is more Bengali than Bangladesh. He's just being formal.

"Are you okay?" I ask.

"Huh?" M looks startled. "Yeah, it's just... I wasn't going to say anything. Not just yet, anyway. I wanted to get the scan out of the way."

"What is it? Has something happened? Is it your mum or dad?" I'm not sure why it's my first thought but after the worry about H2's head, the only thing I can imagine being just as scary is something happening to one of his parents.

"No, nothing like that. I didn't want to worry you, especially as you had enough to worry about already. I wasn't sure when to say but... oh man, it's just, the reason I was late was because my manager called me in for a meeting. She had HR with her. Basically, she's not happy with my performance and doesn't think it's working. So they're terminating my contract."

I'm still high after the relief about my baby and it takes me a second to process what he just said. "What do you mean?"

"Like I say, I didn't want to worry you. Not today. But they're getting rid."

Still struggling to process this. "Okay. When?"

M drags a hand across his face. "That's the thing. I'm on contract. They don't owe me anything. I don't have a notice period. So I'm done. As in, they literally fired me today."

Despite M's good intentions, he has indeed got me worried. Very worried.

18th December, What now?

Seriously, what now?

I can't sleep. My mind is doing somersaults in sync with H2's constant acrobatics. I've been warned that a lot of nocturnal movement in the womb suggests that the baby will be active and awake at night when it's born. As in, I won't be able to get any sleep. That's not on. I'm not getting much sleep now as it is. Surely, things should ease up after the baby comes?

M is sleeping soundly as ever. Despite delivering the news yesterday, he seems relatively at peace with things. Once he told me, he was visibly relieved. Gone was the five-mile stare. The look of death behind the eyes. It's as though my relief upon hearing that baby H2 is okay has been transferred to M, while he passed on the stress about his current unemployment situation to me. It's not a fair swap.

Yesterday was weird. We didn't talk much. Instead, the TV provided all the noise for us. Daytime TV is so shit. It's like it's designed to get you off your arse and get to work. This is why, despite my very flexible work situation, I barely watch TV during daylight hours. It's too depressing. Too much of a reminder that there are things to be done. There's a whole world out there.

M, however, was engrossed. He has a particular penchant for gameshows. He was watching a show where people play a sort of arcade game. They choose which section from which to drop a counter in the hopes that it pushes out more. Counters equal pounds, apparently. We could do with some of them.

How is my husband sleeping so soundly when my mind is going crazy?

Maybe I was too understanding. Immediately after he delivered the news that he was fired without any further notice, I put my PR hat on. I cheered him along, saying things like: "It'll be okay. You can just get on the job hunt. At least one of us is working!" That was a silly thing to say. I'm hardly working.

My God, how did it come to this? He should've stayed in his safe job. He should've put up with the crap from his manager. Don't all of us have to at some point or other? I've had shit bosses in the past. I didn't throw the towel in because of them. He should've done the responsible thing and stayed in permanent employment, rather than going for a risky contract. He played his card and it failed. It failed miserably.

Right, stop it. Stop it! Stop it right now! Anger breeds resentment, which breeds bitterness, more anger, and then life will be difficult. We're not the arguing couple.

I just wish he'd told me. I could've helped. Obviously, I know sod-all about finance but I could've helped maybe on the people pleasing side of things? I could have suggested ways to get in his boss' good books. I don't know. I've just got a lot of feelings right now.

M is snoring. What is it, three, four 'o'clock? I'll check my phone...

Bloody hell, it's 4am! I shouldn't be wide-awake right now. It doesn't help that sleeping on my back is out of the question, and my side is not that comfortable, either.

Also, when did Sonali message me? I didn't even notice. Oh, it arrived at 1am. What is she doing awake so late? Let's have a read:

Hey, how are you doing? I just thought I'd check in... I know you said you'd come to the wedding but I wanted to double-check that's still the case. We're finalising numbers and my parents are being tight on head count. I told them we shouldn't have gone for the bloody hall in Wimbledon! Anyway, get back to me when you can.x

Oh yes, I forgot that non-Bengali people RSVP properly when it comes to weddings, instead of a quick fire text reply saying: *Can't wait!*

M and I still have to figure out the logistics of how we're going to go to two weddings in one day. Also, how much should I gift? What is the etiquette these days? Sonali and I haven't spoken in years but I'm pretty close to Reena. Would it be bad if I gave Sonali less? Would she even know? I'll have to figure all this out, whilst factoring in our current financial situation.

Oh, man. M's unemployment changes everything. He's snoozing peacefully, unaware of how much I'm fretting. I'm wide awake while the rest of London is asleep. Well, those Londoners that work in the day, that is.

What will we do? I have savings, though I don't really want to dig into them too much. I don't want to shout about having money to be used. Won't that emasculate him?

This procrastination is driving me nuts. I'm going to watch some TV. Maybe the sofa in the living room will be more comfortable.

No matter what time of day, we never shut the blinds in our flat. There's no need. Nobody can see into our home from that high up, anyway. Okay, maybe the neighbours across the road can but I doubt they're looking. Everyone is too busy in their own bubble to nosey in to our flat.

Oh dear, oh dear. Oh dear. I sit on the sofa and rub my belly. I read somewhere that talking to the baby helps. I guess I'll chat to H2 then, since I've got no one else to speak to.

"I know you can hear me in there." I gently tap on my belly. I receive what feels like a punch in return. "I think we'll be good friends. Anyway, your dad is in a bit of a pickle but nothing we can't sort out. So don't you worry about that. I will try to be relaxed for you and not stress you out. But I'm just going to warn you now, worrying is in my nature. Anyway, you keep growing, preferably around the skull, so those doctors don't say odd things about your head. I'm trying to sleep and you should, too. You should be moving during the day, not at night. That is not going to fly when you're born."

I turn on the TV and flick through the channels. There are a bunch of infomercials selling Peletons, steam mops, and other tat I couldn't care for. It turns out that TV in the early hours of the morning is just as bad as it is during the day. Perhaps that's another reminder that I really, really shouldn't be awake right now. I lie down on the sofa. It feels hard and cold, like the room. It's not worth putting the heating on, as it's early in the morning. I'm not worried about the heating bill but it seems like the wrong time to put it on. The blanket will keep me warm enough. And, on the down low, I am a bit worried about the heating bill.

22nd December, Comparison-itis

Neetu is a trooper. There is no other way to describe that woman. She comes into the office, throwing down Tupperwares full of curry and foil wrapped flatbreads. All this, while her bump is only getting bigger. Despite being due after me, she is sporting a protruding belly, made all the bigger by her five-foot frame. She carries out her job with the same rigour, the same ballsy hustle that she's done since the day I met her.

Me, on the other hand... I'm already thinking about winding down. I am so tired now. Even getting to the office feels like a mission. The bus is a pain and the Baby on Board badge is so small that hardly anyone notices it. I got all the way to Fenchurch Street before someone had the good grace to offer me their seat. Bloody Londoners.

Anyway, since we're on the cusp of Christmas, I figured I'd make one last visit before the office closes for the holidays.

"What can I get you today?" Neetu asks me.

"I'll just have a chicken curry with rice." I don't sit down as I'm about to head into a meeting.

"How's it all going?" Neetu talks to my bump, rather than my face.

I instinctively rub my belly. "It's good. Just tired these days, that's all."

"Tell me about it." Neetu looks down and I notice the darkness around her eyes. "I am beyond exhausted. But what to do? The bills won't pay themselves."

"True. When do you finish?"

"Finish?" Neetu cackles. "You never really finish when you are running your own business. I'll probably take a couple of weeks off and then I'll get back to it. My mum is coming over from India next month, which will be a huge help. She'll be staying for six months at least." She hands over the container of chicken and rice. "What about you? Will your mum come and stay?"

I hesitate. I've never even thought to ask my mum. I know it wouldn't be easy for her. "No, she won't be coming. My dad doesn't really like staying anywhere that's not home. Plus, my little sister still lives with them. So it's hard to leave."

"That's tough. I'm lucky, because my younger sister is 20 now, so she can fend for herself. And my dad, well, he'll get by as my grandmother lives with us. He won't be short of a roti or two."

My mouth trembles. I can't let any emotions get to me but it's hard. I don't elaborate on the fact that my sister is 22, therefore should be able to fend for herself. Mum would never leave her like that. She thinks that's something English people do, as she puts it. Kicking the kids out once they're 18. For mum, her children are her responsibility until they're married.

A lump forms in my throat. I swallow it down. It's probably just hormones. It's probably everything. I know I should count my blessings. I whisper a prayer to myself whenever I harbour thoughts full of negativity, of a half empty glass.

They're coming more frequently now. The feeling that everyone else has it so good.

Glass half full. Glass half full.

"You are lucky, Neetu," is the only thing I can manage to say.

"I guess you could stay with your mum. The 40-day rule and all that," she suggests.

I smile and say nothing. I have vaguely heard of the 40-day rule in the past, where women do nothing but look after the baby while everyone else takes care of everything else. It's not really practiced in my family. I haven't asked mum if I could or should stay over when the baby comes. Why would I? She's never asked me.

"I'VE BEEN WORKING IN theatre production publicity, mainly. Or should I say, my background is in theatre. Then I had all these producers and playwrights coming to me, asking if I could do publicity for their shows and things like that. That's how it started. Then I ended up drafting press releases and speaking to the local journalists and getting these producers and playwrights on the radio. After that, I thought, hey... I kind of like this. Why don't I make this my gig?" Meera laughs at her latest career pivot.

While she's taking an awfully long time to explain her credentials and how she will provide PR for my clients while I'm on maternity leave, all I can think to myself is: *So you're not a real PR person? You've just winged your way here by writ-*

ing stories for some people and getting lucky with the local media?

I am full of snark this afternoon.

It's lucky that we're on a Zoom call and her screen is pixelated. Hopefully, mine is the same, with darkness descending in the large downstairs meeting room at my office space. The mahogany panelled walls don't reflect much light, nor does the Christmas tree in the corner, with its tired tinsel and dim fairy lights, so I'm hoping she can't see my many eye rolls.

"That's great," I say with the fakest smile I can plaster on my face, "but do you have any experience in B2B publicity? A lot of my clients feature in the trade press. It is boring and not very sexy compared to the theatre but that's just how it is. Have you worked in those areas?"

Meera looks off into the distance. "Not exactly. I have done something similar, as I worked for the franchise of an electronics retailer. Well, it was my family business, actually. Anyway, I did lots of publicity for them. I managed to get the Lord Mayor round for the grand opening. The buzz was huge. Like, literally the talk of our village."

"Yeah... um... so that's still not really B2B. As in business to business. I'm guessing the buzz was amongst consumers? I mean, I do some of that. For example, I've got a slimming coach on my books but the majority of my work is getting clients into industry magazines and peer-to-peer publications."

"Ooh," says Meera, as if she's had an a-ha moment. "You mean business to business. Sorry, I couldn't hear you properly. It's a bit crackly here."

Sure, Meera. Blame the reception.

"I haven't done a lot of that but I think, in publicity, everything is kind of transferable, isn't it? I've got such a breadth of experience that I think I could turn my hand to whatever you need."

"Hmm." I don't hide my cynicism. "Okay, and what would be your day rate?"

Meera takes a deep breath. "I can be flexible. I'd say anywhere between £250 and £375, depending on the job."

"Right, well I've briefed you about the job so, which is it? £250 or £375?"

"Erm... I'd say for what you need, it would be the upper end."

That would leave me with very little change at the end of each month. "Great. Thanks for your time and I'll get back to you."

"Fab, okay. Also, I should mention... I can send you the newspaper cuttings I've achieved for my clients. We've had some amazing local coverage."

"I'll let you know if I need anything but I've got another meeting happening any second now, so I'll just say a quick bye now. I'll be in touch." I wave at the screen for half a second before ending the call, while Meera is still mid wave.

I know I was being a cow, though I'm not sure why. I've been on the receiving end of that call. Needing to fill my pipeline with paid work. I know what it's like. I know what it feels like when someone doesn't give you a chance. I now know what it's like to be on this side. The kingmaker (of sorts). And as a sort-of kingmaker, I could've been nicer. But honestly, there are so many aspects of my life which I don't have control over right now. This is the only place I feel I can exert some power. Also, and I don't really like myself right now for feeling like this, but there is something intoxicating about being the one who holds the cards, when all my life it's been the other way round.

I wasn't lying to Meera, though. I am interviewing one other person today.

The next candidate has arrived, I have been alerted by Graham.

Vanessa, a slim, curly haired woman, sits opposite me with a broad smile. "I didn't expect you to be so young," she says. "No offence!"

I like her already. "None taken! I don't often get called young these days, so that's nice."

"Really?" She sounds surprised. "I can tell you're younger than me. I've got bags for days. And the grey hairs, let me tell you." She ruffles the front of her fringe, highlighting some silver strands. "That's what happens when the kids become teenagers. I guess you'll find out soon."

Vanessa is personable and I can tell she'll be good on the phone to clients. The glass half empty side of me is worried that she'll be a little too good. They might want to poach her when I'm back from leave. However, the glass half full side is reminding me that not only is she capable, personable, and has worked in the B2B public relations sector, she's affordable, too. So I can enjoy a small income every month while not working. Now *that* is being a boss bitch.

I HEAD BACK INTO THE kitchen to find Neetu packing away her Tupperware. She must've had a good day, as she's only got about four or five on her pallet.

Jasdeep walks in. "How's business?" he asks as he runs his mug under the tap before turning it upside down. He didn't even bother scrubbing. It'll be covered in tea stains.

"Erm... yeah it's good," I reply, surprised at the interaction. I thought he was still avoiding me as I all but outed him as the creepster on the online dating site.

Now that he knows I know, I'm not sure how to react to him. Must say something to make him squirm. Come on... fire back with some sass. I am in snarky mode today, after all.

"Have a good day!" he says, before I can decide on my next move.

The slippery eel. I didn't even get a chance to tell him about my new freelance hire. That would rival his many houses and businesses in India.

AT HOME, M IS IN THE same position as I left him. Please don't tell me he's not moved all day.

"Hi," I say, walking towards the kitchen to find this morning's mugs and cereal bowls still in the sink.

"You alright?" he says, not moving a muscle.

"Yeah. What did you do today?" I ask, though I'm afraid of the answer.

"Nothing much. Just been watching Tipping Point and taking it easy. I thought I'd make the most of it while I was off. I never really had the time to watch daytime TV."

He is grinning like he could get used to it. He better not. And take it easy from what? I never realised that M worked down the mines digging for diamonds. It's only that kind of job that could warrant needing to take rest when he's off.

I won't ask him about job-hunting yet. It's clear he hasn't done any. However, the temptation to bring it up is overwhelming. I mean, isn't there a sense of urgency given my impending due date?

Don't ask. Don't ask. Let him have one day. I'll be busting his balls tomorrow.

I bite my lip to stop myself from further interrogation. I sit on the adjacent sofa, flip open my laptop to send a terms of engagement letter to Vanessa. After that, I log onto a mum forum. I know I shouldn't. It goes against my whole don't-tempt-fate-you're-not-a-mum-yet mantra.

I type into the search bar: Lazy husband.

It's throws up several pages of posts from disgruntled mums. The first one looks the juiciest.

It reads:

Before I share my story, I just want to say that my husband is mostly great. He is generous, caring and loves his kids. But, here it comes... We both work full-time, yet I do 90% of the childcare. I pack the lunches, do the school run, ferry round for the after-school clubs. He does watch them from time to time, but that's usually with one eye on the football and the kids mostly being ignored. They walk past him to come to me for things. But he does work longer hours and earns more. I'm not sure if he's a lazy husband, or is that just men for you? AIBU asking him to step up?

This is just the reading material I need.

I open up several more posts. All from wronged women who want advice on what to do about their husbands. I've deduced that AIBU stands for 'am I being unreasonable'.

The questions could've been written by the same woman as they all paint a similar picture. The answers aren't much different, either. Almost unanimously, the advice is: N*o, you're not being unreasonable, leave him!* There is some counsel that isn't quite so blunt, which suggests talking it out, sitting down and going through an action plan but overwhelmingly, the feedback is to kick the husband to the kerb.

I wonder whether these women would heed their own advice, or it's just something that they're glad to suggest anonymously on a forum. Perhaps it's easier to plant the missile and watch it crash, rather than dealing with the debris.

I look over to M. His stubble has grown. His T-shirt has a new hole in it. He's engrossed in his TV programme. I take a deep breath and return to my mantra. He's a good husband. He's a good husband. He's a good husband.

28th December, A tale of two weddings

IT MADE PERFECT SENSE at the time. Two weddings in the same city, just a few miles away from each other. Attending the religious ceremony of one and the reception of another. What could go wrong?

Oh yeah, I'm heavily pregnant. The perfect plan is not so perfect now that I'm tired, bloated and generally uncomfortable. Sitting in M's car, my back is sore, my legs ache, and even my lady parts are throbbing. What is that about?

Still, there are some silver linings. After a period of dormancy, M has kicked-started his job hunt. He is now on the books of several recruiters, as well as having applied directly. Luckily, this was of his own initiative, and he didn't need any nagging from me. Though I did make my feelings known in other ways. I am the master of passive aggressive silences, one-word answers and side-eye.

As we roll up to wedding number one, I am taken aback by the picturesque castle in front of us. The expansive country road which leads us up to the building looks like something from a Bollywood movie. You know, the sort where they pretend that the protagonist lives in a stately home or castle. Those very realistic films.

Then, after parking near what looks like the stables, we see scores of saree-draped women and sherwani-wearing men making their way towards a nearby marquee. Silly me, of course Reena isn't getting married in the actual castle. She's not royalty. Though I have to say, the large white tent with no windows is fairly anticlimactic.

Just like when I was at Reena's hen do, I am wondering whether I'll recognise anybody from university. Obviously, Sonali won't be here. She's busy having her own wedding ceremony as we speak. I'll be seeing her later.

"Do you think they'll have canapés?" asks M.

"I don't think so."

"Damn. I purposely had a light breakfast, thinking there would be some good samosas and stuff."

I tut. "First rule when going anywhere, always eat properly before you leave as you don't know when your next meal will come. I thought I taught you better than that."

As we enter the marquee, my thoughts are confirmed. There aren't any drinks to be drunk or food to be snaffled, so M and I head through the double doors to what seems like the main hub of activity.

Hundreds of people are milling around, brightly dressed in orange, yellow, green and turquoise. It's a kaleidoscope of ethnic wear. I now wonder whether my biscuit coloured saree, with subtle gold embellishments, was the correct call. Right now, clothing choices in general are a compromise. Today's deciding factor was what petticoat would fit around my waist. Even the blouse needed adjusting, as it sits across the top of my bump. The gold heels also weren't my best choice.

However, I challenge anyone to wear a saree with flats. It's not possible. You'll be tripping over for days.

There isn't the usual table seating that is custom at Bengali weddings. Instead, all chairs are arranged in a line, so we can sit as spectators, observing the main event unfold in front of us.

"What's that?" M asks me, pointing at the canopy-like structure on the main stage.

"It's a mandap. You know, when they walk around the fire?"

"Learn something new every day," says M.

"To be honest, I don't know much myself. Just snippets I've learnt from uni friends. And Bollywood movies, of course. Julia is probably more clued up as she dated a Hindu guy once."

"Julia? As in your mate?" M stares at me in disbelief. "I wouldn't have expected that. She gets weirded out when I eat with my hands."

"To be fair, her ex-boyfriend probably didn't eat with his hands in front of her. Plus, it was a long time ago. And Miles probably doesn't even eat crisps with his hands. I bet he uses salad tongs."

"Or tweezers!" M offers. "I can imagine him pinching them like this." He pretends his hands are pincers and we both laugh.

Yeah, we're childish.

Everyone is speaking loudly in Gujarati, so it's one big foreign muffle. There is the distinct aroma of incense. M spots a non-Asian on the main stage, who is holding an adorable mixed-race baby on his shoulders. I think the baby is keeping him company throughout this unapologetic Indian-ness.

Reena looks regal. She is wearing a maroon and diamanté lehengha. I could never imagine her as a bride. She's always been a tomboy, choosing jeans and trainers over a dress and heels. Then again, there was a time I couldn't imagine myself as a bride. For different reasons. Namely, the pickings were slim.

There is so much activity around them that I'm struggling to get a glimpse of the groom. Finally, a few aunties budge out of the way and I get to have a nosey. He's not bad. Not bad at all. He's tall-ish (as far as Gujarati boys go), has all his hair, with a few grey flecks, and is bespectacled. He looks kind, which I've come to learn is a very important trait in a husband.

I catch Reena's eye and offer her a wink. She does a coy laugh, one I've never seen before from her. Among the groom's party, there is the one white guy with the baby, who looks bewildered by it all. He's dressed in a traditional tunic and baggy trousers, with an orange scarf draped around his neck. Perhaps he's a brother-in-law? I'll have to get the who's who from Reena later.

M and I take our seats two rows from the front.

"How long do you think this will take?" asks M.

"It shouldn't be too long. From what Bollywood has taught me, they go round the fire seven times and then it's done."

There's some commotion as people start taking their seats. It's like you're at the cinema. There are some aunties on stage saying things in Gujarati, with the occasional English translation. Something about promising to look after Reena, that sort of thing.

Then they walk around the fire. Reena walks behind her husband, with a scarf between them, intertwined in their outfits. It's quite romantic, really.

"Here we go," says M with satisfaction. "Let's get the show on the road so we can have lunch."

I CAN'T BELIEVE THEY'RE still at it. All those years of watching Bollywood movies, I feel like I've been cheated. They don't walk around the fire seven times consecutively. There are various breaks, speeches, blessings, etc. It goes on for a while.

M is getting tetchy. He really should've had a snack beforehand.

"I might have to pop out in a minute. I'm expecting a call."

"Okay. From who?"

"It's about a potential job," M says quietly, as though my fear of jinxing things has rubbed off on him.

My heart swells. "That's good news. On a Saturday, though? And in the Christmas holidays?"

"Finance never stops, plus they have clients in America so work different times."

They could have clients in Antarctica, for all I care. It's a lead. A prospect. M leaves to take the call and I am alone. I'd talk to Reena's sisters but they're busy speaking to various aunties, passing around baskets of flowers, offering glasses of water to the elders, and other such duties bestowed on immediate family members.

An old lady is sat next to me with a walking stick. She's wearing a burnt orange saree, paired with black plimsolls.

"Nice wedding, *he na*?" She smiles at me.

"Yes, it's lovely."

She then proceeds to speak to me in Gujarati. Needless to say, I don't understand a word. A few sentences in, she notices my blank expression. "Gujarati hai?"

"No sorry. I'm Bengali."

She nods her head from side to side. "No worry. We all be same, no? You be expecting?" She looks at my undeniable bump.

"Yes, auntie."

"Lovely news! I have seven children. Twelve grandchildren." She holds out both hands, fingers spread out, even though there aren't enough to emphasise her point. She then reverts to Gujarati, perhaps forgetting that I am Bengali and do not understand. After telling me something rather profound, judging by her facial expressions, she looks back to the stage.

I see the bride and groom take what I'm estimating is the third walk around the fire.

M returns with a look of relief.

"How was your call?" I ask, trying not to convey the eagerness for an employment breakthrough in my tone.

"Yeah, it's okay. They want to interview me next week."

"That's great news," I say, clutching his hand. He squeezes my fingers tightly.

We've got this.

I'm worried about how long food is going to take. On the invitation it said that lunch would be served at 1.30pm. In typical Asian timing, it's gone 2pm and they're still walking around the fire. We're going to be driving across London to Sonali's do later. At this rate, we will probably only be there for the final dance.

One thing I have to give credit for is that these Gujarati weddings know how to make it all about the couple. I've been to countless Bengali weddings where the connection was so distant, I didn't even know whether I was related to the bride or groom. I just went along for the ride. And the tandoori chicken. Sometimes we wouldn't even get to see the bride as we'd leave early or they'd make their grand entrance late.

Even my own wedding had a bloated 600-person guest list. I didn't know most of the people there. Many didn't know me, either. They wouldn't be able to pick me out in the street. Yet, they were there by invite. No gatecrashers.

At Reena's wedding, all eyes are on them. Bar a few small children running amok, everyone is focused on the bride and groom as they do their thing. Between walks around the fire, there are various asides. Conversations between what looks like Reena's father-in-law and brother-in-law, and her mother-in-law and mum. There is no scramble for food (much to M's annoyance), no distracting music, no other form of entertainment to deflect from Reena's big day. It's all about her and her husband. As it should be.

Once they have completed the ritual, I spot a chance to head over to the newlywed couple. I give Reena a hug and sit next to her.

"You look amazing," I say, stroking her net dupatta.

"Thanks man. I can't wait to get out of this get up, though." She guffaws. I'm glad to see Reena is still there, hidden under all those layers of makeup and sparkle. She turns to M. "Thanks so much for coming, you guys. We really appreciate it."

Reena's husband nods in agreement and offers a handshake to M.

"No worries," says M. "We didn't want to miss it, even though it meant doing two weddings today!"

Reena pulls a face and M realises he's said too much.

"Uh, so what do you do?" He asks Reena's husband in an attempt to deflect.

"I'm a software engineer." Her husband is so softly spoken and quiet. He's the opposite of her and it's hard to hear him over all the hubbub. "What about yourself?"

M falters. Damn, we hadn't anticipated being asked this. I've not briefed M at all.

He shrugs. "I'm not doing anything at the moment, to be honest with ya."

Oh God. Why did he say that? It sounds like he's on the dole. Reena looks at me, as though M has revealed that he's had an affair.

I look at M, with an expression that I'm hoping conveys that he should add some context. Preferably favourable, PR-friendly context.

"I'm between jobs at the moment," he adds.

Good save, I think to myself, breathing a sigh of relief. Now, we just need to work up an agreed story for when we go to Sonali's wedding. We can think it up in the car.

"SHOULD I NOT TELL PEOPLE I've lost my job?" asks M on the drive to wedding number two.

Oh, how I wish I didn't have to spell these things out for him.

"I'm not saying you should lie but you don't need to offer up the information, do you? Everyone else puts their best face forward. You don't hear about all their business."

"How would I hear about that? I've never really spoken to your friend, Reena."

"I don't mean literally. Just in general, not everybody shares everything. Like, you don't need to tell Julia and Miles that our salad tomatoes were from the reduced aisle. It makes us sound cheap. With the job front, I think what you said was fine, that you're between jobs. It's just people are nosey. Sometimes sharing isn't the best thing."

M keeps his focus on the road ahead. "Whatever you say, boss. Sometimes, I can't keep track of the different secrets and stories we've got going on."

He laughs and so do I but we both know it's true.

I shuffle in the passenger seat, trying, and failing to get myself into a more comfortable position. The truth is, at this stage of pregnancy, there is no such thing. Especially in this car. When I recline the seat, it hurts my lower back. If I bring it forward, I squash my belly.

"Did you like the food?" I ask, distracting myself from the discomfort. "Or did you miss meat?"

"I did miss having some chicken or something but it was okay. Shame we couldn't get seconds. I'd quite like to have served myself extra helpings of potato curry rather than having dinner ladies give us a spoon each. If I'm going to queue up for my food, I want to make sure I'm getting a good amount."

"True. I don't exactly know what the food situation is at Sonali's, so is it worth getting a drive-through en route? I am eating for two, after all."

"Sounds like a plan, Batman," says M. "Especially as I'm growing a food baby to complete my unemployed look. I might get a wife beater vest, too."

He laughs. I don't.

"I'm joking, man," he says in his fake Geordie accent. "I got options now. And a job interview next week."

"Thank goodness for that," I say under my breath.

I'm glad to see that Sonali's wedding is in a proper building. A banqueting hall, so to speak. I was feeling a bit chilly in the marquee. Freestanding electric heaters are no match for gas central heating, especially now, as the winter's first frost has started to settle on the ground.

Sonali looks glamorous in her teal green Swarovski encrusted lehengha, which I'm assuming is the second outfit of the day as she would've been wearing a more demure, traditional look for the religious ceremony. This outfit, with the scarf pleated thinly over one shoulder, reveals both her cleavage and a hint of midriff. Her hair is styled in bouncy waves, and she stands taller than me in her vertiginous heels.

I wish I'd cut my hair before the wedding. I styled it long and loose, securing the front in a quiff which, to my mind, looks pretty good. Except my mane has become leggy, limp and shapeless. At this reception, everyone is dressed to the nines, wearing figure skimming outfits that would never fly at a Bengali wedding. The only thing I'm flaunting here is my belly and that's by circumstance rather than choice. Nothing will hide it these days, not even six yards of saree material.

I am also now at that stage of pregnancy where I'm bloating all over. My cheeks are puffy like a squirrel and my fingers are officially sausage-like. I can no longer wear my wedding ring. Or most of my other rings, for that matter.

Needless to say, being at a wedding where everyone is in full glam mode wouldn't have been my first choice of things to do. Top of the list would've been lying down in whichever position is comfortable, with my v-shaped pillow, gifted from middle sis, stuffed between my legs.

M looks dapper, though. It's actually nice seeing him suited and booted, as it's been a while. Even whilst working, he didn't have a super strict office. Chinos and jumpers were fine. However, now he's entered his unemployed era, all good dress has gone out of the window. His grey stubble has been anything but designer and his home clothes have developed more holes than I care to count. Put it this way, his T-shirts are more like string vests and his boxers are like thongs. He's been like a caricature from a movie when someone hits rock bottom and they change beyond recognition. Therefore, seeing M today, clean shaven and showered, is most welcome.

As it's the evening reception, Sonali is walking and talking more freely as the religious ritual has been performed earlier in the day.

She comes over and gives me a warm hug. "I was worried you wouldn't be able to make it, though I would've totally understood with the clash and all. I'm still in Reena's bad books. You'd think I had a say in the wedding date, the way she's in a mood."

"She'll get over it in good time. We all turn a bit bridezilla when we're getting married."

Sonali laughs. "I sure did. Anyway, you've come just in time as food is about to be served and then you can get your dancing shoes on."

I look down at my belly. "Maybe my waddling shoes."

Sonali's reception has a sit down table service, much like all Bengali weddings. M is relieved that he can get seconds without feeling like a naughty schoolboy. I'm relieved, too. I didn't fancy queueing up, buffet style, twice in one day. The heels on my feet are not playing ball.

After the starters of cassava chips, chilli paneer and some other vegetarian delicacies, the lights dim low.

"Looks like it's boogie time," says M. "Do you want to go and dance with your mates?"

"I might sit this one out," I reply.

M is not a dancer. I realised that quite early on in our relationship, so I needn't ask him if he wants to join the disco.

An old school Bollywood song, called Meri Yaar Ki Shaadi Hai, is being played while the bride and groom's sides take opposite ends of the dancefloor. Oh, they're having a dance off. It looks like it's rehearsed as people vaguely seem to know what they're doing. The departing sea of people makes way for Sonali and her husband to take centre stage, hand-in-hand. They're having their first dance. They hold each other and sway from side to side, to a chorus of music and wolf whistles. The elders remain sat at their tables, some watching the dancing, others lost in conversation. There's an old guy with his arms folded as if he's ready to call it a night. That's exactly how my dad would be at such an event. My mum, on the other hand, would be throwing me dirty looks if I were to dance with my husband in public. It's not something we do.

I see Sonali's husband, Krish, whisper something in her ear. She giggles in response. She looks happy. Truly, truly happy. She's found her person.

I look over to my person. I was whingeing about going to two weddings in one day but it's M who encouraged me to see off my friends. He's the one that did the driving across London as he always does. He's a good egg. He may be an unemployed bum at the moment but I hope and pray that this is a temporary blip and...

M puts his arm around me and rests his head on my shoulder, suspending my thoughts. For a moment, I forget about my worries. I forget about M's job or lack thereof. I forget about what the future might look like. M helps me focus on the now by simply putting his head on my shoulder.

The mains are taking ages to arrive and it seems that nobody else minds. They're making the best of the free bar. M is on his second glass of Coke, while I've treated myself to a strawberry mocktail. I keep wondering whether to call it a night but M keeps saying we should stay as it's not often I get to do things with my friends.

Sonali comes over and grabs both M and I by our arms. M doesn't know what to do, apart from follow her onto the dance floor.

"Come on! We can do a slow, pregnant lady dance together."

I gasp. "Sonali, are you telling me you're pregnant?"

"No, but I've got a belly, haven't I?" She pinches an inch of her stomach, which has shrunk since I last saw her at Reena's hen do. I guess she's been on a wedding diet.

As we get on the dance floor, Krish goes next to M and both men do an awkward, holding drinks, swaying kind of dad dance. Krish whispers in M's ear, leaving my husband looking unsure what to say. I can bet he's being quizzed on his career. One thing I can say is that M is not a natural liar and I am grateful for that.

The mains arrive by 9pm, and I wolf down the daal, roti and vegetable curry.

"Is it socially acceptable to dine and dash?" I ask M.

"It should be okay as we've been here for ages and you are pregnant. Though you might as well say goodbye to your mate. Speak to her properly before you go."

I head over to Sonali. "Sorry, but this baby mama is wiped. Let's meet up again soon?" I offer.

"Yeah, definitely. Are you having a baby shower?" she asks.

"Erm... I'm not sure yet."

"Fair enough. I'd be hesitant, too. Don't want to jinx it and all that."

I smile as if in agreement though, for once, my hesitancy isn't about superstition. It's because I haven't got anybody to throw me a baby shower. Or at least nobody has offered.

Sonali sighs. "If you do end up having one, let me know and I'll try to come. But you know how these things are. There'll be so many occasions and family invites and dinners now I'm married, there'll barely be time for anything or anyone. I have to schedule in family visits."

I hug Sonali, fully aware that everything she said is true and it will be a good while before we meet again. It's been nice to see her and witness her happy ever after.

"Are you sure you don't want to stay for dessert?" she asks.

"It's super tempting but I don't think I'll be able to stomach much. Baby H has taken up most of the space in my stomach, leaving little room for anything else. The mains have filled me up to here." I put my hand just under my chest. It's true, the baby pushes every other organ and now I am fit to burst.

Also, I think to myself, *I've quite had my fill of Indian weddings for one day, and I mean that in the least racist way possible. Even though it does still sound a bit racist.*

As I clamber into the car, and I mean, literally clamber, I reach for my phone to check for any messages.

There's one from little sis:

Could you message me when you get home from the wedding? Mum's been doing my head in with worry. She said you shouldn't be attending two weddings in one day, or even one. So just let me know that you're alive and haven't gone into labour.

There's also a message from big sis:

Hey lady, how much do you get your eyebrows done for in London? I found a new parlour here, but the lady is charging £6. Isn't that a bit much?

Finally, there is a message from Naila. What does she want?

How's it going, man? I've been meaning to message you for time but been so busy with bookings and stuff. Mum told me you're pregnant. Welcome to the club! Come round to mum's it'll be nice to see you. Haven't caught up in ages.

What is her game? Why is she asking me to come over now, when she's never cared before? I've been pregnant for months. She could have reached out any time.

"Could you change the tune?" asks M. "I've heard enough Bollywood songs for one night."

"Sure."

I hit shuffle on his phone, which is synced up to the car stereo. The next song to come on isn't a song. It's a musical score. The most stunning symphony orchestra.

"Where's this song from, again?" I ask.

"I can't remember the band, but it's from that Stephen Hawking movie we watched, The Theory of Everything."

I check the name of the track on M's phone. It's Arrival of the Birds, by Cinematic Orchestra.

"Are you okay?" M asks as I smile to myself.

"Yeah, I'm fine. I think I've found my birth song."

9th January, Sophia's books

Sophia is an absolute sweetheart. She has posted out all her books on parenting, which I will happily devour. It will save me a packet on buying books that I will only read once.

The first has a very dated front cover with a 90s model in a pink vest, with her ponytail swished to the side while she closes her eyes. I don't think I'll look that serene whilst in labour. The book talks about having a pain-free birth. I never knew there was such a thing. It mentions a technique called hypno-birthing, where you apparently breathe your baby out. I'm sceptical but interested.

There are three more books. One is about how to get the baby to sleep at night and eat well. There's an awful lot of focus on the sleep side of things. Maybe the horror stories about sleepless nights are true? There's also a book of Muslim baby names. Maybe M and I can go through that together one day. The final one is about the various stages of development a child goes through in the first 18 months of their life. It gives a week by week breakdown of what to expect. I never knew children were so formulaic. What happened to the thing about every child being different that keeps being spouted on mum blogs and forums?

"What's the plan today?" M asks breezily as he comes into the living room.

"Working?" I don't mean to sound snarky and I instantly regret my tone when I see M look down, embarrassed. "What about you?" I ask, trying to match his earlier breeziness.

"Same shit, different day. I've seen four jobs advertised today, so I sent my CV off to the recruiters. One is in Westminster, making it quite an easy commute. I'd be getting the District line again. It's decent pay at around 65K. Then the other is in..."

I look with my eyes, though I don't listen with my ears. M is so glass half full and so different to me. He talks things up before they've happened. My cautious heart can't cope. I'd rather not know until it's a certainty.

"See what happens. It sounds promising, though," I say that with complete honesty, but it's just scary. I'm reluctant to even think about getting excited about these prospects, talking through the commute, the pay and perks, until they are real prospects.

"Also, I should be hearing from the recruiter today about how the interview went on Monday. They want an immediate start, which is good."

"That is good," I say. "Fingers crossed. Also, we'd better start doing some proper baby shopping. There's not long now and we've still got loads to buy."

M does a lip grimace like my mum's. "Don't worry about that yet. There's time." He walks into the kitchen.

Why is he grimacing? Is he worried about money already?

"We can't leave it too late. Soon, I won't be able to even go to the shops. I already hate the Tube."

"Don't worry," says M. "We'll sort it."

It's easy to say don't worry but quite another thing to cause the worry. Right now, I need actions, not words.

"Also," I add, "I better look at booking myself onto an NCT course. I'm sure I was meant to do it ages ago."

M brings my mug of tea through and places it down on the coffee table in front of me. "Is that the baby class thing?"

"It is. Sophia has been going on about it. Reena mentioned that her sisters did it. That's what most people do. Most people that can afford to, anyway." I realise what I said and quickly add more words to smooth it over. "I think it would be nice. I'm not sure where the nearest one will be. I can't imagine there being one in Tower Hamlets. It's not a very typical Bengali thing to do. At least not according to my sisters."

I open up my laptop and go on the NCT website. I look for a local group. I can't see anything, apart from lots of information about how important the classes are to help give a good start to pregnancy and impending motherhood. I can't find a simple booking form online, so I head into the spare room/office to speak to someone directly.

"Hi, I'm looking to book your NCT course. I'm based in E1 and I was wondering how to go about it?"

"Right, well great. I'm just looking at the system..." the friendly voice on the other end of the line informs me. "It looks like your nearest one is in Islington."

I knew it wouldn't be in Tower Hamlets.

"How many weeks pregnant are you?"

I do some mental maths. "I'm 29 weeks. Actually, nearer 30, I think." I must sound terribly half-arsed.

"Oh, you are rather far along."

"Have I missed the boat?" My heart sinks. Is this one of the things I'll miss out on as I've been busy procrastinating?

"No, no. It's just a lot of people tend to book the course a few weeks earlier. Let's see when the next slot is. Right, okay, there is one actually starting near the end of this month, which will be ideal for you."

"Perfect." I breathe a sigh of relief. I know it sounds irrational but I really wanted to do the NCT. Not just to learn about giving birth. From what I hear, the course is a normal thing to do for most people. Julia would do it. It's like baby showers. If you don't, you're left out of that circle. That circle I've always wanted to be in. The circle I've worked so hard to be in.

"Great. I'd love to join the class. How much does it cost?"

"It's £300 for the full course."

I gulp.

"And it's several sessions spread over about four weeks."

My throat is dry. She lost me at £300. How can I justify that, when M can't even bring himself to buy a pram?

Perhaps noticing my hesitation, the kind lady adds: "We do have a discretionary discount available, depending on household income."

As I'll never meet this person face-to-face, I don't need to lie. Instead, I'm going to swallow my pride and tell her about our dire current situation.

"Okay... we're not on benefits..." I guess there is a little pride there still. "But... my husband is between jobs at the moment. I mean... he's currently out of work. He's going to get something soon so he's not bothered signing on to any Jobseeker's Allowance or anything like that. And I am working but I run my own business so that means that one month I might earn around £2000, whereas another month it might be just £800. That means over the course of the year..." I swallow hard, desperately in need of water, "I think I meet the minimum threshold."

I have to stop myself from shouting: '*We are not poor!*' It takes me back to when I was in school. Dad had retired early and we were on Income Support for a brief while. I still remember feeling that thin veil of pity. It was shit. All these years later, having climbed up the greasy corporate pole to be the same as my white peers, here I am again, negotiating for a discount.

"That's absolutely fine. We offer a concession, as I mentioned. So, for you, it would cost £60."

I nearly fall off my chair. £60! Is that it? That's far too generous! Would it be weird to say that? It probably would.

"Okay, that's great. Do you need to see proof of income? I'm happy to send screenshots of my bank statements or anything else you might need?"

"Nope," the lady replies without taking a beat. "I'll take your word for it. So, if it's okay, I'll get the payment from you now to get you booked on?"

I'm elated. If I could hug this woman I would. No othering. No pitying. Just straight down to business. I hastily grab my bank card, relieved to part with this small sum of money. I hang up before she changes her mind or asks any further questions in the name of due diligence. To be fair, of all the things to swindle a discount for, getting a reduced course on childbirth would be an odd one.

Then, my delight is replaced with worry. What if the people on the course find out I'm there on a discount? That I'm not truly like them? That I shouldn't be in the circle? That I'm not middle class, affluent or white enough? God, will I have to queue separately when attending the course?

Glass half full, glass half full, glass half full. There's no reason they should know. It's certainly not something I'm going to offer up. I stuff those worries down and replace it with complete gratitude that I have got onto a course I really want to join for a ridiculous bargain, without having to beg for scraps. I'll take the win.

"H-hello? Yeah, speaking." I hear M take a call in the living room. It must be the recruiter about that job he interviewed for. I shouldn't eavesdrop but I obviously will. "Yeah, I've been looking at a few other jobs."

Wait, what? Why is he telling them he has other prospects? That's like telling someone you're dating that you're seeing other people when you're looking to get married. You don't do that. You make that person feel like they are the one true choice.

"To be honest with ya, there is a finance job in Canary Wharf that would be better, because it pays more."

It's getting worse. I want to go in the room and mouth: '*Stop saying that!*' but then it would give away that I'm listening.

I casually walk through the living room and head to the kitchen to get myself a much needed glass of water. I turn the tap ever so slowly so as not to disturb M's call and also ensure

I can hear properly *and* to buy me more time to eavesdrop. I'm a genius.

M gets up and heads to the spare room, perhaps aware of my nosiness. Rude.

"If your client can offer more, then that would be of interest but yeah, I've been looking at a few so I'll have to see."

He's playing hard to get. Is that a tactic? Will it work? If it does, I might have to rethink my whole strategy in life.

"Yeah, okay. That's fine. Right." M pauses. I wonder what they're saying to him. "Sure, just let me know."

Shit.

M returns to the living room, looking crestfallen. I don't jump down his throat and instead wait for him to come and sit next to me. My stomach is in knots and H2 is currently spinning around above my bladder.

He collapses on the sofa and exhales deeply.

"How did it go?" I ask in the most cheery voice I can muster. Which, to all intents and purposes, isn't that cheery.

"Fine, I think. It was just the recruiter. They were asking me if I'd been looking elsewhere. I told him I had and that I've got prospects, that sort of thing. Then they said it's between me and one other guy. They are going to speak to the client now and then get back to me."

Don't jump down his throat. Don't get involved.

Despite my internal instructions, I can't help it. "It's probably best not to tell them that you've got other prospects and that they're not your first choice."

M looks at me, as if I've revealed something novel.

"It's just that, in my experience and I've probably been bouncing around jobs a bit more than you, employers want to hear that you're only interested in their job. That you're available for them. If they hear that you have other options, or you're looking elsewhere, they might think that you're more of a flight risk and not worth hiring. They might go for the other guy who is more dependable. Not to say they will in this case, just a thought."

M doesn't say anything. He sits back on the sofa, his body sinking into the soft cushion. "Oh man. I didn't think about it like that."

I bite my tongue to stop myself from getting too involved. I might be wrong and his strategy may work. M, however, looks dejected. I need to stop micromanaging and let him figure things out. After all, he does earn more than me. Or at least he did.

His phone rings again. He looks up at me and says: "I guess we'll see."

"Good luck!" I'm trying to hide the nerves in my voice.

He retreats to the bedroom to take the call. I, of course, bend my ear closer.

"Yeah, okay. No worries. That'd be great. Keep me posted."

M comes back into the living room like a guy walking to the gallows. This time he sits on the adjacent sofa, which is faux leather with cracks on the armrests. "I didn't get the job."

I try my best to hide my disappointment, and say: "Never mind, something better will come up."

I try my best to believe it.

15th January, What's in a (baby) name?

"Hey, shall we call our baby mountain goat?" M teases.

"What? Give me that!" I pull the book of Muslim baby names out of his grasp.

I need to see this for myself. M points to the name in question.

Arwa, meaning Mountain Goat. Though the name seems unflattering, it denotes independence and an ability to leap over obstacles easily.

"Let's put it on the reserve list," I say.

Just for the fun of it, M and I look at the names of baby boys and girls, despite knowing we've got a little lady growing in my tummy. The thick tome offers up names I had never even heard of, such as Yusha, Luluah, Qitara.

Hassan, means handsome. Zayn means beauty. So, why be handsome when you can be a beauty? However, having a name that sets a high aesthetic standard could either become a self-fulfilling prophecy, or set poor baby up for a fall. It's like when Bengali aunties are called Beauty or Lovely. It seldom ends well.

The book details some English sounding names, which would be good for assimilation. Rebecca, Jennifer, Shelina... no issues with mispronunciation there.

On the other end of the spectrum, there are names that would leave many a non-Muslim tongue tied- Aa'eedah, Afreedah, Maimoona. I remember middle sis complaining of how everyone mispronounced her name. It was during her *wanting to fit in* phase, in those awkward teenage years. She resorted to shortening her name, to make it easier for everyone else around her- school friends, teachers, the receptionist at the doctor surgery. She abbreviated it to accommodate them.

I'm torn down the middle. On one hand, I want my girl to have a name that will be easy to pronounce. That nobody will struggle with. A name that will, dare I say, help her in this western world. That won't separate her out, when there already will be so many differences assigned to her from birth. However, I don't want to erase her ethnicity. I don't want to whitewash her background and fade her colour. I've done enough of that for myself. I'd like it to end with me.

"What about this?" M asks, pointing at a name in the book.

It can be both Anglicised and desi-fied. The name means joyful, happy. And after all, beyond everything else, beyond health and wealth, beyond beauty and intelligence, isn't being happy the most important thing in life?

I run my index finger across the name, as if I can feel it calling out to me.

"Well, what do you think?" M is eager for my thoughts.

I smile at him. "It's perfect."

20th January, The things you do for love

"These benches aren't getting cleaner, are they?" I manoeuvre my way onto the only unsullied patch on the seat.

Julia blows a puff of cold air. "No, these pigeons will continue to poo, outliving us all, now that us humans have committed to destroying each other."

I look at Julia, aghast. "That was a bit morbid."

"Life is." She holds her cup to her lips. Her diamond ring is jutting out of her purple leather gloves. "At least that's how it seems when you turn on the news."

"I've not watched the news of late," I confess, stroking my stomach. "My threshold for bad news, particularly anything involving children, is very low these days."

"It's probably for the best. The world isn't being kind to children right now. Anyway, how come you're not watching the news? Isn't that part of your job?"

"It was when I had plenty of clients to service and I needed to be on top of the news agenda. It's not so much the case these days."

Julia offers a sympathetic pat on my knee. "Sorry to hear that. Business isn't going great?"

My pride kicks in. "No, it's fine. I wanted to have a lighter client load anyway, at this stage. It's better to have less work so I'm not stressed out and worried about getting my freelancer to cover it. Everything works out for a reason, I suppose."

She nods and sips from her cup.

I can't do this. It's Julia. If I have to put on a PR front with her, what hope is left?

"The thing is," I'm hesitant. "M lost his contracting gig."

"Oh no!" Julia gasps, making me feel worse about the situation than I already did. "The timing, too."

I frown as she raises her hands in the air. "Sorry. Not helpful. I'm sure he'll be fine. I mean, he's totally employable and there are always jobs coming up. Miles is constantly seeing new contractors join his place." Julia looks as though she's had a brainwave. "You should ask M to send his CV over to me. Then I can forward it on. The more irons in the fire, right?"

I feel a glimmer of hope. Julia is right. When I was made redundant, I hit my emails hard. It paid off. M needs to try everything. Be everywhere.

I try to tell M this in my least patronising voice, as I'm very aware that even with my best attempts, I'm still very patronising. I also don't want to micromanage his job hunt. That way lies trouble. He pretty much left me to it when I was looking for work before I decided to build my business. At the very least, I should afford him the same courtesy but it's tricky. When I was made redundant, he wasn't heavily pregnant. It's comparing apples and pears.

"I hope it's not stressing you out too much," says Julia. "Remember, stress is not good for the baby. Or making a baby, in my case." She looks up from her half empty cup of coffee and moves her fringe out of her eyes. "Anyway, we should do something to celebrate. We never really did a dinner or afternoon tea or anything in honour of your pregnancy. I've been rubbish and so busy, especially as I was back up north last week, to make up for spending Christmas with Miles' family."

"And how was that?" I ask.

"Different. Can't say I loved it. Miles' parents are a bit, dare I say, stuffy. So it was hardly a raucous affair."

I bite my tongue, as it sounds like Julia has described her own family. I guess there's a sliding scale of stuffy.

Julia sighs. "Miles insisted on an extended stay at theirs as a sort of dry run before we get married. That's my life now, alternating Christmas' between his family and mine. The compromises you make for love, right?"

I smile at Julia's predicament, which is so familiar. "Indeed."

26th January, Learning about childbirth

M and I are on the bus, en route to our first NCT class, when my phone pings. It's Reena:

Alright, how's you? Thanks so much for coming to my wedding and for the incredibly generous gift. Things are good here but proper hectic since we've got back from honeymoon. Just let me know when you're having your baby shower, I'll try and shuffle what I can as I wouldn't want to miss it.

What I want to reply is:

I would let you know the date of my baby shower, if I was having a baby shower. If I had someone to throw me a baby shower.

Instead, I text back saying:

No worries, will do. I hope you had a great honeymoon x

"Who is that you're messaging?" asks M.

"It's Reena. She's asking when I'm having a baby shower."

"Are you having one?"

"No. Someone's supposed to throw you one and nobody has offered. My sisters obviously won't do anything like that. And Julia hasn't mentioned anything."

"Could you ask her?"

"It would be a bit awkward. Probably a bit desperate, too. She hasn't offered so I can't exactly impose it on her. Plus, she might not be up to it after her.... you know."

M stretches his arms out and yawns. Why's he tired? He's not had a busy working week. "I bet she'd love to throw you a shower. It's not like she'll resent you having a baby. If Jam had something I didn't, I'd be happy for him."

"I'm sure Julia is happy for me but I think that's where men and women are different. You guys are a lot more straightforward with your feelings. I don't want to be rubbing her face in it, asking if she can organise a celebration of my baby's arrival, when she..." I lower my voice, "lost hers."

"That's true. Would it be really weird if you threw yourself a baby shower?" M asks what seems like a ridiculous question but then I wonder whether anyone has done that.

A quick consult on one of my mum forums tells me more.

User19247 says: *I don't know why in Western cultures people expect friends and family to throw them baby showers. Here, we do it ourselves. It's much nicer as you can plan it how you want to. Just like if you were planning a birthday party.*

Meanwhile, Hotmama1234 says: *I think the idea of a baby shower is bizarre. Why would you want to have a big celebration before your baby arrives? It's bad luck jinxing yourself before the baby's come. In some countries, they don't even have a pram in the house before their baby's due date as they're so superstitious.*

Clearly, Hotmama1234 and I are kindred spirits.

It still feels weird, though. I've not met someone in real life who's not had a baby shower out of superstition. I also don't know a single person who's hosted their own baby shower. It's usually done for them. God, this is when I wish my sisters were more proactive. I don't get anything from them these days, except questions about eyebrow threading from big sis.

Maybe I could ask little sis? I fire her a quick message:

Hey, totally random but do you reckon you could throw me a baby shower? I could organise it all, but you can be the officiator.

This is a new level of desperation.

Little sis, to my surprise, replies straight away. I thought she'd still be asleep at 9.30am on a Saturday.

She says:

Yeah, that's random. I could do but I wouldn't know where to start. Would you want it in Manchester or London? And who'd come? Would I have to be there?

Oh, forget it. It's just too much hard work. Like other things in my life, a baby shower will be something that will retreat to the recess of my mind. I'll deflect attention onto M, by asking about his job search.

"I could get in touch with Julia and see if she can pass on your CV to Miles, if you like? I remember at dinner, he mentioned his company is always hiring."

M shrugs. "You could do."

"It's good to have options, isn't it?" I ask, mildly annoyed at his nonchalant nature.

"No, yeah. It's good. I just don't know what will come of it."

He looks out of the window. I wonder if beneath this chilled out nature, M is worried about the future. Is he concerned about finances? Is he thinking about needing to tighten our belts? Is he afraid of how long it will take to get a job? Or are these worries that only I carry on my shoulders?

We disembark near Old Street roundabout and spend five minutes figuring out where the actual meeting place is. Despite this area being so close to us, it is so unfamiliar. We have no idea where we are and what direction to head.

Finally, M's phone map negotiates us to a black box of a building, which looks anything but inviting. Standing outside, we contemplate whether we've got the right place but then a heavily pregnant woman and her partner slowly make their way inside. It would be silly to ask if they're here for the NCT class, as they so obviously are. We follow them in.

Another lady arrives, shuffling along ever so slowly. God, she looks ready to pop. Once again, I feel like I've got it easy with my neat bump and lack of joint pain.

We are invited to sit in a circle made of blue plastic chairs. We are among the last to arrive and the only brown faces but, at this point in my life, I've come to expect it.

"Welcome to this NCT course," a curly-haired lady announces with glee. "I am Carmen and I'll be running this course for you. I've been working with the NCT for nearly 20 years. So it's fair to say I know my way around a nappy."

This is greeted by polite chortles from everyone.

"Right, well, I'm sure many of you can't wait to get into the different modules. And we're going to make it as enjoyable as possible. Well, as enjoyable as childbirth can be."

This is received by generous chuckles from the men and nervous giggles from the heavily pregnant women, myself included.

The first order of business is to go around the circle and introduce ourselves, share our due dates and a fun personal fact.

"Hi, I'm Jean-Patrice," says a smartly dressed man with a French accent. His nose is sharp like an arrow, with flared nostrils. His dark hair contrasts with his ice blue eyes. Not that I'm looking. "We are due on..." He looks to his partner.

"3rd April," she helpfully adds.

He nods. "Yes. Now, let me see...... Fun fact? I speak three languages."

That doesn't sound very fun. Impressive but not fun.

"I'm Claudia, and apparently I hold the Guinness World Record of being the longest baby born that year."

Claudia does indeed look very thin and elongated. Her poor mum.

And it goes on. Jim loves fishing and every New Year's Eve he goes to Scotland in search of salmon. Melinda enjoys fell walking. Peter is into darts, while Josephine has visited 26 different countries.

When it's M's turn, he shrugs and says: "I don't have anything particularly interesting. But my hobbies include golf and watching the football."

Thankfully, I've had enough time to prepare when the spotlight turns on me. "When I'm not doing my day job of running my PR consultancy, I write a lifestyle blog that's kind of morphed into pregnancy stuff recently." I smile proudly, happy to have plugged my diversified blog to a captive audience.

"I'm Rory, and like my man over here..." he gestures towards M, "I do like a round of golf."

"I'm Cindy," says the last person in the circle, "and I'm really glad to be here and looking forward to learning about this crazy next stage of life. My interesting fact is, I can tread water without doing anything. My friends think it's mad but I don't even need to move. I think it's my size, I'm very buoyant." Cindy pretends to lift her bump but inadvertently heaves up her bosom instead.

M does a great job of keeping his eyes focused on her face, as do all the other men in the room.

Carmen proceeds to share some pictures of her daughter, Kerry, who gave birth last year. The projector presents a slideshow of Kerry with her partner.

In one shot, he is inhaling the gas and air, which was meant for Kerry. They are holding hands in the inflatable paddling pool. Her in a sports bra and him in a soaked t-shirt. It's all smiles until the pictures take a turn. The next slide shows the poor girl bent forward, face contorted in pain. Another one shows him rubbing her back while she is mid-scream. They go on like this, with Carmen's daughter exhibiting expressions I never knew possible, as though the pain of it all brings out previously unused facial muscles. Finally, the last photo in the slideshow of horrors is of the couple smiling, holding a newborn. Those are just minor details as there is one thing none of us can take our eyes off.

"You're all looking at the pool full of blood, aren't you?"

In the space of a few photos, the water turned from clear to deep red.

"I want to reassure you that it looks a lot worse than it is. It's actually only about a shot glass full of blood but the water makes it look like more. Now, what I really want you to do is not fixate on the blood in the photo, but instead look at the family."

It's hard to focus on the couple when they're sitting in the Red Sea.

"Right." Carmen clasps her hands as though we haven't just been traumatised. "Who has thought about their birth plan?"

Claudia raises her hand. "We've discussed it and I'd quite like to have a home birth, if that would be medically possible."

Carmen smiles and ruffles her grey, curly hair. "Yes, a lot of mums prefer to have home births. It's much nicer to be in your own home, rather than a clinical hospital. It's all the medical equipment and machines, they make you nervous. When you're at home with the midwife, it's much more comfortable. There's not much hanging around. And generally, statistics show that women who have home births tend to have fewer interventions. It's a lot easier and less stressful. After all, stress is a big hindrance when it comes to childbirth."

I've heard similar suggestions from midwives before. Is there a shortage of hospital beds or something? Why do they keep pushing for home births? That would be the last thing I'd want to do. I couldn't stand the mess, all the fluids sloshing around, not to mention being so far away from hospital. I would feel much more comfortable with a medical professional hovering around, just in case things got tricky.

"I'd like to know about other options," says Melinda. "I'd be scared about complications. I've got pregnancy diabetes so I'd prefer a hospital setting."

"That's fine." Carmen nods earnestly. "I'll run you through all the options and interventions available."

In a whistle-stop tour, I learn about gas and air, inductions, forceps and sutures. It's quite an education.

"Now, let's talk about birthing positions." Carmen strokes her hair. "You don't have to take part, if you're not comfortable," she tells Genevieve, who is struggling just sitting.

The rest of us are invited to take part in what I can only describe as an amateur yoga session. All us pregnant ladies, with our bellies hanging out, are summoned onto all fours to rotate our hips, forwards, backwards and in a circular motion. M, along with the other partners, is advised to rub my shoulders and stroke my back while I writhe around. It's all very surreal.

"Another thing that really helps relax you is swaying around. Come on, let's all try it. Onto your feet! Grab hold of your partner and do a slow dance. Sway from side to side, that's it. Yes, Rory! That's how you do it. The movement, motion and gravity helps to relax mum and baby."

"This is the only time I've got you to dance," I whisper in M's ear.

"I know. What would my dad say if he saw us? I'd probably get a clip round the ear."

As we rock in silence, I feel baby H2 doing pirouettes inside me. I think she likes it. Jean-Patrice looks slightly uncomfortable, holding Claudia at the waist with flexed fingers. Meanwhile, Rory and Cindy are re-enacting a scene from Dirty Dancing, looking lost in the moment.

"Let's never speak of this again," M mumbles.

After working up an appetite with the world's slowest dancing, it's time to eat. Everyone in the group has brought their own packed lunch. Sandwiches covered in tinfoil, pieces of fruit and water bottles. M and I feel rather guilty with our supermarket bought meal deals complete with fizzy drinks. We never think to make our own sandwiches. It's just not in our DNA. Perhaps it's because our main focus is on making curries, which are quite the process, we decide to leave anything involving bread to the experts.

"What is it you do?" Rory asks M.

M slowly chews on his tuna baguette to buy extra time for a response. "Nothing much at the moment." Then he looks at me and I share a glance that suggests he should provide some subtext. "I'm between jobs at the minute. But when I'm working, it's in finance."

"If you can take the time off, make the most of it. It sounds like when baby arrives, there won't be any respite."

"I know," says M. "It'll be hard work."

I roll my eyes. It will be hard work for me. M won't be breastfeeding round the clock. It'll be on me. So don't encourage my husband to have a rest, Rory.

I look around for bits of conversation and learn that amongst us are lecturers, bankers, analysts, doctors and lawyers. All middle-class and white. With M not working, and me barely freelancing, I am sat on a knife edge, constantly worried that we will be ousted from the group as we don't belong. I always wanted to be in this room. Figuratively speaking, that is. I didn't actually want to be heavily pregnant, sat around a lot of other ladies who are struggling with indigestion and achy limbs. I mean, I wanted to be part of this conversation with very grown-up people with very respectable jobs. Now I'm actually in the room, now I've made it, I'm scared it will be snatched away through one wrong foot by M.

After lunch, Carmen shows us an electronic device that looks like an instrument of torture.

"This might be worth you getting. It's a Tens machine. You can either buy it outright, or you can rent it. It's rather genius. It sends electric signals, like little shocks, to the area you stick the patch on, and that helps reduce the feeling of pain during labour. It can make the contractions seem less intense. Can I have a volunteer?"

It's the machine middle sis told me about.

"I'm not doing it," M hisses in my ear. "The pad will rip off all my arm hairs."

I cover my face. M can still make me giggle, I'll give him that.

Rory is a trooper and offers himself up for sacrifice.

He roles up his sleeve and Carmen sticks a pad on his forearm.

"This might pinch a bit," she says with a glint in her eye. "However, it's only fair, given what you ladies are going to go through soon."

There's a buzzing sound, then Rory flinches. Carmen presses the button again. Another flinch from Rory. Another glint in Carmen's eye.

"In a sense, it's replacing one form of pain with another," says Rory, between shocks.

"Sort of, yes," says Carmen, pressing the button harder.

What fresh hell is this? Why would you, when you're already in pain, inflict more pain in a bid to deflect from the initial pain? Who wants to electrocute themselves? No, thank you. Not for me.

"Okay, the session won't be much longer as I imagine you all want to get home. I'll just cover a few more aspects of birthing. The next time you come in, we will be exploring the stages of labour and possible after effects, such as perineum tears," says Carmen, as though it's nothing at all.

4th February, An obligatory call

"I tell you something and you no be angry, okay?" says mum.

This doesn't sound good. "Go on," I say, with trepidation.

"Your auntie Jusna call. She been pestering me so long to get your number."

"Why does she want my number? Since when does she care to call?"

Mum huffs. "You know, soon as you get married, your value rises. Then pregnant and value go up even more. Suddenly she all caring auntie. More like nosey lady want to know everything about your business. Hmmmph!"

"Of course she does. You didn't give it, did you?"

Mum goes silent.

"Mum! Did you give her my number?"

I can't see mum's face, as we're speaking on the phone but I can just feel her doing a lip grimace. "You see, she kept asking. In the end, how could I say no? How bad it look? So maybe just speak to your dad's sister this one time? You only have one."

"What? Are you guilt tripping me about only having one auntie? She's a bloody nosey one!"

"*Dooro!*"

"You said it yourself! She's nosey."

"When I say that?" Mum goes all defensive.

"Literally just now, mum. You're always saying she's nosey. I can't believe you gave her my number."

"Okay, okay. But what I supposed to do? She act like she might die if she never get to speak to you. Anyway, you have nothing to hide. Just tell her that you're okay. Keep things short and simple. Maybe no mention about your work. Don't tell her you got own business."

"Mum, I've never understood that. What's wrong with me having my own business? It's still in the field I built my career in. It's not like I'm sewing knickers or something."

"You forget what she like? She make it sound small. As if you run coffee shop or worse... being beautician."

Mum utters the last profession as though it's a dirty word. I should inform her that Asian makeup artists charge a fair whack for bridal makeovers. Eyebrow threading isn't cheap, either.

"Fine, I won't say anything about my job."

And I definitely won't say anything about my husband's lack of job, I think to myself. That would really get the rumour mill going.

"Good, good. I better go because she call you now."

"What? Now? Mum, I'm not ready. I need to think about what I'm going to tell her when she asks me 101 questions."

"No need to be ready. Just your auntie, remember?" I'm getting whiplash from mum's flip-flopping. "Also, no need to mention about renting, either. If she does ask, say you just waiting for right house."

"What's our housing situation got to do with anything?"

It's too late. Mum has hung up and, like clockwork, my phone rings again. I brace myself.

Me: "Salaamalaykum, how are you?"

Auntie Jusna: "Walaykum Salaam Warahmantullahi wa barakatu. I be okay but you forgot about me! Do you know who I am anymore?"

Me: (Laughing): "Sorry, I've just been busy."

Auntie Jusna: "Yes, your mum tell me you've been very busy. Still working? When you going to take time off now you having baby?"

I laugh nervously.

Auntie Jusna: "I've no stop thinking about you. I been so worried. How are you coping over there, all alone? With no family to help you?"

That hurt a bit.

Me: "I do have some support. My uncle Tariq and auntie Rukhsana aren't too far away. They sent food over last week."

Auntie Jusna. "Oh yes. Uncle Tariq be your mum's cousin? They the ones who daughter married English man?"

Me: "That's the one."

Auntie Jusna: "And what of their sons? They have two boys, no? Are they married?"

Me: "I don't think so."

Auntie Jusna: "You don't think so? How you live near them and not know?"

Me: "I mean, I do know. They're not married. It's just they don't live at home. They work elsewhere, I think."

Must stop saying 'I think'. I'm giving her more ammunition to dig holes.

Auntie Jusna: "What your plans when baby born? Are you going to come to your mum's for stay?"

Me: "I'm not sure. We haven't made any plans yet."

Auntie Jusna: "You mean your mum not ask you yet? I spoke to her other day. I said: *'You must tell your daughter to stay. First time baby, she can't be alone over there in London.'*"

Me: "They might come and stay with me."

Auntie Jusna: "Stay with you? In your small flat in London? They no be able to cope without proper kitchen. And my brother won't be comfortable there. I can't believe she not ask you. I told her to. Let me ask her again."

I never knew my dad's sister would be a conduit between myself and my mother.

Me: "I better go. I've got some work to do."

Auntie Jusna: "Oh yes, of course. I know how hard it is for you. You must go. And tell your husband make more money. Work harder! You need to take your rest."

Me: "Will do. Anyway, I-"

Auntie Jusna: "I know, I know. Young people are very busy. Never got time to talk to old auntie. How much you pay in rent?"

Well, that wasn't a natural segue.

Me: "I think...... About £1800 a month?"

Damn, I said 'think' again. Maybe this isn't such a bad thing, as it suggests M covers the rent, which is why I'm vague.

Auntie Jusna: "Only £1800? That cheap? Hassna husband has family in London. They live in... I think... West London? You hear of Kensington?"

Me: "I have heard of Kensington, yes."

Auntie Jusna: "They say rent in that area be £3000 a month. Can you believe? For small flats?"

I spy an opportunity.

Me: "Property prices are crazy. How much do they pay, then?"

Auntie Jusna: "Heh? Who?"

Me: "You said Hassna's husband has family in Kensington. How much are they paying?"

Auntie Jusna (mumbles): "Line keeps going funny. Can you hear me?"

Me: "I can hear you fine, auntie. You were saying that property prices are around £3000 a month in Kensington. Is that how much they're paying, too?"

Now it's auntie Jusna's turn to laugh nervously.

Auntie Jusna: "No, they in council flat."

Me: "Sorry Auntie? What was that?"

Auntie Jusna: "I say, they live in council flat! I'm just glad my Hassna bought her house when she did. Now, there's no way they could afford a four-bedroom semi-detached house. Anyhow, you keep working. But remember to take rest, okay?"

And with that, my beloved auntie hangs up and I, for the first time in my life, feel satisfied that I got her all tongue tied.

16th February, I hate shopping

Shopping is only fun when it's hypothetical.

When you're doing it for real, exchanging real money, it's a different ball game. We walk straight past the golden egg highchairs and head to the clearance section of the department store. I'm not proud.

"Those throne type baby chairs are a bit ridiculous, anyway," says M.

"Hmm," is all I can respond with.

I know he's right. They are ridiculous. It wasn't even about the highchairs. It was about wanting more for baby H2 than I had for myself. Just like mum wants me to buy new things for the baby, because she wasn't always able to. I get it. I understand where she's coming from. Growing up, my sisters and I were used to making do with less. Not having the best trainers or the nicest new coats. We expected our fashion to be a season behind our friends in school. I wanted better for H2.

I worked so bloody hard my whole adult life to be able to do more. I didn't expect this. I didn't expect to be rifling through the sale section in the hopes of finding a newborn outfit.

Yes, I'm stingy by nature. Yes, I shop in the sales but for my little girl, I wanted more. At least at the beginning. I wanted to give the best start to level the playing field for her when it was so imbalanced for me.

M, however, is less frugal. He is admiring an oak effect cot, with a matching cupboard and chest of drawers.

"What do you think of this?" he asks.

"It looks nice. How much is it?" I have to ask the million dollar question.

M goes hunting in search of a price tag. There isn't one. We need to ask the saleswoman, readying our best poker faces for when we learn it's way out of our budget.

"Do you need any help?" The smiley, mousey-haired saleswoman asks, inching towards us.

"We wanted to see how much this set is?" says M.

"Or just the cot?" I add.

The girl examines the priceless cot with as much confusion as we do. "Ah ha," she says, having an epiphany. "It's ex-display. That's why there isn't a price tag. I'll check on here." She taps into a device attached to her hip.

Her eyes widen in surprise and I'm not sure if it's genuine or all part of the sales pitch. "This is actually reduced quite heavily because it's previously been on display and it's the last one. So the full set is £595. Ordinarily, it would be £999." She looks to us, expecting gasps in shock and awe.

M is impressed and so am I, to be honest. It's a pretty good deal, especially given that the golden thrones were the same price.

"Do you think we should get it?" I ask M. "We weren't planning on getting a full nursery set, were we? Don't we just need a cot?"

"Yeah, but it is a nice set. And she'll need somewhere to put her clothes, won't she? Our cupboards are full and our flat pack drawers are bursting. They are probably more useful than the cot, to be honest with ya. She'll probably end up in our bed."

"No she won't! I'm not going to be one of those mums who doesn't put her baby in the cot," I bite back unintentionally aggressively.

"Well, it's still worth getting the set."

"Can we afford to, though?"

M laughs in disbelief. "Course we can. Why wouldn't we?"

Does he really need me to spell it out?

"The fact that you're out of work," I say, lowering my voice. "And that I'm barely working so between us, things are pretty grim."

M's eyes dart from side to side. I can see the look on his face. It's indignity. I went too far. I don't mean to hurt him. I don't mean to emasculate him. It's just... I don't know where we're headed. It's hard enough being out of work in London when it's just the two of us but with a baby on the way? I can't be as relaxed as M. I can't.

"I suppose we need to get something and it's a good price," I say.

After the incredibly lengthy sales process (which seems unnecessary. The store really ought to rethink that), M and I get the bus home.

I suggest we look for some more essentials, like a pram and a car seat. M says it's worth waiting for that. There is still time, according to him.

"I'll get back on it, work-wise, this afternoon," M declares. "I need to email those recruiters and give them a kick up the arse."

"Shall I chase Julia about the job at Miles' place? I've not heard anything back yet."

"Don't bother," says M. "There will be plenty of other opportunities. Things might be a bit quiet at the moment because of the time of year but they'll pick up. Anyway, we've got more exciting stuff to look forward to. Haven't you got your doctor's appointment?"

"Oh yeah, I'm going to listen to my new favourite sound, baby H's heartbeat. But look, as it's at 4 'o'clock, you might as well head back to the flat and get on the case with the recruiters. I can do this appointment by myself. We are in the safe zone now."

"Are you sure?"

"Yeah, it's fine. I'll keep the baby cooking in the oven and you can fill the pipeline."

"Or should that be the piping cream line?" M laughs.

"Huh?"

"It's just you said about a bun in the oven, so I thought I'd continue the baking theme. As in piping the cream on the cake. Now that I say it out loud, it doesn't work."

I frown. "Not one of your best jokes."

"DID YOU MANAGE TO GET a urine sample?" asks the doctor.

I pull the small plastic tube out of my bag. "Always."

I no longer flinch at peeing on my hand, as it's become so synonymous with this pregnancy. I do feel that my ick threshold has greatly increased over these past months.

The doctor takes the warm sample of wee and dips a stick into it. After swirling it round a couple of times, she concludes that all is well.

"Now let's have a look at your blood pressure."

As she pumps away, expanding the armband and squeezing my bicep, she raises an eyebrow. "Hmm. Your blood pressure is a little high. Nothing major but it's just something to be aware of. Are you getting enough sleep?"

"Not really. I'm not that comfortable these days."

She sighs. "I know. It's a nightmare, isn't it? I've had three children. They're still terrible sleepers. Is there anything else? Have you been stressed out lately at all?"

I don't think that dishing all to the doctor about M's work situation is going to help matters. I mean, what is she going to do, offer him a job? There is no cure for worry, is there? I just have to ride this one out. "No, nothing in particular is stressing me out."

I lie on the examination table for the umpteenth time. I know the routine off by heart now. Piss sample, pressure check, prod baby bump.

I wince in discomfort as the doctor presses her fingers sharply around my stomach to feel the baby's head. "Sorry about that," she says, continuing to dig away. "There we are. The baby's head is where it should be. The back seems fine. There's the little feet."

"How can you even tell?" I ask. "Isn't it all like one big blob?"

The doctor laughs. "It comes with practice. When you've done it as long as I have, you learn to make out the body parts. Okay, would you like to listen to the heartbeat?"

I close my eyes. "Yes, please."

Throughout all of this pregnancy, H2's soothing, pulsating heart beat has been medicinal. It always sounds a little quick but the doctor assures me, every time, that it's perfectly normal.

I thank the doctor as I leave, comforted by the fact that I am inching closer to having the baby and there is less and less chance of there being any problems. Dare I say, I'm starting to enjoy the pregnancy. If only I could continue to keep that niggle of worry at bay.

The low winter sunshine bathes my face as I head out into the cold. I pop in my earphones and load up the audiobook that Sophia recommended on hypno-birthing. The narrator, a birthing doula, has a nasally, shrill voice. It's not the most pleasant of listens, but I persevere.

You'll have an amazing birth. You will have an amazing birth, she repeats like a chant. She's giving me ear worm but I am trying to focus on her words, instead of her delivery. It's helping ease my worry and wash away negative thoughts around M and his work situation.

Speaking of which, I enter the flat to find that my husband is lying down on the sofa, watching TV.

I don't want the job hunt to be the first thing I ask about. I sit on the adjacent sofa. "What are you watching?"

"Tipping Point."

M looks forlorn, dejected. He watches so much TV these days. I'm worried. He should be working now. As modern minded as I like to be, I well and truly believe that men need to be outdoors working. I think it comes down to the notion that is as old as time. Men go out hunting and bring home the spoils, while women stay home to cook it. I believe that, fundamentally, in our DNA, we haven't changed much since the cavemen times. Men still do the lion's share of work. Women, even if they hold down a full-time job, do most of the housework and parenting. It's not fair but who made the rules? It seems that's always been the way.

Despite having my own money, I am all too aware that I am the one that's going to be birthing a baby and staying at home, raising it for the first year, at least. Seeing M like this, sluggish on the sofa, only cements my belief further that this isn't his natural state. He needs to be out there, hunting for animals. Or the modern day scenario, earning money to buy halal meat so I can cook it.

"Any news on the job front?" I finally ask. I can't take the suspense anymore.

"No," he replies, still looking at the TV. "I called a couple of recruiters while you were at your appointment. One didn't answer and the other one told me that the job I applied for a few days ago has already been taken."

"Oh. Have they got anything new on their books?" I feel like I already know the answer.

M is still fixated on his programme. It's like every other daytime gameshow. The formula remains the same, only the people are interchangeable. It's like watching the same thing, over and over again, with only the slightest variable being altered. "No, it seems really quiet at the moment." His voice is monotone, like he's resigned himself to this. He's giving up.

I get up off the sofa and head to our bedroom. I close the door so M can't hear me cry.

20th February, A lie is but a lie is but a lie

"It be nice of you to stay for few days," says mum. "I missed you."

She is currently adding spices to the chicken curry. The extractor fan is on full blast and its abrasive whirring is numbing my brain. "Has he taken time off?"

"Yes," I lie. "He had some annual leave to use."

"Tell him not to take too much holiday now. He will need it for later, when baby come."

I say nothing and instead fish out four potatoes from our makeshift pantry under the stairs.

"How much holiday do men get from work?"

I'm glad mum has asked in generic terms, so I'm not outright fibbing. "It's usually two weeks."

"And for him? Will he get two weeks as well?"

Okay, I guess I am going to have to lie, again. I wish mum wouldn't probe so much. "I think he gets two weeks."

Middle sis walks into the kitchen. "I thought contractors didn't get paternity leave?"

The cow.

"I mean, he's going to take two weeks off." I look away from both nosey ladies.

Middle sis then says: "If you were a teacher, you could've coordinated it around the school holidays."

I tut. "Sure, because fertility is magic like that and you can just pick whichever day you want."

Middle sis shrugs. "Well, I guess not for everyone. But I had mine in July, so..."

I don't need to be reminded of her super fertility, or her husband's stable, generous holiday giving, very-unlikely-to-get-fired-from job.

"Have you bought all your bits?" middle sis asks.

"We bought a furniture set the other day. A cot, wardrobe and chest of drawers."

"That's good. Anything else? Clothes? A Moses basket? Or a car seat?"

I cut the freshly washed potatoes in half. "I've bought a couple of things but want to wait until later. Sophia said she can give me her Moses basket."

"Heh?" Mum looks up from her pot stirring. "You still talking 'bout getting second-hand Moses basket? I told you, need to buy new things for baby. Honestly, earning so much money and being so stingy. Doesn't baby deserve new things?"

I can feel tears prick my eyes but blame it on the onions that middle sis started slicing away at.

"Does it really matter if it's second-hand? How long do babies sleep in those things, anyway? I'll obviously be getting a new mattress for it."

"*Dooro!* It still not nice. These things you only buy once. Then you can use it for your other children. They're not even too expensive, either. I'll give you money."

"I don't need money." My voice shrinks.

"Then just buy it! These things not worth being stingy for. That's not what we do. Or you shouldn't, anyhow. It not like old time when people had no money. What people say?"

"It's not always about what people will say, mum. What have people ever done for us? Are people going to come and look after the baby? Are people going to help me? No, nobody does anything, yet everybody has something to say."

Mum frowns. "Okay, do whatever. I need to pray now. Watch the chicken no burn. And you want to make a roast chicken today? I bought parsnip. But you need to go to Cash and Carry to get whole chicken."

"No," I say, to the surprise of mum and middle sis. "I can't be bothered."

As mum shuffles away, middle sis rubs my back. "You know how she is. And, you won't like me saying but, she's right, we don't really do the hand-me-down thing."

"Mum is very choosy about what we do and don't do based on tradition. Aren't we meant to do the whole 40-day thing where everyone looks after me so I can focus on raising the baby? Isn't that a tradition? How come she hasn't said anything about that?"

Middle sis turns to face me, knife still in hand. "None of us had that. I had all three of mine by myself. Mum visited but she didn't stay."

I take a step back. "That's what other people do. It's normal. We don't do normal things. Like having a baby shower. People's sisters do that for them. Not mine, though."

Middle sis sighs. "Again, girlie, I didn't have one, either. And if you're so bothered, I'll throw you one the next time we come. It will have to be in the next school holiday so we can do it here and-" she pauses, no doubt doing mental arithmetic.

"Yeah, and I'll either have had the baby or be way too pregnant to travel back up north. Clearly, you lot wouldn't go out of your way to come to London for such a thing, would you?"

"It's harder with kids. You'll know when you have your own. You have to do everything around them and their school. Even then, it depends on when your brother-in-law can take me. It's not like you're close to us, living down south."

I breathe out heavily, hoping to calm my racing heart. "Doesn't matter. I'm just saying. I wish we did things like other people sometimes. Rather than picking and choosing what's the done thing."

Middle sis squeezes past me. "The chicken is burning. I better give it a good stir."

I go to the living room to find big sis and little sis in a compromising position.

"Ow! Bloody hell." Big sis pants as if she's in labour. "Okay, do some more."

Big sis is leaning back, upper lip red raw, flinching every time little sis drags the thread across her moustache to pull out the hairs.

"Since when did you get so good at threading?" I ask.

"Since I started doing my eyebrows. Do you want me to do your 'tache?" asks little sis. "It's looking luxurious."

I raise my hand to the side of my mouth and feel some spiky hairs brush against my finger. God, I really have neglected all forms of grooming. And I mean, *all* forms of grooming. I will have to address the lady parts very soon as I don't want the midwife to be judging me when I go into labour.

"Where is the fella?" asks big sis.

"He's gone to his mum's."

"His mum's?" Big sis furrows her brow. "I thought he'd be going straight home on a Sunday night?"

Why is it that when M had a job, nobody cared for his whereabouts? Yet now, everybody is forcing me to lie? It's like they know our secret.

"He's got a bit of annual leave to use," I say before realising my mistake. In contracting, you don't get annual or paternity leave. Good job middle sis didn't hear my tall tale.

"Tell him not to use it all," big sis warns. "After all, he's going to need it when the baby arrives."

"So I keep being told."

Big sis examines her upper lip in the mirror. "I think you missed a few strands but I'll leave it. It's too painful." She turns to me. "On the subject of babies, remember my friend, Laura?"

I have to think. "Laura... Laura... Laura... oh, eternally single Laura? Is she having a baby?"

"Yes, but not with a fella."

"What do you mean?" I ask.

"She's still single and would struggle to have a baby even if she did meet someone. That's why she's having a baby on her own with the help of a..." big sis pauses as she looks at little sis.

"It's okay. I know more than you think," says little sis.

Big sis swallows hard. "Right, well missy, you better not let mum hear you say that. Anyway, Laura said she's had enough of waiting for a man, so decided to have the baby with the help of a donor." She whispers the last word.

"She's going to have the baby all by herself? Wouldn't that be really hard?" asks little sis.

"It's going to be very difficult. She thinks she can do it, though. She'll have her mum nearby which will be a big help. I couldn't imagine it myself, though. Raising kids isn't easy, even when you've got a husband."

"Good for her," I say. "Why should she miss out on kids just because she hasn't got a man?"

Big sis applies cold cream to her upper lip. "I don't know, lady. I mean, obviously I'm happy for her as it's something she's always wanted. And anything is possible these days. You hear of people having kids in all sorts of situations. It'll just be a shock for her, that's all. She's used to having so much time for herself. That will go out of the window. Count yourself lucky that you've got a nice boy to have your baby with. I bet he'll be good at changing nappies too, your fella. He seems the hands-on sort."

"I do count my blessings," I reply, knowing full well that I haven't been counting lately.

"Did your *fella* change nappies?" little sis teases.

Big sis rolls her eyes. "He tried his best, but he was never very good in that department. I guess it's not a traditional man's role so I didn't expect much."

She looks at me, searching my face for offence. However, there is none taken. Big sis' idea of offending is more of a compliment to me. I'd much rather have a husband who seems the hands-on sort.

IN THE PRIVACY OF MY former bedroom, I get Googling. There are things I need to know, namely, how much it would actually cost to have a baby and where I can make savings. I need to be more practical and, dare I say, this is my comfort zone. I'm appealing to my core nature, my inner stingy bitch. The recent years of London living made me deviate from my true self. The fancy meals. The nights out. Barbour coats. Heck, even hiring a cleaner. All of that isn't me and I was fooling myself to think it should be otherwise for baby H2.

A quick search of 'how to save money when having a baby' is informative. Front and centre is the obvious– you can save a packet by breastfeeding rather than giving a baby formula milk. This is music to my ears, as I already believe breast is best. Apparently it's not only best for baby, it can save me thousands each year, too.

Another option is not so appealing. Reusable nappies. The website says reusable nappies are an amazing way to help the planet and your pocket. I'm sure they are but I have questions. What happens when the baby does a poo? How do you clean it out? Do you just tip it upside down into the toilet? What if it's a runny poo? Then what? Do you have to rinse it in the bath? Like the olden days? I'm not sure if I can do the whole reusable nappies thing. I'm all for saving the planet but that just reminds me of what people used back in the day out of circumstance, not choice. I'm going to put that on the back burner. It's a maybe, but unlikely.

The rest of the options are second-hand clothing, hand-me-downs, and the like. Mum would have a fit if I went down that road.

I message M.

Me: *I've seen how we can save money when the baby comes. Apparently, you can save up to nine grand by doing some simple hacks.*

M: *What are the hacks?*

Me: *Reusable nappies, for a start.*

M: *Eww! What about when the baby has a dump? You'd have to clean it out. Would you want to?*

Me: *Not sure. I'm going to look into it. It might not be that bad.*

M: *I wouldn't bother. My mate was saying you can get supermarket brands that are just as good as Pampers.*

Me: *Which one of your friends has a baby?*

M: *Billy.*

Me: *Who?*

M: *You know, Bilal. He likes us to call him Billy. A few of my friends have babies, remember? Didn't I tell you about Akbar as well? He's got three kids.*

Me: *I forget because I only ever hear you talk about Jam (Heart shaped emoji).*

M: *(Grinning face emoji)*

This is nice. Recently, M and I haven't been the best of friends. Or should I say, I haven't been too happy with him, while he seems to be none the wiser. The stress of being pregnant and M's job situation has meant our relationship has taken a backseat. I miss this. Joking with M. Maybe being apart for a few days at our respective parents' houses will help. Having him at home the whole time is a bit much.

M: *What else are you up to?*

Me: *Mainly dodging questions about your work.*

M doesn't reply. I shouldn't have said that. His unemployment is at the forefront of everything these days, which is neither helpful nor healthy.

He finally replies: *I guess we both have to get used to being better liars.*

Me: *Hopefully not for too long.*

M: *InshaAllah.*

Me: *InshaAllah?* God willing? Look at you, asking for blessings.

M: *We've got lots to pray for. And be thankful for.*

Me: *We do.*

M: *Seriously babe, I don't want you to be worried about anything to do with money or my work. It'll all come together. Remember, my mum says you're my good luck charm? People have it worse. I don't want you to feel like you have to compromise by getting cheap stuff that's gonna make your life harder.*

The tears glisten in my eyes again. I think it's hormones, making me cry at the drop of a hat. I just hope, truly, deeply, that what M says is true. And that we will be okay.

24th February, Bloody M

One positive about being heavily pregnant is that my mother-in-law has eased up in the kitchen.

Correction, she hasn't eased up. I have removed myself from a lot of the heavy duty work. Any tasks I need to perform, which are minimal, I can do sitting down.

Right now, I'm bashing the life out of a thumb of ginger. It's quite therapeutic. My mother-in-law is trying her very best not to say what she's thinking which is: '*Can you bash it as you have done in the past, putting the pestle and mortar on the tiled floor and squatting over it, as there is a risk of damaging the table with the heavy pummelling.*' I know her of old now and can be confident that she won't suggest such a thing. In my current condition, if I do anything squatting, I might just give birth.

M has upped his game in the kitchen. He was always good when we were at my mother-in-law's, bursting in to save the day when he sensed that I might be burdened with a task too far. However, pre dad-to-be M would often come to the rescue a little too late, when I've already started grinding flour, or cutting onions, or shaping kebabs into round patties. The end result would never be pretty. Now, he is front and centre in the kitchen, assuming domestic God duties. He's made a cup of tea for his mum and offers me one.

"Do you have decaf?" I ask.

M searches in all the cupboards.

"Just have a normal tea," my mother-in-law advises, as she is leaning over the daa, cutting through the bones of frozen fish.

"I'm not supposed to have normal tea more than once a day, I think."

"Really? We were never told that!" My mother-in-law giggles. "You all turned out okay."

She looks to M for confirmation. He says nothing and instead squeezes the teabag until there are no more drippings.

"You probably won't be able to come again, no?" M's mum asks her son.

"She won't be able to come anymore, as it's not comfortable to travel. I'll be able to, if need be," says M.

What? M coming up north without me? When I'm due any day soon?

He looks at me. "Only if it's an emergency. And only for one night."

That's better. I lean back in my chair, then H2 head-butts the bottom of my spine. I guess I'll sit back up then. There is no pleasing this baby.

"We came up not so long ago anyway, when-" M stops himself from saying more.

"When you come?"

Damn.

M falters. "I-I had work. Not in Manchester. It was in Bradford. We only stayed one night."

My mother-in-law looks hurt. We've broken the unwritten rule of not visiting her when we're in the north of England.

"It was a really quick visit. She didn't even come with me. We met at her sister's."

Damn, M. Damn you.

"How she come? Train?" My mother-in-law looks at me.

Damn. Double damn.

"No, she came up with... Jam." M stares down into his teacup.

"Oh. Anyone else?"

Triple damn.

M pops the teabags in the bin. "No, just them two."

After a brief silence, my mother-in-law says: "Ah, okay. Yes, trains not safe now you're ill."

Thank goodness for my illness. Otherwise, I'd be seen as the loose woman who travels with her husband's unmarried friends, minus her husband.

27th February, Annoying friends

Do you know what really grinds my gears? It's when people fleetingly offer a glimmer of hope, only to take it away. Miles was adamant that there were jobs going at his place all the time. I've passed M's CV over. And since then? Nothing. Absolutely nothing. Not a peep from Miles or Julia. Why did they bother mentioning it in the first place?

It reminds me of when I was single and looking to get married. I'd go to those charity events, hoping that either I see someone, or someone recommends someone. I remember meeting Heena, who promised to set me up with a pharmacist. Then she went quiet and let me desperately chase her for more information. It's sad what she did. It was cold.

The job world feels even more frosty. It's everyone for themselves.

Right, stop it. Stop it right now.

It's time for positive thinking. My affirmations and gratitude journal has gone to pot since I had my third scan, receiving good news about the baby and then the bad news about M's work. I just couldn't be bothered keeping it up.

However, I know I'm wrong. I need to get back on it as I really do believe that putting positivity out into the universe breeds more of the same.

I slide across the sofa and pull out my journal from underneath the coffee table. It's hidden within a bunch of opened letters, gathering dust. That's how much I've not been bothered with it recently.

– I am grateful for having a healthy pregnancy.

– I am grateful that M has prospects and job opportunities.

I write that point down through gritted teeth, as I'm not thoroughly convinced that M has a lot of prospects right now.

– I am grateful to be able to afford to have a lady to clean my house, even if I haven't hired her in the last two months and our entire home is a mix of limescale, dust, and hairballs.

That reminds me, I must hire her again soon except, suddenly, £15 an hour seems like a whole lot of cash when you've not got a lot to go around.

Right, the next bit.

I scribble down... what would make today great?

- M getting a job.
- Someone buying my online PR course.
- Did I mention M getting a job?

If I write it down twice, is it more likely to happen? Come to think of it, can I do affirmations for somebody else? Does gratitude only work when you're journalling for yourself? I've never thought about that. There is a fat chance of M doing this. He thinks this is all a bunch of woo woo bullshit.

Okay... onto affirmations. Let's have some positive thoughts:

I am happy, healthy, and strong. My baby is happy (judging by her somersaults), healthy and strong (based on her kicks to my pelvis).

Deep breath. Deep breath. Deep breath. I trace my hands along my bump and it feels like H2 is doing the same inside me.

I take another deep breath and... dive into my work. Did you expect I was going to stay in this state of Zen forever? I've got bills to pay, you know.

I have to write the final press release for Joy. It feels quite cathartic. I once was boastful, having a roster of clients on my books. Now I have two, and one has given me notice. I could be worried about it and upset. Is it worth it, though? I might as well resign myself to the fact that everything happens for a reason and this is perhaps nature's way of telling me that I need to take it easy and prepare for the new life I'm about to bring into the world.

Let's polish this one last turd and make it extra glittery. Joy wants me to write a press release off the back of the news that obesity is on the rise. I'm not sure how newsworthy it is. Hasn't obesity been on the rise for years? Anyway, what do I know? She is the client, I am the supplier.

These days, I'm so tired that it's an effort to string a sentence together. Even sitting on the sofa is dangerous as I end up slouching and wanting to fall asleep, mainly because there's such little sleep happening at night. Even with middle sis' gifted V-shaped pillow, it's very hard to get the right position to allow for some shut eye.

I close my eyes as they feel heavy. *Stay awake, stay awake, stay awake.* Let's push out the press release. Then I'll allow myself to sleep.

My phone rings. It's mum.

"What you do?"

"Nothing much," I reply. "I'm just writing up a press release."

"A what? I can't hear you properly. This phone so crackly."

"Are you in the kitchen again? You know there's no reception there." I've lost count of how many times I've told mum this.

The sound of the kettle boiling confirms my theory.

"Okay, you wait. I go to front room."

There's a few seconds of what I can only describe as brown noise as mum muffles and mumbles, making her way into the front room.

"*Heh?* Phone for me?" I hear dad ask. There is no sound of the TV blaring. He must be reading the newspaper as I can hear some brisk rustling.

"No, who call you?" Mum is harsh as ever.

"*Eh-heh*, maybe Rashda maa."

"Because she always be calling you, no?" says mum in response to dad's hopes of auntie Jusna calling. It's not only Brits that do sarcasm. My immigrant mum has it nailed down. "Your sister always be calling me! And only when she want to brag! Or be nosey about our family! It's your daughter on phone now."

"Which one?" dad asks.

I feel I need to interject. "Erm, shall I call back later?"

Mum and dad continue speaking as though I'm not on the other end of the line. Once dad has established that it's his heavily pregnant, London-based daughter on the phone, he asks: "She coming this weekend?"

"How she come?" Mum gasps. "In her condition? You think she be able to travel?"

There is a brief pause.

"Then when we see her next?" Dad asks in the smallest voice imaginable.

"Mum, can I speak to dad? Or even better, can I video call so I can see you both?"

"Video call? Oh okay, but you have to show me," says mum.

TEN MINUTES LATER, we are up and running. I see two cute, yet slightly annoying, Bengali elders on my phone screen. Mum is wearing an olive green scarf, loosely draped around her head, with lots of raggedy grey hairs peeking out the front. She needs someone to help dye her hair. She can't do it by herself. The instructions are confusing enough for someone fluent in English. She doesn't stand a chance.

Dad is wearing a prayer hat, as he increasingly does indoors nowadays. I think it's to keep his bald head warm. He looks smaller. He's always been a little shorter than mum. I don't know how he passed the suitor test back when mum was looking to get married. Then again, he had a British passport, so I guess that sealed the deal. It's not just the height difference, though. He looks shrunken, thinner. Whenever I go and visit, dad is a fleeting presence, popping in and out of the room and generally avoiding eye contact. As a result, I don't get to look at him often. I keep hearing that he doesn't eat much these days and now I can see it. Now we can all see each other.

I feel a pain in my stomach and this time it's not from baby H2's flying kicks.

"Where is *damand*?" asks dad.

"He's at work," I respond to dad's queries about where the groom is.

Though it's a lie, it's not a big one. M is meeting a recruiter. There are times when I wonder whether it's worth telling all to mum. After all, I usually tell her everything. Even in my 30s, I look to her for input on every aspect of my life. Even though she's never had a career of her own, or lived in London, or could drive, or shares any other similarities to my life, her advice is heeded. She just knows the right thing to say. She is my mum, after all. Yet, I can't tell mum or dad this. I can't burden them with all my worries. Looking at their faces, older and etched with time, I can't tell them that I am so, so worried about what will happen. To me. To the baby. To M.

"Have you eaten?" asks mum.

This is the default question I've been asked since the age of 18, when I left home with two squeaky suitcases. It's the most important question of all. The question that surpasses any other queries about my welfare and well-being. At all times, mum needs to know that I am fed.

"Yes, I've eaten. Have you?"

"I'll eat later," says dad. "We had KFC on the way home from shop, so no hungry."

"KFC? Isn't that the second time this week?"

Dad grins, revealing tea-stained teeth. "I like the *seef*."

"They do make good chips," I agree.

"So you good?" Dad checks his watch. It's nearly 1pm. Time for the Bangla news headlines, which arrive on the hour, every hour, without fail.

"Yes, I'm good. All is well here."

"So when you coming next?" asks dad.

Mum sniffs. "*Dooro!* Didn't I just say she can no come now? Not until after baby born!"

Dad thinks. "Okay. I forget. Anyway, think news on now. How do you turn this off?" He looks at mum for tech support.

"I think it be here."

I watch them for a moment, pressing the screen in the wrong place and fiddling with the sound button, adjusting it higher and lower.

My parents.

Usually, their lack of technological know-how would drive me nuts. I'd have to dictate to them how to make a call, send a message, or open a photo that's been sent to them from a relative in Bangladesh. I used to get frustrated about how long these simple tasks took them, and therefore, me. It was taking away from my time. Taking away from my work. Taking away from me scrolling on my phone. Me living my life. Yet now, I wish time would stop for a brief moment. I just look at them, as they are blissfully unaware that their every clumsy move is being watched.

I've never had the kind of parents that I have long chats with. Don't get me wrong, I talk to mum when there's something to talk about. When there's gossip about a family member. When I have news to share, or something else of note. We don't just... talk. We don't spend ages on the phone every day. It's usually very transactional. Have I eaten? Are they well? That's about it.

Something about this call feels so final. The reality is, I don't know when I'm going to go back up north next. How easy will it be to travel with a new baby? How easy will that already punishing four-hour trip be? I'm drinking in this moment while I can. I feel it and I think dad feels it. Possibly even mum beneath her tough exterior. It's the feeling that next time I see them, life will be drastically different.

While my parents bumble their way through ending the call, I'm wishing it would last longer. Finally, dad's thumb slips into the right position, rendering my screen black.

3rd March, Dirty flat

"You need me to come every two weeks. The flat is very dirty. Me cleaning once in a few months is not enough. Need to keep it clean for baby," Ana admonishes me, while spraying the tiles of my bathroom with toxic cleaning products.

I don't dare argue with her. She's scary.

"Before I leave, book me in for two weeks. And then, if we do every two weeks like contract, it be better for you."

"Okay," I say, but I won't be committing to any such contract. I am too poor to invest in fortnightly cleaning. Instead, I'm dragging my waterlogged legs across the laminate floor, alternating between hoovering and mopping once a month. M does the rest in between, including the elbow grease of bathroom and kitchen cleaning (as he should, as he's neither pregnant, nor working).

It was only with M's insistence that I got Ana round today. The nudge came due to the fact that uncle Tariq and auntie Rukhsana are visiting us. Yes, you read that right. They'll be coming to *us*. The reason being that I'm far too pregnant to go to them.

Hosting is the last thing on my mind. Even though they won't expect anything, I still ought to do something. At least offer a cup of tea and good biscuits.

Ana finishes up and I make some excuses for not being able to commit just yet, because I'll be going to my parents' house when the baby is born. Another lie to add to my web of lies. I don't even know what the truth is these days.

Within minutes of Ana leaving, uncle Tariq and auntie Rukhsana knock on the door. Auntie Rukhsana greets me with a hug. Her headscarf smells of fresh linen. However, I can still detect traces of cooking oil and spices in her hair. She must've been preparing food just before she came here. Food for me, as I can see uncle Tariq holding a blue plastic bag, loaded with containers. He cups my head with his free hand. So much warmth emanates from them. As I'm hundreds of miles from my own family, uncle Tariq and auntie Rukhsana have become like surrogate parents. I don't see them as much, despite their calls to come over, but at least I know they're there. Always.

Upon entering the hallway, Uncle Tariq wrinkles his nose at the smell of bleach.

"Don't use strong chemicals when cleaning," auntie Rukhsana says. "It will be no good for you, or baby."

Uncle Tariq nods, putting his cigarette lighter back in his shirt pocket.

"How's Naila?"

Auntie Rukhsana giggles. "Same. She got work. Bridal makeup job."

I spied on Naila's Instagram earlier. She was getting ready to go to an influencer event. The opening of a restaurant or something. Darren must be at home with the baby. Just last week, she was at the launch of a new clothing range for babies, helmed by some z-list celebrity but no doubt stitched together by someone less famous.

"And the brothers? Are they okay?" I ask.

Uncle Tariq looks out of the window of our living room, onto the traffic of Commercial Road. "They be busy working. Never get to see them these days."

I never fully understand what the deal is with Naila's brothers. Since I've moved to London, I've barely seen them. There was one fleeting moment at a wedding and that was it. I've never known such secrecy. And that is saying something. Obviously, I can't ask uncle Tariq or auntie Rukhsana directly. That would be disrespectful. I might have to see if mum can find more intelligence.

Uncle Tariq plays with the window handles. He wouldn't dare smoke in here, would he? I get that he's old school and a law unto himself, but surely lighting up around a pregnant lady is a step too far.

"Good windows. Very good. Nice ventilation. They don't give you that with houses," he declares, having inspected the insulation around the window frames. "Naila bought a house and the windows all need changing. House is always cold. It's big old house. High ceilings, need lots to heat. Flats don't need so much."

"Because we have heat from every side, you see. Floor below, floor above," auntie Rukhsana adds. "When I go to their house, I always need my thick shawl." She plays with the dial on my electric heater.

Uncle Tariq and auntie Rukhsana continue, debating the pros and cons of Naila's house. Apparently, the garden is too big and they don't know how she will maintain it. Especially now that she's pregnant again, they let slip. The kitchen is too small, so how is she expected to cook in there? Though, they add, it's still bigger than the pokey one auntie Rukhsana has to cook in. Then they joke about how little the kitchen would be used anyway, as Naila is more of a Pot Noodle and coffee girl.

All of this washes over me. I feel as though I'm not there. Because all I heard was that Naila has her own house. We've been renting since we moved here. It's been years. M was renting before that, before we got married and I moved down. When will we ever get to buy a house? The exorbitant rental prices didn't matter so much when we were both earning good salaries. Now, the numbers on our joint account dwindle every single month. I've needed to dip into my savings for general expenses. M didn't have much savings to start with.

I wish we bought when we first got married. We fleetingly discussed it but there was always a question mark hovering over when we would go back up north. Buying a flat that we might not stay in for long seemed an investment too big to make. Plus, we couldn't afford a deposit. However, had we known that in the space of just a few short years, house prices would skyrocket, we could've begged, borrowed and stolen to scrape together a down payment for a flat.

That's the other thing. Naila has a house. Not even a flat. How does anyone afford a house in London? How much is she making as a makeup artist? What does Darren do? How much does he earn? I've always, for my snobby sins, dismissed their careers. She uploads on Instagram so often that it seems that Darren's main role in life is to take pictures of his wife as an Instagram husband. Now who is the one with the jobless husband?

The heat rises from my belly through to my chest. It travels up my neck and settles in my cheeks. While uncle Tariq and auntie Rukhsana complain of cold, I am all fired up.

Don't cry. Do not cry.

"Do you want a cup of tea?" I ask, trying to steady the tremble in my voice.

Auntie Rukhsana grabs my hand and squeezes tight. "I'll make it. You sit."

"Actually..." My voice is still trembling. "I need to go to the bathroom. I'll be one minute."

NOT ONLY DID AUNTIE Rukhsana make the tea, she also decanted the curries that she'd cooked and brought over, boiled some rice and served up lunch. It was 4pm, so a late lunch but that suited me fine. I can only eat little and often so was happy to chow down on meat and potato curry. I didn't eat the prawns and instead popped them in the fridge for M.

I am grateful that auntie Rukhsana did all the washing up after we'd eaten. I'm grateful that she washed my plate, even though I am capable of cleaning my own. I am grateful that they didn't linger for too long after they'd eaten. I'm grateful that they didn't ask too many questions about M's work, or mine. I'm grateful they didn't probe into what my plans were after the baby is born, as I have no idea myself. I'm grateful that M didn't come home while they were still here and have to lie about work, or put his foot in it, as he sometimes does when he can't think of what else to say. I'm grateful that they didn't mind me excusing myself to go to the bathroom three times in the one hour that they were sat here.

Most of all, I'm grateful that uncle Tariq and auntie Rukhsana didn't pay any attention to my puffy, tear-stained face, once I'd finally emerged from my first bathroom visit. Even though their faces were full of worry, they knew better than to ask. And for that, I'm grateful.

There's a knock on the door. Has M forgotten his keys again?

Through the spyhole, I see it's my neighbour, the Bengali lady that lives on the same floor.

"It's just a super quick one but I've been meaning to pop round for ages," she says, coming through our tiny hallway into the living room. "I'm not stopping but I wanted to drop this off..." She holds up a family sized dish of lasagna. "I did a bulk cook, so eat it tonight for dinner, or put it in your fridge or whatever. I just thought it might help as cooking is probably the last thing on your mind. It certainly was for me when I was pregnant."

I'm floored by the gesture. The lady who I barely know and spoke to properly once, has brought the most thoughtful gift. Food. Nothing quite beats it.

I offer a cup of tea but she refuses, citing the million jobs she has to do, including unloading the washing machine, picking up the kids from Arabic class and ironing for the week. She sounds like superwoman. I'm so glad I found such kindness on my doorstep. I always wanted a Bengali friend, now I'm grateful for such a helpful person to have come into my life, when I feel I need it the most.

I place the lasagna in the fridge, manoeuvring a few items as we are now rich in containers full of food made with love. I am grateful for that. It's helping put out the fire burning through my heart and I don't mean pregnancy heartburn. However, all these gestures, all this kindness, hasn't quite managed to extinguish the flames.

I hear the key twist in the front door and M comes in.

"Hey babe, you okay?" He rubs my shoulder while I remain sat in the same spot on the sofa.

"I'm fine."

"Have I missed uncle Tariq and auntie Rukhsana?"

"Yeah, they left not long ago. And our neighbour knocked on with food."

"We have a neighbour that gives food?"

I don't look at him, but I can see his gleeful face in the corner of my eye. "It's the Bengali lady I told you about." I stare at my hands.

"Cool, are you okay?" M sits down next to me.

Don't cry. Don't cry. Don't cry.

Despite being married for years and M being my person, I don't like to cry in front of him. I don't like to cry in front of anyone, for that matter. It feels like a sign of weakness.

My jaw begins to shake. My hands tremble. My eyes prickle with water. I'm furious but I can't be furious with him. He's my boy. But... I'm just so pent-up frustrated.

"How are you getting on, on the job front?" I ask.

M rubs my back but looks down at his shoes. There is a scuff in the leather. He should've worn his better ones. The ones reserved for weddings. "It's going okay. It's just hard. And frustrating."

"Why is it frustrating?"

"You probably know from when you were looking. It's hard work. Are you okay? Why are you crying?"

He puts his head against mine but I move away.

"How can I not cry? How can I not be worried? You don't know this, as I didn't want to put it on you but I've been having little cries by myself a lot recently."

M looks worried. "When? Why? I've been at home all this time and I've not noticed."

"Exactly. You've not noticed. Actually, that's not fair. I've been hiding it from you but it's because I'm scared. Aren't you worried about what will happen in the future? You've got no job. I'm barely working. If you've not noticed, I'm going to have a baby any day soon."

"Of course I'm worried. There's no point me telling you that. It would only make you feel worse. It will happen, babe. It will come together. I'm doing my best."

M puts his arm around my shoulder and pulls me in for a hug. I don't resist and sink into his embrace. However, it doesn't feel the same. He doesn't feel like my safety blanket.

The one thing I've learnt from years of marriage and from the advice of others, is that I should never share my dark, inner thoughts. Especially not when I'm emotional and I may say something that I would regret that can never be taken back. I can't share my inner thoughts. I can't share my resentment that other people have it better. That Naila has bought a house. That my other cousin Hassna's husband has bought her a house. That Adnan took the financial lead when Sophia had her kids. That both my older sisters don't need to worry about paying bills. That M's sister-in-law doesn't have to worry about bills. That other men seem to be doing better, earning better, providing better.

Is this my just desserts for being a modern career woman? Have I instilled so much of this 50-50 notion that now, when the balance is shifted, I can't fix the scales? Have I created a situation where I will have to be the financial lead, even after having the baby? Have I failed to manage our very modern life with some traditions that I hold on to, one being that I wanted to be a full-time mother for at least the first few years? Have I fucked it all up?

I can't say all this to M. I can't share these thoughts that I stuff deep down under H2. It's too hurtful. Instead, I have to carry them alone. Like I've been carrying so much.

They say comparison is the thief of joy and boy, is that true. It's stealing my happiness. Because the one thing all of this comparison-itis has done is make me think the unthinkable. It's made me wonder whether, if this is M doing his best, what if, after all the effort, it's not good enough?

14th March, An eventful bus ride

"It's quite normal for you to be swearing at your partner during labour. I called my husband every name under the sun when I had my daughter." Libby lets out the dirtiest of laughs.

She is the replacement for Carmen, the NCT lead we've had the past few weeks. I must say, I don't mind the change. Libby is upbeat, funny and has just enough of the South London swag for my liking.

"Also dads, if you see a floater in the birthing pool, you're going to turn a blind eye to that, okay? It's more likely than not that your wife is going to do a little poo as she gives birth. You are not allowed to bring that up to her, ever again. We'll just sweep that away and pretend it never happened."

This nugget of advice is greeted by giggles, grimaces, and looks of denial. Jean-Patrice looks horrified at the thought of his well-heeled wife toileting in front of him, even if it is a by-product of childbirth.

"I'm going to remind you every single day, if you poo while giving birth," M whispers into my ear.

I smile tightly, as I'm still lowdown annoyed with him. I know it's not fair. He is trying his best but I've got a muddle of mixed feelings. There is resentment, frustration, impatience, and a whole load of irrational hormones thrown into the mix. It's not good.

More than anything, however, is the overwhelming urge to get this pregnancy over with. I'm huge, heavy, and fed up. Everything is a chore. I need the toilet more frequently than my swollen ankles can take me. And while I escaped morning sickness, I find that even bending over to pick up a pen has me refluxing like a baby.

"Can the poop be attributed to meconium?" asks Melinda. I can't tell if she's joking or not.

Libby shakes her head. "Sorry, no, meconium is the baby's first poop. The floater will absolutely belong to you, mum. Can't go blaming the poor baby when they can't speak for themselves, can you?"

"Worth a try." Melinda laughs.

"And mums, you will feel angry and frustrated at times." Libby reads my mind. "Fellas, sorry to say, you are going to bear the brunt of it. Especially in the labour ward. Just remember, it's nothing personal. Also, you did get them in that situation, so you have to grin and bear it."

Melinda and her husband, Jim, exchange knowing looks at each other. Peter and Josephine put their heads together, as though nothing could break them. Not even a surprise poo, or a few labour induced expletives.

"Honestly, mums..." Libby shakes her head and looks down at the ground in disbelief. "I wish I could prepare you for what it's going to be like after the baby's born but nothing really prepares you. And there's nothing I can say that will be able to tell you how life is once baby arrives. You just have to go through it."

Libby quickly shifts gears and hands out some baby grows as gifts to all the expectant parents. She asks everyone if they know what they're having, before giving either a blue or pink striped sleepsuit. M and I tell a lie (why break the habit of a lifetime?) and stick to the script that we don't know what gender our baby will be. It turns out to be a clever con, as we get gifted two baby grows. Given our dire financial straits, I'll happily take them both.

I look around at all the couples, brought together by the fact that we are due several weeks apart from each other.

Cindy and her partner coo over the blue and white striped baby grow. She mentions how she plans to go back to work two days a week at the University where she is a lecturer. Her husband will be able to make up for the shortfall as he is gunning for a promotion.

Jean-Patrice, who looks pretty hot in his sky blue shirt (must be the pregnancy hormones making me thirsty), rubs the thigh of his wife, Claudia. When they've not been conversing with the group, they've been locked in conversation, speaking in French to each other. He works in finance, like M. He's self-assured and confident.

Josephine, a pharmaceutical sales rep is talking to Cindy, while their significant others share a joke together.

Then I look at M, who is going to remind me that I've pooed during childbirth. He is easy-going, laid back, passive.

"I'm just thinking," says Cindy. "Shall we exchange numbers? Then I can create a WhatsApp group for us?"

Finally, someone suggested it. That's pretty much the reason that most people join the NCT course, isn't it? So you get to make mum friends who are in the same boat once the baby is born?

"And maybe we could have a group one with all of us, not just the mums," offers Jean-Patrice.

He's so commanding. He says what he wants and just goes for it. M would never do that.

Am I allowed to be annoyed with my husband now, or do I have to save it for labour?

"WHEN WE WERE PRACTISING nappy changing in the next room, I found a dead spider and put it in the nappy, so the next person would have a fright," declares M, proudly, on the bus home from the course.

"Who was the lucky person who discovered your spider?"

"The French guy. Is it Jean-Patrice? He jumped out of his skin!" M is so proud of his achievement.

I can't face him. "Why did you take on that contract job?"

M looks startled. "What?"

"I mean, why did you think of taking on a contract job when I was pregnant? Wasn't it always a risk that you'd lose the job?"

"I didn't expect to lose it, to be honest with ya. Some people contract for years and years. It seemed like too good an opportunity and my current boss was pissing me off. You told me to go for it at the time."

"Did I? I don't remember that."

"Yeah. When we were at one of your appointments. I told you about the role and you said I should apply."

I scratch my head. "I really don't remember saying that. Even if I did, you shouldn't go on my say so. My head has been all over the shop these days."

M says nothing but I'm not done. "We all have shitty bosses at some point or other but you can't just up and leave because of that. Not everyone has that luxury. We certainly didn't."

M leans away from me. "What made you think of this now?"

"I was thinking of this all along. I always thought you contracting wasn't a good idea."

"Why didn't you say at the time?"

"I did!"

"You didn't."

"I'm pretty sure I asked if you thought it was a good idea."

M looks out of the window.

I take a deep breath. He's a good husband. He's a good husband. He's a good husband.

"We need to think about what we're going to do."

"About what?" asks M.

I point at my stomach. "Hello? About this baby? And how we're going to fund it?"

"You always do this. You always make me feel like I'm not good enough. You do it in front of your friends, too. Pulling me up about the reduced tomatoes I bought. Telling me not to eat one of those shitty small canapés at Julia's engagement. They didn't serve food! The canapés were *the* meal. What else was I supposed to do? Chew on my fingers?"

I feel we're going a little off subject now.

A few people look over their shoulders to witness our domestic. I can't believe we're doing this. I can't believe we're having it out on the number 15 bus. We have become *that* couple. That couple who argues in public. I should be mortified but the words keep rolling out. All PR politeness has evaporated to make way for a raging pregnant bull.

"I've pulled you up on these things because they're stupid things to do. You don't have to tell people tomatoes are reduced. You don't have to tell your mum that I got a lift with Jam, your unmarried friend. It's common sense and I shouldn't even have to tell you but that's beside the point. The bigger issue is I haven't been able to sleep for the last few months because of worrying about how we're going to support this baby. You don't even want to do proper baby shopping because you're so skint and at the same time you keep telling me I shouldn't worry? What else should I do?"

"Do you think it's been easy for me?" says M. "I've been awake at night, worrying about what I'll do for work."

I snigger. "No, you haven't."

"Yes, I have!" says M, his voice louder as though he's a pantomime villain.

I make my voice even louder, too. "You haven't! I know you haven't because I've been actually awake at night, hearing you snore."

M stalls. I've caught him out. I shouldn't be gleeful about it but I am.

"I have been worried." This time, his voice is barely a whisper. "I didn't want to tell you, because you'll worry even more and where will that get us? It won't be good for the baby. I've been trying so hard, looking every day for jobs. What more do you want me to do?"

Now it's my turn to be lost for words. What do I want him to do? I just want him to get a bloody job. That's all.

"You should've stayed in your old job. At least until the baby's born. Then you could've started looking for a permanent position that has job security."

M turns his gaze from the window to look me square in the face. "When you lost your job, I didn't make you feel bad. I supported you when you were looking for work and getting nowhere. I was fully on board when you set up a business. I never made you feel like shit for any of it."

"Well my dear..." I poke him in the shoulder, like a 19th-century headmistress scolding a schoolboy. "You weren't pregnant at the time."

M says nothing. Neither do I. There's nothing to say. The silence continues as we get to our bus stop. I press the button, then M gets up, while I shuffle my way past the other people on the bus who are no doubt enjoying the show.

This is a new low. How did it come to this? This isn't us. We don't argue. We've never been this annoyed with each other. Yeah, on the down low, we get frustrated but we've always managed to squash any issues. We've never had it out like this.

M walks a metre ahead of me, like my dad does with mum. Every so often, he looks over his shoulder, not making eye contact, to check I'm still behind him and haven't gone into labour on the street or something.

When we get to the door, M says: "You got the key?"

I rifle through my bag in search of the flat key. I don't want to add to the argument but I can't help thinking why doesn't he have his keys with him? How unchivalrous, expecting me to open the door in my condition. I bet sexy Jean-Patrice would never do that.

I step into the hallway to find rose gold confetti on the floor.

"Surprise!" I hear lots of voices yell.

"What the f-" I come into the living room to see Julia, my old school friend Helena, Reena, Bushra, Sonali and even my former work mate, Bryony, standing there with eager, excited looks on their faces. This is in stark contrast to the flushed, angry faces that M and I are sporting.

Julia comes over and gives me a hug. "I can't believe we pulled this off!" she says to M, while offering him a high five.

What is going on? Was M in on this?

"I really wanted to do something for you as a surprise but couldn't figure out how to bring it all together without you finding out. So when you sent over M's CV and it had his mobile number on the top, I seized the opportunity to reach out to him. We've been plotting ever since. It's as much his effort as it is mine so I can't take all the credit. M filled in the gaps by getting the numbers of your friends who I didn't know and coordinating with your sisters."

I look around. Where are my sisters?

"They couldn't make it," Julia states the obvious. "But they wanted to be a part of the occasion so sent over presents."

I look at M. He doesn't meet my eyes but says: "That's why I put off doing the baby shopping. They wanted to get most of the essentials."

Oh God. I feel awful on so many levels.

Julia looks nervous, unsure of my reaction. "Do you like it? Sorry about the mess. We can help clean up the confetti afterwards."

I take in the scene. There are rose gold balloons trying to escape through the ceiling. Shiny confetti is everywhere. Our coffee table has been taken over by cupcakes. Not just any cupcakes, Lola's Cupcakes. On the floor, there are some boxes. Big boxes.

Reena is having words with Sonali in the corner of the room, no doubt about their wedding date clash. Bryony, Bushra and Helen smile at me, waiting for a response.

"This... is... amazing," is all I can muster.

There is so much more I need to say and a few dark thoughts I need to atone for. But first, cake.

TWO CUPCAKES LATER (don't judge me, I'm pregnant), I sit down with Helen, who I haven't seen since my hen do. She's not changed a bit, even down to the same full-fringed haircut she's had in school.

"I can't believe you're here," I tell her.

She shrugs. "I was in London anyway, so when Julia messaged me about your baby shower, I figured I might as well show my face since I'm in the area."

Yep, she really hasn't changed at all.

"What brought you to London?" I ask.

Helen grins. "I'd rather not say too much but I'm seeing someone."

"That's amazing news!" I don't mean to sound dramatic but I am shocked. For as long as I've known her, Helen has never had a boyfriend. She was so prim and goody two-shoes that I felt she was more Bengali than me.

"Finally, it's my turn." She crosses her fingers. "It's early-ish days. As in, it's only been a few months."

"That's not early days in my book! I was married within months."

"I know, but your lot are different-" Helen stops herself and adjusts her glasses.

I laugh away the awkwardness and she looks relieved. To be fair, in multicultural, liberal, central London, it's been a while since someone said something a little racially suspect. Perhaps it was due.

"Awww... I can't wait to hear all about him but I better catch up with Reena. She's been giving me side eye all this time."

I think Reena heard, as she pushes in next to me on the sofa.

"I didn't expect you to be here, Reena, especially with you being married now. I didn't expect any of this." I grab some confetti and sprinkle it on the table. In amongst all the sparkle, there are lots of Baby on Board badges dotted around. How did Julia get hold of so many? I thought they were hard to come by.

"Honestly man, I needed a break. Living with the in-laws ain't no picnic. You're lucky you escaped that shit. I had to use the excuse that I was seeing my sister to be able to come today."

"Really? Would they not approve?" That feels so strange coming out of my mouth. It's like I'm in some parallel universe where Reena's under lock and key and I'm the footloose one. Ever since I've known her, it's been the other way round.

"My mother-in-law wouldn't say anything outright but she'll be in a huff about me not being there this weekend. Since we got married, she's lined up a queue of guests to come and see me. Like they all didn't get to have an eyeful at the wedding! Honestly, I can't wait to be done with these newlywed formalities, let me tell ya."

"What does your fella say about it? Can't he have a word?" I ask, thinking of the times M has fought my corner when his mum had gone rogue in the kitchen.

Reena tuts. "As if! He's a proper mama's boy. There's no way he'd dare get on her bad side. Mate, I'm just counting the days until we move out."

"You and me both." Sonali slides to the back of the sofa.

"Hold on. You don't live with your in-laws, do you?" I ask.

Sonali sighs, reaching for a red velvet cupcake. "No, but we're close enough for them to be frequent visitors. Very frequent visitors. I'm going to work on Krish and see if he'd be willing to relocate to my ends."

"You don't know you're born, mate," Reena interjects. "At least you're not all under the same roof. You can shut the door to them at the end of the day. We can't even have noisy sex as his mum and dad are in the next room. That doesn't work for me. I don't know any other way."

Reena cackles, Sonali snorts, Bushra giggles, Bryony blushes, Julia coughs, Helen rolls her eyes and M excuses himself to pop to the shops. I don't think we actually need anything, it's just to escape this coven. I don't blame him.

Reena heads to the toilet and Bryony takes her place next to me.

"Well, hello there, stranger." I put an arm around her shoulders.

"Same to you, stranger!" says Bryony. "We're both as bad as each other but it's been crazy busy with work. Since I've handed in my notice, they're making me do extra as punishment."

"You handed in your notice?" I'm so surprised that Bryony is leaving the company that made me redundant a couple of years back. Had I not been ousted, I'd probably still be there now.

Bryony tucks a strand of hair behind her ear. "Yeah, I'd been looking for a while. I feel like I've outgrown that place and needed a new adventure. And more money, to be honest. They hadn't given me a salary rise in two years, so I figured I might be more appreciated elsewhere. Even if elsewhere means big pharma."

"You're going to the pharmaceutical industry? Well, I bet that does pay well."

Bryony raises her mocktail in the air. "It certainly does that. Once I've made a six-figure salary, I can leave the industry and work on my scruples. For now, I'm focusing on getting my own place and moving out of my parents' house. I am 32, after all."

"As am I." I rest my hand on her knee. "For what it's worth, I'm still generation rent and probably will be for a long time."

Bryony sighs. "I don't know. From what I see, you've got it pretty made. And your M is so sweet. When he first messaged me on LinkedIn, I wasn't sure what to make of it. I thought it was just some weirdo." She laughs. "No offence but it's not everyday someone messages you saying that their wife worked at your company with someone called Bryony, and they want to check if you're the same Bryony so they can invite you to her baby shower! The lengths he went to!"

I say nothing. M did all that for me?

"Honestly, you've got a keeper. Hold on tight. Not all blokes would collude with their wife's best friend to do all this." Bryony gestures towards the foil balloons and plastic champagne flutes filled with non-alcoholic beverages.

"As for generation rent," Bryony adds, "living in a high-rise apartment in zone one, with a concierge, isn't that bad."

"It's not," I agree. "I just forget to see the good stuff sometimes. I suppose it's true, comparison is the thief of joy. I reckon we all need to get that stamped across our foreheads."

"Comparison is the what?" Bryony asks. "I've never heard of that phrase."

"Don't worry, I'm just thinking to myself."

M comes back in but before I have a chance to say anything, Bushra comes into view. "You're the Belle of the ball today. It's like your hen do all over again," she says.

"Hardly. More like Cinderella. But enough about me..." I raise my eyebrows.

"Yeah, I know what you're gonna ask me. And yes, Ahmed and I are doing the meet-the-parents thing."

I throw my hands to my head in disbelief. "What? I was not expecting that much progress. I was just going to ask if you are going to see him again. Tell me everything."

Bushra holds out her palm, as if to stop further interrogation. "I will but not today. Today is your day. And I don't think it's a conversation I really wanna have in front of everybody. But yes, let's talk at some point."

"Definitely. I need all the details."

My phone rings. It's Sophia on video call.

"I couldn't be there in person, hon. You'll know how hard travel is when you have your own baby but I am here with you virtually. I even brushed my hair for the occasion." Sophia fluffs up her bouncy waves. "Did you like your present?"

I glance over at the pile of boxes in various shades and patterns of gift wrapping.

"I haven't opened anything yet."

"You haven't? Perfect! Prop me somewhere. I mean not, literally. Prop the phone somewhere so I can see your reaction as you open them all. I'm gutted to be missing this so I want to at least get some of the action."

I follow Sophia's instructions and lean my phone against a grazing board, so she can be part of the festivities. Everyone sits around on the sofa, the floor and wherever else they can find a space in my small flat.

"Do mine first!" Sophia is as bossy as ever. "It's the one in green and white stripes."

M arrived at just the right time as there is heavy lifting to be done. He pushes the large box along the floor towards me.

"Careful! You'll tear the wrapping." Sophia shouts to M. Her voice crackles through the phone to make her presence felt.

M puts the box on its side so I don't have to lean over to open it. There's lots of anticipation as I unwrap the parcel, not least for me.

"It's a Moses basket!" Julia squeals.

"I was going to give you my old one," explains Sophia. "However, when I fished it out of the attic the other week, it looked a bit well worn. I figured your baby deserves something new."

"Thank you." I try my best not to well up, as I've been doing far too much of that lately.

There are quite a few to get through and everyone is standing on ceremony waiting for my reaction. Must do my best poker face if I get a rubbish or inappropriate gift.

I unwrap the next present. A smaller package in a shiny red wrapper. It's a set of baby grows. "I saw those and thought they're right up your street," says Bushra.

I take a babygrow out of the plastic packaging. It's emblazoned with the words: *Mum, dad, I know what you've been doing.* Innuendo-laden babywear? I never knew there was such a thing.

Julia hands me another parcel. This one's a neat box in matte gold wrapping. "This is from me," she declares.

I open it up. It's a baby monitor.

"Julia..." I stare at her, my mouth quivering. "It's too much."

"Nonsense! You're my best friend. It's not too much. I asked M what's still on your list and he mentioned a baby monitor."

M looks sheepish. "To be fair, we've got a pretty long list."

He pushes over two more huge boxes. They've not been wrapped but they both have green bows stapled to their side. M hands me a pair of scissors so I can slice through the tape of the first box. It's a car seat. Who is this from?

"This is from your big sister," M explains. "She asked me what we needed when we were last up north." He nudges the other box in my direction. "This is from her, too."

I tear through the cardboard to find an ISOFIX to fit under the car seat. Together, it would have cost big sis hundreds. "Did she add the bows, too?"

M's face reddens. "I added that to make it look like a present."

"Where have you been hiding all these boxes?" I ask M.

"They've been with the concierge for weeks, in their post room. I didn't bother to collect them, or that would give the game away."

Julia and Reena look at each other and smile. They know M's a good one. If only I did, too.

More gifts come my way.

I unbox a pram. It's from mum. It's not the shiny, leather-trim pram-porn prams I've been lusting after but it's a good pram. It has a solid frame, chunky wheels and a foam handle. It's sturdy and it'll do the job perfectly.

Middle sis has bought enough clothes for baby H to wear for the next year. Concealed within the clothing, there's also a Tens machine. She's left a handwritten note saying she used that machine during all her labours so it should come in handy. She also says the proper present will come when the baby is born. What proper present? What more is there to give?

Bryony has gifted an ivory keepsake box and photo album, Reena hands me a handful of gift vouchers. She hasn't had a chance to shop, she reasons. I understand. I was once a newlywed, too.

Helen passes me a powder blue gift bag. "It's nothing much but I didn't want to come empty-handed."

I peer inside the bag to see some Johnson's baby oil and talcum powder.

"Thanks, you shouldn't have," I say.

"Don't mention it." Helen grins proudly.

I'M BURSTING WITH GRATITUDE but also bursting to go to the toilet every few minutes so, for efficiency, I decide that a group family call to say thank you would be the best bet.

My phone screen is divided into four, with a beloved family member taking up a square each.

Me: "I wanted to thank you ladies for my presents."

Big sis: "Which ones, lady? Did you get the car seat? Or the ISOFIX?"

Me: "Both. And you spent way too much money. You didn't have to get that."

Big sis: "It was expensive, lady, but I wanted to give something useful. Not a silly novelty bib."

Middle sis: "Hey, I got a novelty bib for her!"

Big sis: "I'm just saying. They have their place but I wanted to get something that you really need."

Middle sis sniffs.

Big sis: "Where's the fella?"

Me: "He's in the bedroom. Probably asleep."

Big sis: "Ah, okay."

Little sis: "The decorations look nice."

I look behind me at the backdrop of bunting and glitter strewn across my living room.

Little sis: "I didn't have a chance to get you a present yet but I will once the baby's born. I just haven't been to town in ages."

She yawns. I didn't realise I was keeping her awake.

Me: "That's fine. I can't believe you all managed to keep this a secret and worked with M. I was thinking he was being stingy and didn't want to do the baby shopping."

Middle sis: "Well, you're always moaning that we don't do anything to surprise you like a normal family. We thought we'd try this time."

Big sis: "I'd like to have come for the party but train fares to London are so pricey. It made more sense to put that towards your presents and get something useful as babies are expensive and your budget is probably being stretched."

I do a lip grimace like mum. Does big sis know M doesn't have a job? Has he told her when they were planning my baby shower? Or is she speaking in general terms? There are so many secrets floating about, I can't tell fact from fiction these days.

Middle sis: "Clothes are useful, too."

Mum: "What you say? I can't hear anything? All I can see is lots of mouths moving."

Mum puts her ear to the phone.

Me: "Mum, you don't need to do that. Just look at the screen normally. Did you press the button to make the sound come on?"

Mum: "Which button? I don't know these things."

Little sis: "The audio button, mum. I showed you before."

Me: "Are you not at home?"

Little sis: "Yeah, I'm upstairs."

Middle sis: "Why don't you and mum get on the call together? It would make it easier."

Little sis: "I'm in my dressing gown now. I don't fancy going downstairs again."

Mum: "Heh? What you say now. *Dooro!* Wait. Let me get your sister."

Mum walks away, as the screen flashes across the ceiling, across the door and what appears to be the bottom of the stairs. Then I hear the soothing sound of mum banging her hand against the banisters.

Mum: "*Heh!* Help me with call. I speaking to your big sisters."

Little sis: "I know, mum. I'm on the same call. Hold on, I'll just come downstairs. For God's sake."

Little sis' phone screen turns black (she's probably put it in her dressing gown pocket) as she huffs and puffs her way downstairs. Then, she ends her call and appears next to mum in our dining room.

Me: "Anyway, the baby grows are really nice, thanks. Clothes *are* important."

Middle sis: "When are you due again?"

Me: "In a couple of weeks but it could be any day now."

Big sis: "You never know, lady. As it's your first time, it's quite common to be overdue. I was and I had to be induced."

Little sis: "What does that mean?"

Big sis: "It's when they have to start your labour for you... artificially."

Middle sis: "I'm glad I didn't have to do that. My kids all came on time. I didn't fancy having a tablet shoved up my lady parts."

Little sis: "Gross."

Big sis: "It is rather gross. Anyway, if you want to avoid that, do plenty of walking. Not too far, just in case you go into labour and you're not near home. You won't want that."

Middle sis: "I think I did too much walking first time round. You need to get your rest, too. I laboured so quickly, I ripped my bum."

Mum: "*Dooro!* Have shame. You shouldn't say all this in front of your little sister. She's too young to understand."

Little sis smirks.

Me: "Right, so I should walk but don't walk too much and make sure I get rest but not too much. Got it."

Middle sis: "If you think that's conflicting information, just wait until you have the baby."

Me: "Can't wait."

I stifle a yawn.

Me: "I'll say goodbye now as it's 11 o'clock. I might as well lie down in bed, even if I won't be able to actually sleep."

Big sis: "Baby still keeping you awake at night?"

Me: "Baby and everything else. It's just a pain."

Middle sis and big sis both pull the same face. It's a look of knowing.

Me: "What?"

Silence.

Me: "What? If there's something to say, just say it."

Big sis: "It's just that... if your baby is keeping you awake at night now, it's likely it won't be a very good sleeper."

Me: "I've heard that loads before."

Big sis: "Oh, well good. Anyway, are you going to get your eyebrows done before the baby arrives?"

I slide my fingers across my coarse eyebrows.

Me: "Are they really that bad?"

Big sis: "They are a bit bushy, lady. I'm just thinking, you won't want to post any new baby photos on social media looking like that."

Ouch.

Middle sis: "Make sure you also shave before you go into labour."

Mum: "*Dooro!*"

Me: "I can't even reach down there."

Middle sis: "Get the fella to do it."

Mum: "*Dooro!* Have shame!"

Middle sis: "Why shouldn't he? He got her in that situation in the first place."

Me: "I don't feel like doing anything right now. I stopped wearing my wedding and engagement ring as my fingers are like sausages."

Middle sis: "Yeah, your nose is all bulbous as well."

Me: "Hmm. Anyway, I'm not sure how many photos I'll be taking as I'll be in the birthing pool."

Cue lots of looks of disapproval, and one look of confusion from little sis.

Big sis: "You're not going to go in the pool, are you? Why can't you just have your baby in the ward like a normal person?"

Mum: "Pool? Like swimming pool? Is that safe? What if baby drown?"

Me: "Yes, it's perfectly safe and perfectly normal."

Big sis: "It sounds odd. Will you be in the pool with other people?"

Me: "No! At least, I doubt that. The midwife never mentioned others. I should be by myself."

I look to middle sis, the marginally more modern of my elder sisters.

Middle sis: "You do you, girly. I was in the ward for all mine 'cause I didn't want all my bits floating about in the water."

Big sis: "It wasn't even an option when I had my kids. They tried to offer a home birth but I said no thanks! As if I'd have my baby at home. Imagine the mess!"

Me: "Well, water births are quite common now. I even get to choose my birth music."

Cue more looks of disapproval.

Mum: "*Yalla*, what she saying? This not be disco! You should be saying, '*Allah, Allah*,' when you give birth, not having concert."

Me: "I won't be dancing. It's just classic music, to calm me down. I'll be praying, too."

Big sis and middle sis smirk.

Big sis: "Golly lady, you really do everything differently, don't you? You'll be eating your placenta, next."

Little sis: "Ugh... gross."

Me: "On that note, I'll say goodbye."

FIVE MINUTES LATER, my phone rings. Who the bloody hell is it now? Then I realise it's mum.

"I just be thinking. Do you want to have baby here?"

I sit up. "What? Mum, do you mean at a hospital in Manchester? Or your actual house?"

"*Dooro!* Not in the house, silly girl! I no want the watery mess. I mean, local hospital here. Maybe that would be easier. Then you've got us around. I can help with baby."

"Mum, that's a nice idea but it's a bit late now."

"Is it?"

I have to think for a minute. I haven't even factored in going back home. "Yeah, I think it is. I've got my hospital here. I'm registered. I've got my birthing book. A birth plan."

"What plan?" asks mum. "You just plan to give birth, no?"

"Yeah, but... I think there's a bit more to it than that." I daren't mention the birth pool and music again. "I'm due in two weeks. It's a bit late bringing this up."

Mum falls silent.

"I'd love to come home," I say. "Maybe after the baby is born. And you are going to come here straight after I give birth, aren't you?"

"Um... we'll have to see. You know what it's like with your father. I'll have to check train times and prices and all that."

"Mum, I'm really hoping you can come. I don't want to hear about train times. I don't want to worry about that. I need to be really selfish right now. I could have the baby any day. I need you to come. Or at least tell me you'll really try."

"Okay, I'll see."

"No, mum. You can't just see. Please try and make it happen."

"That's why I say you come to me."

"I can't just come like that! I shouldn't even be travelling far this heavily pregnant."

"Hmm. That be true. Okay *InshaAllah* we try come."

I hang up the phone. I am still in the living room, clearing up some of the debris from the earlier baby shower. I am both full of love and frustration at the same time. I love Julia for throwing me the baby shower. I'm annoyed at mum for being so noncommittal. As for M, we haven't had a chance to unpack our feelings yet. And honestly, I don't have the energy or the fight in me. I need to get through these next couple of weeks before baby H2 arrives.

1st April, Due date

"I wasn't sure if you'd make our meeting today," says Graham. "Aren't you due soon?"

I gesture towards my now expansive bump, before realising he can't see it properly as we're on a Zoom call. I stand up for full effect. "It's actually my due date today."

Even though the picture is grainy as Graham is no doubt in the dark, dimly lit boardroom of my office space rental, I can still make out his startled face. "Crikey! Should you even be on the call? I wouldn't know what to do if you went into labour."

I laugh. "Believe it or not, most women don't actually give birth on their due date. It's more of a guesstimate, so you're safe. Plus, you'll be glad to know I live right near the hospital and M isn't too far away as he's gone out for... err... an errand."

I still can't bring myself to tell everyone that M is out of work. I could do without a raised eyebrow. A look of concern. A well-meaning question about how we're managing financially. I don't need it from Graham. Not today.

Though, in fairness, M could well be out on an errand, as he's been very elusive these last couple of weeks. Since we had a slightly embarrassing public spat on the number 15 bus, we haven't properly talked. Of course, we've talked but not *talked*. We haven't acknowledged what was said and how we felt. We've sort of been co-existing.

While M hasn't been as forthcoming with updates on the job hunting front, I've known better than to ask. I've shoved my worries down to the bottom of my gut and choose to trust that he's doing his best. After all, my main focus now should be on the safe delivery of H2. I don't have the capacity, physically or mentally, to take any more on my plate.

"Honestly, you ladies are like super women." Graham sips from his mug. "Though I'm glad you could make the time as we can box off some admin around you going off on maternity leave." Graham shuffles some papers, making himself look very official. Well, as official as someone as jolly as Graham can look. "The way it works here is that you can pause your contract but, to be honest, it's not like you have to come back in nine months or a year. We can just restart things when you're ready to come back, or if you're ready to come back, I should say." Graham pauses and looks at me. I think we both know this is the end. I won't be going back to that workplace. I just know it.

"It's like the end of an era," says Graham, wistfully. "Loren, the telesales whizz left just last week and there's been a shakeup in the boardroom."

"Really? Who's left the boardroom?" I ask.

"Well, I shouldn't really say as it's not appropriate but since you're leaving..." Graham leans into his laptop screen. "Jasdeep has had to step down from the board."

This makes me lean into my laptop, too. "Had to?"

"Unfortunately, yes. There have been a few complaints from some of the female coworkers regarding his behaviour. Oh God, I've said too much." Graham throws his hands in the air. "Far be it for me to gossip. But anyway, he reckons it's a load of hot air but we have to take these allegations seriously and he's agreed to stand down from the board. We sort of let him leave discretely, turban held high." Graham covers his face with his palm. "Oh God, I didn't mean to say that. Is that racist?"

"Possibly, Graham, but it's okay."

After tying up loose ends at my office workplace, Graham and I say goodbye. I'm still reeling from the news about Jasdeep. However, I'm glad that justice has been served in a roundabout way. Truthfully, I was never going to do anything. I've read many books where the heroine exacts revenge on the man who wronged her in the most spectacular of ways. Whether it would be a punch to the nose or a knee to the nuts, the payback would always be sweet. It's a nice fantasy but that's not how it really works in life. For all my talk, I wouldn't have kneed Jasdeep. My knees can't reach that high.

I decide it would be strange to call my freelancer on the day that I'm due because, from the sounds of it, I should be doing nothing but waiting for the baby to arrive. But what exactly does one do on one's due date? I cannot, for the life of me, just sit around for the entire day.

I consult my parenting book. Let's figure out how to get the baby sleeping through.

The book I'm currently reading is about a nanny who has helped many Hollywood stars get their babies to sleep at night. I'm not sure about this one. She's very pro-bottle and pro-dummy and, as I'm hoping to breastfeed, I'm not sure if her advice would work for me. Still, I indulge.

She talks about 'the village' helping take care of you in the first forty days of the baby's life. Funny, I thought that was an Asian thing. A key underlying theme in this entire book is how hellish the lack of sleep can be, if the baby isn't trained properly by the parent. She suggests several methods. The first one is 'the disappearing chair'. This is where you sit next to the baby while it's in its cradle the first night, then move the chair slightly further away the following night. You continue moving the chair further away each night until you end up outside the door. From the baby's perspective, that must be freaky as anything.

Another suggestion is the 'pick up, put down' method. This is when you literally pick them up every time they cry and put them down straight away. Rinse and repeat until the baby eventually stops crying and just goes the hell to sleep. Then, there's the 'shush-pat' concept. It's quite simple, you shush and pat them to sleep.

The whole emphasis of this book seems to be on not picking up, cradling or holding the baby for long periods of time. Feeding whenever the baby wants is frowned upon, too. It all sounds rather militant.

One thing the book does suggest, which I rather like, is the idea of showing your baby around your home, like they're a grown up, when you bring them back from the hospital. Then, after their whistle-stop tour, you plop them down in the Moses basket and have a cup of tea with your partner. If it's as easy as that, bring on parenthood.

I pick up another of Sophia's books. On the cover, there is a mother cradling her baby with love. That's a bit more me. The writer explains how the first three months of a baby's life is actually a fourth trimester. The baby isn't quite ready for the world so you should carry them at all times, give them cuddles, respond to their every cue. It's a very nice idea, except I will have to figure out how to write press releases and respond to media requests between all this snuggling.

Both books, though very different in their approach, are confident in one thing– that they know all about babies and have all the answers. The glass half empty me wonders whether babies are really that conventional, while the glass half full me is confident I'll have this motherhood gig nailed now I've read a couple of books on the subject.

I think I need a lie down. I head to the bedroom (which could do with a clean), pop my earphones in and listen to the nasally not-so-dulcet tones of the hypno-birthing lady. She is adamant that I will breathe my baby out, as long as I keep practising her techniques before the labour itself.

I sit on the edge of the bed, put my hands to my belly and gently breathe out, feeling my fingers spread apart. I then breathe in, letting my hands come together.

Okay, I'm bored of this now. As sleep will be scarce when H2 arrives, I might try to store some now.

OH, WHAT IS *that?*

The most unusual churning sensation wakes me from my sleep. What time is it? I look out of the window to see it's raining but still light outside. I, therefore, didn't nap for that long but long enough to end up with a patch of drool on the side of my cheek.

It feels like someone is opening and closing a zip around my abdomen. Shit, that's painful. I have to sit up.

I do my deep breathing and hope to breathe away the pain. Breath in, one... two... three... four. Hold, then deep breath out, one... two... three... four... five... six... seven... oh God! I can't do it. It's done nothing to quell the intense pain.

I breathe in again, heavier this time. It's more like a pant. That doesn't do much, either. Sod it, I'm going to need the Tens machine. I head to the bedroom and the pain subsides. Good, this gives me time to rifle through the top drawer to find the instrument of torture.

Nestled between my knickers, I find the Tens machine. My heart feels heavy as I realise that without M, I'll have to electrocute myself.

I drop my missing husband a message:

Can you come home? I think I'm going into labour.

He could be anywhere. On the Underground. In an interview. Having a comforting hot chocolate without me. I'm going to have to figure this out for myself.

I place the sticky pads on my back. Two at the bottom, two at the top. I can't bring myself to press the button. It feels like some sick masochistic torture. Hold on... the contractions are coming back. Oh no! They are strong. I couldn't even describe the pain. Maybe it's like being awake during an operation. It's stopping me in my tracks. I stand up, put my hands against the wall and push myself down, doing the world's least sexiest twerk. I look out of the window of our high-rise apartment to see if anyone in the flats opposite can see me. Luckily, nobody is watching this most unsavoury show.

Then, just as quickly as it escalated, the pain subsides. I take long, slow, deep breaths, regulating my heart, my senses, my body as I come back to neutral.

Phew. That was a *lot.* Deep breath. Another deep breath.

Is this it? Is this labour? It better not be bloody practice contractions as I can't take too many more of these before warming up to the real deal.

I settle back onto the sofa, catching my breath. It's strange how the pain can be like a crescendo, then disappear into nothing. It's not like the ache you get after hurting yourself, where the throbbing continues long after. It's not like anything else I've ever been through.

My phone rings. I hope it's M.

Nope, it's mum.

"Hello? What you do?" asks mum.

I better not tell her that I'm sat alone in my flat having contractions. That will only make her worry.

"Nothing," I reply, conscious of the breathlessness in my voice.

"Why you sound so tired? You be out running? You can't run far now! It be dangerous. Might end up having baby in road."

"I've not been running, mum. I was just... I went downstairs to check the mail. What are you doing?"

"Watching the news." Mum sighs. "It all so sad."

"What is?"

"You not seen news? I thought you had to for job?"

"I've not watched it much recently."

"You should! Need to know what happens in world. Anyway, I call to check, is everything okay? You're due today. Any pain starting?"

I breathe unintentionally heavily. "None yet."

"Hmm. New mum can take *lit-ool* longer. Most ladies no give birth on due date, anyway. But make sure you don't go on Tube. Don't want to have baby underground. That would not be good."

"No, that would not be good. Was there anything else?"

"*Nah, nah*, just checking. If you have pain, make sure you call husband straight away to come from work. But only when pain gets quite a lot. Not at the beginning. It may take long."

"Will do. Anyway, have you booked your train ticket to come down to London yet?"

She pauses.

"Mum!"

"Yes, yes but no, I not book yet. It be too soon. No point coming now. You might not have baby for another 10 days. Then what we do, sit around in your husband face all day? Your dad no be comfortable there. We wait till maybe you go into labour, or we know baby coming. Or, you be induce. Then we book ticket, good?"

I try to squash the rising anger. Mum is speaking pragmatically, of course, but I'm full of emotions. I just had my first contractions, it's hard not to think emotionally. I wish my parents were more proactive. I wish they could come and be sitting ducks, waiting for me to give birth. It's going to happen at some point, isn't it? It's not like it will be a wasted trip.

Deep breath. Deep breath. I remind myself, my parents aren't proactive. It's not in their nature. They're not like Neetu's. I have to accept the hand I've been dealt.

After I say goodbye, I turn on the news to see what the fuss is about. There it is. Bombs. Bombs everywhere. What is going on? There are pictures of death and destruction. Whole buildings reduced to rubble. There's a grown man crying. A woman in a dusty pink hijab beating her chest and wailing in heartbreak. I see small children, their faces dusted with soot. The screen flashes with captions detailing the number of dead civilians and how many of them are under 18. Under 18? That means they're children. Why don't they just say that? All these people are reduced to being just a number. All these men, women and children from a far off country are nameless. They are statistics on the news. Yet, they're so much more than that. They're someone's husband. Someone's wife. Someone's mother. Someone's daughter. Someone's child. And they are dying.

I have seen conflict and disaster countless times on the news. I've become desensitised. But right now, as I am about to give life, my stomach lurches and my heart aches. The news then shows footage of two young boys, no older than 10, searching for food, except there is none to be found. Everything has been destroyed. People no longer have homes, let alone nourishment. Later, it shows them leave a café with a small piece of bread, no bigger than a slice of toast. They're laughing, happily sharing the morsel. Their faces are matted and their fingernails are black and they're sharing bread like it's a gourmet meal.

Suddenly, the golden egg highchair seems ridiculous. The pram-porn is futile. We don't need a pram with a leather trim handle. Our baby doesn't need to sit in a golden egg. It's our conspicuous consumption culture that makes us want all this.

The pain of contractions is replaced by the feeling of guilt and shame.

Where is this? Why is it that these images look so familiar? Is it because I've seen so much horror in Middle Eastern countries that it's become the norm? Is it because I've seen it so many times before, gotten upset for half-a-day, then carried on as normal? Then the news headline tells me it's Gaza.

Fingers trembling, I grab my phone. I usually make charitable donations via mum, who sends the money to people in need in Bangladesh. I have no idea where to send money for Gaza. However, I can feel a contraction warming up, so there's no time to compare and contrast various charities.

I look at the ticker tape that runs across the bottom of the news story. There are relief workers on the ground. I'll send my money to them.

Okay, how much? £30? No, that's a bit steep right now. God, I feel awful saying that. Right, £25. That'll have to do for now. I'll give more when I'm more abundant. I hit send, then throw my phone onto the sofa seat next to me and stare back at the screen. A grandfather is crying. The translation says that he's lost every single member of his family. His pale green-brown eyes are glassy with tears.

I pick up my phone again and donate a further £25.

The pain is rising in my stomach. I can't look at the TV anymore. I make a bid for the bathroom and, just as M twists the front door lock open, I vomit all over the floor.

The blood drains from M's face.

"Sorry, I tried to get to the toilet but I couldn't make it in time." I wipe my mouth with a tissue.

"It's okay, babe. I'll clean it up." M puts his laptop case down. I go to rinse my mouth in the sink, before my stomach lurches again.

"Don't bother yet!" I manage to say before being sick once again, all down the side of the sink and onto the floor.

"DO YOU THINK WE NEED to go to the hospital?" asks M.

I have my eyes closed, trying to breathe through the pain. "I'm not sure yet. I don't want to get sent back home."

I clutch my stomach as I endure the zip tightening around my abdomen. My fingers then slowly join together and come apart as I breathe through the contraction. Going to have an amazing birth, my arse. This is horrific.

"Hmmmmmm." I'm letting out noises I never knew I had in me. Strange, primal noises.

"Shall I switch the Tens machine back on?" asks M.

"Hmmmmmmm!" I keep my eyes closed, as seeing and talking is too difficult. The pain subsides again.

I go on to my contraction tracking app and log the latest one. It's still saying seven minutes apart. Fucking hell. Does that mean I can't go and get some pain relief at the hospital?

Suddenly, I feel like someone's pressed batteries against my back.

"What the hell? The contraction has gone now. Don't electrocute me when I'm not in pain." I shout at M.

Idiot.

"Sorry, I wasn't sure if you were done."

"If I'm not mooing or grunting, then I'm done. Do not inflict any more torture than necessary."

I sit down on the bed, unable to do anything. Lying down is uncomfortable. Sleeping is impossible. Eating? Forget it.

The books lied. They all lied. That bloody hypnobirthing woman is the biggest crook of all. She said between contractions you can have snacks, laugh with your husband, watch movies. Sleep. As if.

Another contraction is coming.

I can feel it rising. Rising. Rising. That dreaded zip is tightening again, taking all my internal organs with it.

"That's it. We're going to the hospital. You should at least get checked out." M decides after my latest round of farmyard noises. "Forget the app. We're going."

Luckily, my hospital bag has been ready and waiting since I was 37 weeks pregnant.

As M closes the front door, he stops. "Shit. How are we going to get there? There's no parking and you won't be able to walk."

"Damn right I won't be walking!" I declare.

"Let me call a taxi."

The contraction has passed and I have a moment to compose myself. I check in the mirror. Nose bulbous. Face bloated. Mouth dry like a desert. I will not be taking any postpartum photos with the new baby. Not like this.

The taxi is swift. We make our way downstairs through the lift, thankfully, without any interrupting contractions. We go past Sam at concierge, who looks up and asks: "Is it happening, brother?"

"I think it is," says M, holding up the hospital bag to emphasise the point.

Then, as we step outside, another contraction comes.

"Mmmmmmmm."

This is a new low. I have to hold the wall in a twerking position again. This time, out on the main road with many a passerby witnessing the show.

The taxi driver comes out of the car. "Mate, come on, I'm on a double yellow line. I can't stay for too long."

Then he notices me, head down, arse in the air. He doesn't say a word and goes back into his car. Sensible.

The contraction melts away and I climb into the car with M. He holds my hand the entire journey and rubs my back.

We get to the maternity unit and, to my horror, I have to wait in a queue. A queue, I tell you! As if I'm at the supermarket. This is ridiculous. Is it because it's a busy city hospital? Is it because it's central London? When my sisters gave birth, they went to hospital straight away and were seen straight away. I'm not sure if I'm looking back with rose-tinted lenses but I don't recall seeing either of them bent over double, or mooing like cows. The worst I got was big sis being a bit sweary when we visited her at the maternity ward.

"You sit down. I'll wait in the queue," M offers chivalrously.

There is a woman in a black burka sat opposite me, crying in pain. She looks like she might faint. Her head is unsteady. I want to tell her: *'Use the arms of the chair to lean against. Don't sit down. It's the worst position when you're contracting. Stand up and twerk it out.'* There is another woman with her. An older woman, who might be her mum. English isn't their first language and I can hear them trying to explain that they want a wheelchair.

"We can't get you a wheelchair right now," the lady says from behind the reception desk. "We haven't got any available. You don't need one, anyway. This is your second baby."

The woman speaks as though she knows her intimately and, therefore, can say with confidence that she shouldn't be writhing in pain.

The poor pregnant lady gets up and uses the bar across the hallway to lean against to get in a comfortable position until she is called through. Having been denied the use of a wheelchair, she leans onto her mother figure, holding on for support.

While we're waiting, I have another contraction. Should I really be contracting like this in a public waiting room? I've never experienced anything like this in my life. I stand up, turn around and lean against the chair. M doesn't know what to do, apart from rub my back, which is actually more annoying as it's making me hot. I don't have the heart to tell him, though. He's never seen me in this much pain.

Finally, I am called through to enter a sterile examination room, with a bulletin board detailing funds raised for the hospital and yet more leaflets about domestic abuse. After the nurse takes down my details, she gets me to lie on the table. "Can you please bring your ankles together and part your knees? I'm going to see how dilated you are. It'll be a bit uncomfortable but have you had a smear before?"

I nod through the contraction pain.

"Well, it's a bit like that. So just bear with me."

She begins her examination. It is *not* like a cervical smear. I feel like my insides are being scooped out. Oh my life! I wince. My toes curl. I push one hand against the fake brick wall for dear life and grip onto M with the other. He looks helpless, like a child, while I bite my bottom lip.

"Sorry, I know it's not comfortable but I really need you to stay as still as possible."

Why don't I examine you and see how still you can be? I think to myself, angry thoughts coming to the fore. Stop it. Stop it. Positive thoughts. She's trying to help me. God bless the NHS.

The pain is worse than a contraction. I make more unusual noises, surprising myself at my vocal range.

She finally releases her iron grip and takes off her surgical gloves.

"I'm sorry to say but you're only 1cm dilated."

Fucking hell.

"What? Only one?" I ask.

"Afraid so. That means you'll have to go home," she says, as though I've won the consolation prize in a raffle.

Is this an April fool?

I look at M in disbelief.

"It's actually better for you to be at home as you'll be more relaxed. You can come back when you're further along. Always remember that 5–1–1 rule."

"The what?" everything I learnt at NCT or read in Sophia's books has escaped my brain.

The nurse leans forward, happy to impart wisdom. "One contraction every five minutes, and it lasting for one minute each time. That's what we need for when you next come in. You need to be about 5cm dilated before we can admit you into the ward."

"Ward? Do you not have my birth plan?"

The nurse looks at me, dumbfounded.

"I think I have it with me. Can you get my bag?" I gesture to M.

"There's no need." She holds out her hand. "We look at the birth plan when you're admitted but the main thing is getting to that stage of labour first."

I sit up on the bed, pulling up my knickers. "Will I still be able to go in the birthing pool?"

"Let's see how you are. Come back when you're further along. Otherwise, you'll be sat here waiting. You're better off being at home. Get some sleep and rest while you can."

Rest? Sleep? How would I sleep between these contractions? More to the point, if this isn't real, active labour to warrant being admitted into the hospital, how much worse will the pain be?

2nd April, Due date +1

Sheets of rain are thrashing against our bedroom window. I would know, as I've been awake the entire time.

It's gone 2am. My contractions are still seven minutes apart. So bloody close but not close enough. It's driving me mad. M is asleep. He tried to stay awake as long as he could but eventually the lying down position got the better of him, as it always does.

Each time I feel a contraction, I need to sit up in bed, get on all fours and assume some tantric yoga position to push out the pain.

I've had enough. I get up and go to the kitchen. Late night, or should I say early morning, starts have become the norm for me the last few months. It's all thanks to baby H2.

I raid the cupboard in search of goodies. There is an open bag of Maltesers and a box of shortbread. I grab both and sit in the living room. There is bugger all on TV at this time, so I don't even bother trying. I'm also reluctant to invest in a new series as I won't have time to binge watch.

Instead, I eat the Maltesers, one by one. I have to say, there is some comfort in the silence at the dead of night. It is so still that I can momentarily forget that I'm in central London. The rain has stopped. The traffic outside is minimal. Most of the lights in the flats opposite are turned off. There are the odd one or two apartments that are lit, probably by younger, childless people who have painted the town red. Looking out of the window down onto the street, I can see the bus stop is empty. A few people are walking around. It is London after all, the streets won't be completely lifeless. Apart from the quiet, everything else is the same. It's hard to believe it will be dramatically different within perhaps 24 hours. It's hard to believe I will leave for the hospital with one person and come back with two.

There comes a bloody contraction again. I can't believe women go through this. Why? Why do we do this to ourselves? Is it really worth it? It must be. Otherwise, there'd been nobody having multiple babies and there would be far fewer children in the world.

Having finished my Maltesers, I move onto the shortbread. I must pace myself to avoid another vomiting episode.

Then there's another contraction.

Hold on. That came quicker. I log onto the app. Oh, five minutes and 50 seconds. Does that justify a trip to the hospital? Please say it is so.

As the contraction subsides, I head into the bedroom to wake M. He lifts his head, startled from his sleep. I can tell he's had a deep, deep, dreamy sleep. The kind I've been robbed of the last few months. So unfair.

"You okay?"

I sit next to him. "I think we should go to the hospital."

I AM EXAMINED BY THE same nurse, who looks sad to be inflicting such torture on me again. The second time isn't any easier. Once again, I practically climb up the bed to escape from her hold, only to hear the dreaded words: "You're not much further along, just 2cm dilated."

Fuuuuuuuuuck.

"This isn't fair. This isn't fair," I say to no one and anyone.

"Can't she be admitted? It's her first time. She's in a lot of pain," says M.

She shakes her head. "You'd just be waiting. Anyway, there aren't any beds at the moment."

"I don't want a bed I can't sleep in! I want a birthing pool!" I say, like a demanding diva. "Or at least some pain relief? Can you give me something for the pain? Like gas and air?"

"We don't give gas and air until you're in active labour. However, I can give you some paracetamol?"

Paracetamol? The stuff I take for a mild headache? Fuck that, goes my inner monologue.

"Yes, please," goes my outer monologue.

Having taken the paracetamol, which barely touches the sides, M and I trudge through the hospital corridor, in denial that we are being turned away, yet again. It's like I have to be crawling on all fours in pain before they will see me.

Another contraction comes. I turn to face the wall. I hold on to the bars tightly, leaning my pelvis away.

"Hmmmm." Again, more primal sounds come from my body, as if I've been taken over by something else.

"Are you okay?" asks a lady with an Indian accent, upon spotting M and I.

"They keep sending us away but she's in really bad labour pains. I can't believe they can send us home like this," says M.

The woman looks at me with a gentle, smiling face. "Don't worry, I'll speak to them. They'll admit you."

"Really? Could you do that for me?" I manage to ask as the latest contraction melts away. I cup my hands in an unintentional prayer at this fairy godmother. I am desperate.

"It will be okay," M says, rubbing my back, as the lady goes and talks to the receptionist.

I close my eyes. Please, please make it okay.

She returns, defiantly. "Come on through."

To my horror, I am led back to the examination room. The place where I'd been previously mauled.

"At least you've not been sent home," offers M.

Small blessings.

Despite saving on another cab ride, I am more uncomfortable here than I was at home. I'm contracting in all sorts of positions. Up against the wall. Straddling the chair. It's all one big mess.

"Can I go in the pool? Or take some pain medication?" I ask in desperation.

"I'm sorry, dear," says another nurse. "You can't have any of those things unless you're in active labour, which you're not at the moment. I can give you some more paracetamol. Or Co-Codamol if it's been four hours since your last painkiller."

"I'll take anything," I wail.

A man walks in, ignores me and asks for the oxygen monitor. Apparently, he can't find a spare one on the ward.

Call me naive but I never knew labour could be so undignified. Nobody tells you. It's another one of the secrets you don't get to hear. I'm not sure who has seen what at this point. Bizarrely, I don't even care. It's like all general etiquette has gone out of the window. What goes on in the examination room, stays in the examination room.

Then, something erupts inside me. I feel a gushing of water, along with some blood.

The nurse looks at me, aghast.

"I'm sorry," I cry, shaking with fear.

"Don't worry about that," says M, moving me to sit on the bed.

"There's quite a bit of blood in there," the nurse says to her colleague.

"What's happening?" I ask but nobody responds.

What follows is the stuff of nightmares. The nurse is so worried that my waters contain blood, that they do an ECG to check the heartbeat of the baby. I have to lie on my back, the most excruciating position I can be in right now. I cry, struggle to stay still, arch my back in pain. All the while, her colleague keeps telling me I can't move as it's going to take longer. They repeat the ECG again. I collapse into M's arms, crying like a baby.

I read in one of the baby books that the pain of labour is so intense, you could almost faint, or start hallucinating. In my delirium, I start remembering other moments of pain. Flashbacks from childhood. Like the one time I fell in school during a game of tag. The teacher lifted my jumper sleeve, to see there was no graze, and told me to be a brave girl. I spent the afternoon crying, sat at the back of the class during story time. This was much to the annoyance of my teacher, who kept telling me to be quiet and stop being a baby. It was only when I got home that my mum rolled up my jumper a little further, to see a huge gash. It turned out I'd cut and sprained my arm. I wasn't being a baby. I was truly hurt. They just didn't see it.

Other memories come to the forefront. Slicing my ankle on the spokes of middle sis' bike, when she was trying to teach me to cycle. I never got on a bike again and to this day, I don't know how to cycle. That time too, I cried like a baby. When did I stop? When did I start feeling shameful about crying in public? At what age do you realise you have to suck it up and not show emotion?

Through all this pain, I am free of the shackles of polite society. I don't have to be a big girl. Be brave. Be strong. Be a grown-up. I'm stripped back to my core. A crying baby in search of comfort.

"Can I play my birthing song?" I ask between sobs.

"Not yet, my dear. You can do that when you're in the ward."

Why do they keep saying 'ward'? I put on my birthing plan that I want to go in the pool. It's meant to be easier for labour and reduce the chances of tearing. What is the point of me putting together a birth plan if they're not going to even acknowledge it?

"Shall I call your mum?" asks M.

"Not yet. Let's wait until I'm closer to giving birth. Or maybe when the baby is born, as a surprise."

The same nurse who examined me twice, comes back in looking grave. "The results of the ECG were inconclusive. Because you were wriggling around so much, we couldn't really check properly. We need to make sure that the baby is okay and nothing is wrong. Obviously, because you had some bleeding, we need to check the baby isn't in distress."

The baby's in distress? I'm the distressed one here.

"I'm afraid we're going to have to do another ECG," she says.

I turn to M. "Maybe message one of my sisters, just in case I die from labour pains."

No amount of deep breathing and hypno-birthing could help me through that ECG. It's something I'm going to have to erase from my memory when H2 is born.

There are only two hard plastic chairs to sit on, or the hard examination bed. I choose the plastic chair. I sit, leaning forward, my head between my legs. I pray under my breath that this pain passes. I pray for forgiveness for any past sins, including not lowering my gaze around that bloody tease, Jean-Patrice.

I look at M. He's on his phone. What the actual fuck? He better not be playing Lemmings. He sees me looking and puts his phone back in his pocket.

An hour goes by in that room. I feel pain I never knew was possible.

The other nurse, who carried out the initial ECG, looks confused as to why I'm in such pain. She then offers to do another examination, as if the first two weren't traumatising enough.

When she emerges from pummeling me, she looks astonished. "You're actually 9cm dilated. You've progressed really quickly in a short space of time. We can take you to your room now."

That's why I've been in unspeakable pain. I've gone into active labour with only painkillers for comfort.

Between panting, I ask: "Can I go in the birthing pool?"

THE ROOM I HAVE BEEN given is bigger than our entire flat. In one corner, there is a regular bed. Then there's a yoga ball to sit on. There are some balancing bars that a gymnast would use. In another section, there is what looks like a toilet but I'm told it's a birthing stool.

Pride of place is the pool. It looks like a Jacuzzi. I think I was expecting some sort of inflatable paddling pool. This, however, is the real deal. It wouldn't look out of place in a spa.

If I wasn't in active labour, I would have written a blog post reviewing the room.

"Make sure you take pictures of this place," I whisper to M.

"I already did," he whispers back.

I am much more zen here and the pain of the contractions in bearable. Perhaps it's because I've been dosing myself with gas and air.

The two midwives looking after me are lovely. Claire has strong, comforting arms with a chequerboard tattoo down her left bicep. Her short, red hair with black roots and quirky glasses with thick rims make me warm to her. Alison is softly spoken, with narrow shoulders and wispy, textured hair that suggests she is nearing the end of a 12-hour shift.

In between offering me water, encouraging me to pee and making small talk with M, they take turns to make notes. They're writing my birth story.

I have such a huge admiration for midwives. The things they do. The things they say. The things they see. All without flinching. All without judgement. I don't think I could do it.

We are getting closer. With each contraction, I'm closer to meeting H2.

"Do you know if you'll have a boy or a girl?" asks Claire.

M and I look at each other. It's safe to share, as I'm never going to see either of them again. "We're having a girl."

"That's amazing!" Claire rubs my shoulder. She must say that to every single patient, regardless of gender. "Do you have a name yet?"

"We've got a name, but we're calling her H2 for now," I say, still wary of jinxing by saying too much.

"I love that. H2! Right, every time you have a contraction, I need you to think of H2. Breathe for H2. You'll be meeting her soon. At this rate, you'll be breathing your baby out. It's amazing."

Finally, my hypno-birthing is coming into play. The contractions seem to subside without much issue.

The girls hook me up to an IV for some fluids. This is in response to my lack of pee in the last hour. I get out of the pool to walk around, at the request of my midwives. Claire and Alison are concerned that things haven't moved along much in the last 90 minutes. I am, however, enjoying the moment. M has put on my birth music. As the orchestra escalates, I find myself bursting into tears. This time not in pain. This time, it's because of the realisation that I'm going to be a mum. That everything will in fact change. I'm giving life. I'm not even sure what these emotions are. But they're coming in full force.

I look at M. He's wiping his eyes. He comes closer and puts his arms around me. We do a slow dance to the music.

"I thought you didn't do dancing," I whisper, trying to find a moment of humour in all of this.

"Exceptional circumstances. Very exceptional circumstances. I'm not sure what my mum and dad would make of this, though. *Astaghfirullah*!"

"Forgive us, indeed," I say, exasperated.

I'm dancing with my husband, in a state of undress, while hooked up to an IV drip. You couldn't make it up. Again, what happens in the birthing room stays in the birthing room.

I go back in the pool to see if that helps things along. Nothing really changes. I get out of the pool. Go back into the pool. I do this several times. I attempt to wee but nothing comes. They administer more fluids in the IV.

The pain becomes more intense. I'm letting out even more animalistic sound now. Thank goodness I have my own gigantic, sound absorbing room.

"I don't know what to do," I say, fighting back more tears.

"Sweetheart, it's okay. You're doing so well. And you're going to breathe your baby out. Just by breathing. You are a warrior princess!" says Claire.

That's a bit much but I'll take the compliment.

"Do you want to eat something? You have been going at this for a while. You don't want to lose any energy now. You're at the final stretch," says Alison.

"Okay. What we got?" I look at M.

He digs in his backpack. "Here's a chocolate coin. It's from my secret stash."

I wolf it down.

"I need to get out. I need to get out of this pool. I feel like I need the toilet!"

The pain is enough to make me faint now.

"Do you want to try the birthing stool?" asks Claire.

Without answering, I climb out of the pool and slide onto the birthing stool, nearly tripping over my IV along the way. Claire hoists me up. I think she is the warrior. Where is my husband in all of this? I look over my shoulder.

"Will you get off the bloody phone?" I scream.

The NCT lady did warn that I'll be swearing at my husband. He saw it coming. M puts his phone in his pocket and comes over to me, rubbing my back.

"That's not helping, either. It's making me feel really hot." I nudge my shoulder away from him.

"Sorry, babe. I wish I could take the pain away."

"Well, you can't. But you can at least be in the moment while I birth your daughter."

Claire squats opposite me, arms out. I hold on tight, digging my fingers in. Poor Claire.

Alison returns to the desk to take notes.

"Okay, I need you to give a really big push for me, alright? Come on. Push for H2!"

"I can't!" More tears.

"You can do it. I can see her head! Just one big push."

"You can do it, babe."

"It hurts! It's stinging." I feel like H2 is rubbing on an open wound.

"Come on. One big push," Claire pleads.

"Can you distract me? I need something to get me through it," I say to M.

"Alright," he replies. "Do you want to hear some good news?"

"I'll take whatever you've got."

M comes close to my ear. "The reason I've been on my phone so much is because, in between reading prayers online, I've been emailing about work. It's for Miles' company, the one for which he said I should put my CV forward. I had the final interview and I didn't want to tell you anything about it or get your hopes up."

"But you tell me everything! Even when I don't want to hear it!"

"I'm trying to be more like you. Remember? Don't celebrate until you've got something? Anyway, they've been emailing me instead of calling. I thought I'd let you know so you don't think Julia and Miles have been flaky by suggesting a job and not coming through."

"Good." I feel like there should be more to this. "And?"

"They emailed to say I didn't get the job."

"Right. That's not helpful!" I say.

"Yeah but there was another job I've interviewed for and they've been in touch, too."

"You can do it. Give me one big push," says Claire.

"Do it for H2," shouts Alison.

M puts his arm around me. "Babe, they offered me the job. I accepted it. We'll be okay."

"Huh? Really?" I ask, between gulped breaths. I'm gasping now, fighting to get through this pain with the last bit of energy and lift M has provided.

"That's it! She's coming. She's coming. Keep doing that. Push. Push. Big push."

"Wait, I have to say one thing," I plead.

Claire and Alison look at each other, bemused. Of course, they're thinking it could wait until after the baby is born but I need to tell M now.

"I know I've been a hormonal cow but I want you to know, I've never been embarrassed by you. Even when you eat with your hands. And you are good enough. You always have been. Also, I was checking out Jean-Patrice in the NCT group."

"Who?" asks M.

"The French guy. I wasn't perving or anything but I did look. With my eyes. But no rude thoughts. Is that really bad?"

"Babe, it's fine." M rubs my back. "He's a good-looking guy. I'd look, too."

With that atonement, I let out what I can only describe as an ear-piercing yell, as though I'm going into battle. And she slips out.

WELL, THAT WAS AN INTENSE 24 hours.

I can't talk about everything that happened after baby H2 came into the world. I can't think about that. It doesn't matter right now. What matters is that she's here. She's here.

She's finally here. Here she is, in my arms, while M puts his arms around me. Here we all are.

There's more to the story... free reads and more for you

I hope you enjoyed this story. But wait... there's more. As I mentioned, this isn't your average romcom. It's got people talking, challenged perceptions, and hopefully shown that we're not so different after all. As the series grows I'd like you to be part of my tribe, so I can share exclusive content, free reads, and get your opinion on future book covers, etc. Would you like to join my tribe? If so, sign up to my mailing list here: https://halimakhatun.co.uk/newsletter-sign-up/.

Enjoy this book? Want to read more? The power is in your hands...

Firstly, thanks for taking the time to read my book. It makes my heart happy knowing that people are taking pleasure from my words. It motivates me to write more. I want my book to be read as far and wide as possible, and key to making this happen is having great reviews from readers like you.

Reviews are the most powerful tool in my arsenal when it comes to getting attention for my books. I'm not represented by a global publishing house and I don't have a huge marketing team and endless budget.

But I have something better, that money can't buy – a committed and invested readership. And I rely upon this most important asset, to spread the word.

If you've enjoyed this book, I would be grateful if you could spend just a few minutes leaving a review on the store your bought it from. It can be as short or as long as you like.

Books by Halima Khatun – have you read them all?

The Secret Diary of an Arranged Marriage

Winner of the 2021 Bookbrunch Selfie Award for Best Adult Fiction...

A British-Bengali girl looking for Mr Right. A motley crew of men, some hoping it's them. A mum on a mission to match make. And an age-old tradition with a twist. Welcome to the world of the arranged marriage.

The Secret Diary of a Bengali Bridezilla

And I thought finding a husband was hard...

One couple. Three months. 600 guests (most of whom I've never met) and LOTS of opinions. Welcome to my big fat Bangladeshi wedding.

The Secret Diary of a Bengali Newlywed

I found me a man, now I just need to figure out how to live with him...

New husband. New city. New in-laws and new expectations.

Welcome to my life as a Bengali newlywed.

The Secret Diary of a Broody Bengali

FIRST COMES LOVE... then comes marriage... now the nosey aunties are asking when I'm going to have a baby.

In this laugh-out-loud, heartwarming romantic comedy, our strong female protagonist - a British Bengali girl - is contemplating starting a family. But with a blossoming career and a transient life away from family, is she truly ready for the life changing journey of becoming a mum?

Mother of the Bride

THE SIDE OF THE STORY you never hear...

A mum on a mission to matchmake. A daughter with ideas of her own. A suitor that threatens to tear them apart. When it comes to arranged marriages, you never hear the perspective of the mother of the 'bride'. So now it's time.

About the Author

Halima Khatun is a former journalist (having worked for ITV and the BBC), writer and PR consultant.

Since she was a child, she knew that words would be her thing. With a lifelong passion for writing, Halima wrote her first novel - a coming-of-age children's story - at the age of 12. It was politely turned down by all the major publishing houses. However, proving that writing was indeed her forte, Halima went on to study English and journalism and was one of just four people in the UK to be granted a BBC scholarship during her postgraduate studies.

She has since written for a number of publications including the HuffPost and Yahoo! Style, and has been featured in the Express, Metro and other national publications. Halima also blogs on lifestyle, food and travel and parenthood on halimabobs.com.

You can find out more about Halima's books at halimakhatun.co.uk.

You can connect with Halima on instagram: https://www.instagram.com/halimabobs and tiktok: @halimakhatunauthor.

Having spent years in London, Halima has resettled in Manchester with her family.

www.ingramcontent.com/pod-product-compliance
Lightning Source LLC
Chambersburg PA
CBHW011552190726
48287CB00010B/2854

* 9 7 8 1 9 1 6 3 1 8 3 5 9 *